LYBID

DAUGHTER OF THE SUN

Part II of II

MYROLIUBA

This book was published with the kind assistance of the ARATTA International Charitable Foundation

A literary-mystical screenplay

Kovhanych Halia V. (Myroliuba)
Lybid, Daughter of the Sun

The book is a screenplay for a three-part feature film. The events in the book take place 3000 years ago and in the present in various countries of the world. The Daughter of the Sun appears among us in her earthly incarnation in order to carry out her spiritual mission on Earth.

The main goal of the book is to show mankind that the meaning of our life on Earth is to defend evil and cleanse this World, making right our relationship with the Almighty.

Editor and Designer of the Book
Maria Tariq

DEDICATION

This book is dedicated to my beloved Parents-My Mother, Hanna Hnativna Vitranenko-Kovhanych, and My Father, Vasyl Petrovych Kovhanych, and also, to all wise people inhabiting our planet Earth.

LYBID, DAUGHTER OF THE SUN

A FULL-LENGTH FEATURE FILM

Written by

Halia Vasylivna Myroliuba Kovhanych

SCREENPLAY SUMMARY

Based on a mystical legend about real events that took place 3000 years ago and again in our time in Europe and the United States, as well as in other parts of the world.

The main character – in antiquity, as well as in the modern era – is Her Majesty the Divine Empress Lybid Artemida, the most beautiful woman on Earth. It was written in the holy books of old: "And in Kyiv, the City of Kings, the ambassadors of all the foreign lands bowed low before her." The Empress has bequeathed to herself not only the royal grab of Scythian gold but also the mission inscribed on the "Golden Tablets." As a brilliant scientist and spiritual Master, she must bring to humanity the truth about the meaning of life: to conquer evil and thus cleanse this world, in order to establish relations with the Almighty. Only He can give the gift of supreme intelligence! Light is mightier than Darkness!

With the support of the President of the U.S., the International Council of Religious Leaders and the World Masonic Congress, and having emerged triumphant in the September War in Manhattan, Lybid Artemida leads her team to the Sun, to pay homage to the Source of Life in our solar system.

Actual persons of antiquity and the modern era appear in the film under their real names.

Who were these people and what were the events that determined the fact of humankind? The answers are to be found in the pages of the full screenplay of "Lybid, Daughter of the Sun."

PROLOG

The Sun – a blinding, seething, living sun that roils like molten steel in a vat. A solar flare shoots forth from the Sun's corona. No, it's a gigantic, white, majestic Swan, born of Father of Sun. The Swan, soaring on wings of blinding light, hurtles through space towards Earth, as if the Sun had extended towards the planet a long, glowing hand.

The Swan-Flare embraces Earth with luxurious wings of bewitching beauty.

Out of the blinding light emerges the images of Her Majesty the Empress Lybid Artemida, the most beautiful lady on Earth. Lybid sits on a throne in the Royal Place in Kyiv, the Ancient Sun City. Envoys from many lands bow ow before her.

September 2000. New York City. The Metropolitan Opera Building. Day 1 of the World Congress of Masons. Night has fallen. A line of Bentleys, Mercedes and other assorted luxury cars are lined up at the entrance, waiting to disgorge their passengers, predominantly older males dressed in evening wear and Masonic aprons. Dozens of reporters are hustling about, hunting for quotes from the delegates, while photographers' elbow for room at curbside. A line of policemen keeps several thousand curious onlookers at a distance. Television vans, their extended satellite antennas feeding live, hum nearby. A television camera's red light goes on, as Betsy Rosenberg, standing against a background of the arriving dignitaries, begins her report for CNN...

ROSENBERG:

> "Good evening! This is Betsy Rosenberg, live from the Metropolitan Opera in New York. A sensational event for the new Millennium! Empress Lybid Artemida has again exhibited her unique ability to influence global affairs. This amazing woman, using the offices of various heads of state, has called on the leaders of the world's Masonic organizations to come together here today to discuss the problem of the Sun. Actually, we don't have a problem with the Sun. It would be more accurate to say that we earthlings are a problem for the Sun, the major headache for our eternal source of Light. The leaders of international Masonry have responded to the intriguing invitation of the woman who is today as the embodiment of the queen who, 3000 years ago, ruled the civilized world. And so today, here in the Metropolitan Opera Building, have gathered some of the most influential leaders of our time, representing

Masonic organizations in almost every country in the world, leaders who, through their representatives and sympathizers in the temporal halls of power and speaking for millions of their members, yield tremendous influence on issues that affect all humanity. Our CNN cameras are strategically placed at various points in the main hall. My colleague, Philip Gorsky, is inside with the latest. Phil, what have you got for us?"

Philip Gorsky appears on screen in the concert hall. During his report the cameras cut away to show the various goings-on inside.

GORSKY:

"Thank you, Betsy! I feel very privileged to be covering this unprecedented World Congress of Masons here at the Met, which is steadily filling up with a mass of humanity, as you see behind me. As you can hear and see, the orchestra has added to the celebratory atmosphere with a stirring rendition of some of the best-known marches. There are delegates from all over the world, many of whom know each other well. You see by the way they greet one another. A true brotherhood of peoples, a Masonic International! A white delegate embraces his black brother; a Japanese kiss a Hindu; a German embraces a Jew. It is probably accurate to say that all races and all peoples are represented here - from North and South America, Europe, Asia, Africa, Australia, the island nations. I was especially moved by the fact that all of the male delegates, almost without exception, have come dressed in their finest tuxedoes and draped with the ceremonial sashes covered with the highest awards their nations have to give. This is perhaps the largest gathering ever of distinguished and honored people. That sound you hear is the Marine Corps band, playing 'Waltzing Matilda' in honor of the delegation from Australia! Yes! The united Masonic delegations from various countries have begun filing into the hall! Each is led by its oldest and most respected members, carrying its banner: 'French Masonry!' 'Masons of Germany,' 'Irish Orangemen!' And there's a women's Masonic lodge from Great Britain"

There is a camera switch and once again Betsy Rosenberg is on screen from outside the building.

"Phil, excuse me for interrupting, but we just received a report that among those present inside are members of some of the world's wealthiest and most powerful families. Bill Gates is said to be here, as well as members of the Rothschild family, the Morgans, Rockefellers, Dupont's, McCormick. There are also some heads of state and high representatives of many governments. And even superstars of the arts and the entertainment industry. Can you confirm this?"

The interior camera is on again and Philip Gorsky is on screen.

GORSKY:

"I can say with some confidence that some of the most influential people in the world are in this hall. So, it's not at all strange that you are getting these reports. But let's do this: let's ask the director to show us as many celebrities as possible! I think our audience out there will get a thrill out of recognizing so many famous faces! But I want to point out to our viewers that, obviously, not all of the delegates and guests here are necessarily Masons. The Masons are in tuxedoes... Well, just about everyone is in a tuxedo. But the Masons are also wearing their aprons, which are the symbol of Freemasonry. So, whoever is wearing an apron is a Mason delegate. others- without the aprons and other Masonic paraphernalia- are not. Although you and I know that the Masons are considered by many to be masters of conspiracy! it's possible that some of the many internationally known leaders of finance and politics -those without the aprons and the symbols of knightly orders -that our cameras just showed really are not Masons. Perhaps most of the guests are keeping secret their membership in Masonic lodges, so not to advertise the source of their power, wealth and fame? Or, perhaps, the Masons are so powerful that they could invite so many famous guests to provide cover for them. And the famous guests came here to satisfy their curiosity. Who knows? But...OH, my to our audience, I'm getting some feedback from our director..."

Gorsky presses his hand to his ear, the better to hear what is being said through his earpiece. He nods vigorously and, obviously chastened, continues in a subdued, almost tone...

GORSKY:

"What was I thinking, saying all those crazy things? The excitement and the atmosphere obviously have affected my judgment! The people here are just good friend! Everything here is fully within the bounds of the U.S. Constitution! let's give the Masonic organizations their due for their great charitable work, the free hospitals for kids and poor people. And what else I can personally say is – stay away from all that pulp, and you won't be blathering like an idiot like I was... But, in the end, what everyone here – the delegates and the hosts, the Masons and the non-Masons alike - came for is to hear perhaps the most famous person on Earth and to decide the problem of the Sun! And so, we will shortly be seeing the Sun, in the form of a woman!"

A long black limousine is making its way along the streets of New York, in a motorcade of policemen on motorcycles and in squad cars leading the way and bringing up the rear, their lights flashing. Inside the limo, dressed in a sparkling imperial robe, sits Lybid, Robert Oberfell beside her. They are watching the CNN broadcast from the Metropolitan Opera.

LYBID:

"Television is progress and progress are television! Within leaving this limousine you and I can see most of the guests and delegates to the Congress, as if we ourselves were among them at the Met. Now, if Julius Caesar had been riding in a limousine to the Roman Senate and watching television at the same time, he would have seen Brutus and the other conspirators whispering in the shadows and concealing daggers in the folds of their cloaks. He would have been able to tell just from the looks on their faces that they were waiting to kill him without mercy, like a pig might be slaughtered. But Caesar had no television and so he... But I do!"

OBERFELL:

"Pardon me, but you seem to be leading up to something and I'm not quite sure what it might be. Do you suspect something about the delegates?"

LYBID:

"Not at all, Robert. In fact, quite the opposite! I am very pleased by the TV reports from the Congress, so much so that it got me to thinking how great it is that I am not

Julius Caesar. Thanks to CNN I can see from the faces of the delegates that there is a genuine atmosphere of brotherhood and mutual trust at the Congress. Their faces are all aglow. I can see all their medals gleaming. I can sense that they are looking forward to seeing me. it's almost as if the screen is able to show what is in their hearts! And of course, I'm oh so happy to escape the fate of Caesar, when, coughing up blood, he gasped, 'Et tu, Brute?' I'm so happy you're not Brutus and that I, coughing up blood won't have to gasp, 'Et tu, Robert?'"

OBERFELL:

"Never, my Queen! You hold my heart in your hand! Squeeze it, crush it, if you must!"

Oberfell squeezes his right hand into a tight fist...

LYBID:

"I believe you, Robert! I am happy that you and I are together in our service to me Father, the Sun. And that I am about to meet the most powerful and influential people of our planet, the golden elite of humankind!"

OBERFELL:

"This is your triumph! All of these powerful people have just about given you carte blanche for your project, just by agreeing to hold this international Congress in your honor. Irrespective of the results of today's vote, your international approval rating has got to increase by at least 50%!"

LYBID:

> "Even if I get only 51% of the delegates on my side, I will still be able to move ahead with my program for the Sun, going through the leaders of all the countries in the world!"

The TV screen shows Lybid Artemida's motorcade approaching the Metropolitan Opera building.

ROSENBERG:

> "The moment we have been waiting for is here! The arrival of Her Majesty the Empress Lybid Artemida! The thousands of people gathered here hold their collective breath!"

The motorcade comes into full view: first the police motorcycle escort, then the police cruisers with lights flashing, then the limousine. Television cameras are in place aimed at the vehicle's door, from which she is expected to emerge.

OBERFELL:

> "It's time! Get ready – Johnson is about to open the door. God speed!"

Secret Service agent Johnson opens the door from the outside and a radiantly smiling Lybid Artemida steps out of the limousine into the bright TV lights, the gold and jewels of her garb blinding in their brilliance. The throng gathered in front of the building erupts in a roar of excitement and approval!

ROSENBERG:

> "Ladies and Gentlemen! Like the blinding Sun, Lybid
> Artemida has appeared!"

As Lybid enters the Concert Hall the assembled spontaneously rise to their
feet and applauding. She walks down the center aisle to the front and
ascends the stage, where the leaders of the international Masons are seated.
Behind them the stage has been decorated with the symbols of ancient
Egypt, including the all-seeing Eye of Hor, gleaming, radiant, seemingly
alive. Lybid approaches a specially appointed rostrum. The men on the
stage all stand and bow slightly in her direction, while the chairman of the
Congress, an elegant, handsome elderly man-who could be Sean
Connery's double-wearing a mason's apron, walks up to her, kisses her
hand and then turns to the microphone.

CHAIRMAN:

> "As the co-chairman of the Supreme Council of the
> International Masonic movement, and elected
> chairman of this Congress of the Sun, I welcome you, O
> Goddess, in the name of the Masonic lodges of our
> planet Earth!"

The hall again erupts in applause. The orchestra plays the introduction to
the Masonic international hymn, and continues as the delegates sing
fervently and in full voice. The song ends and the assembled sit down.

CHAIRMAN:

> "The Sun! The central celestial body of our solar system,
> in which our Earth spins on an elliptical orbit, third
> from the Sun, after Mercury and Venus. Should the Sun
> ever become angry with us, it could hurl at us a bolt of
> plasma, one of its solar flares, which would vaporize
> every living thing on Earth! In a nuclear explosion, the

10

radiation – a stream of photons -kills people in an instant, leaving nothing but their shadows on the ground. Like in Hiroshima and Nagasaki. But the Sun is a billion times mightier than all the nuclear weapons ever produced on Earth. If the blinding eye of the Sun changes its love into hate and hurls at us the lethal energy of its anger, in the eight minutes and 50 seconds that it would take it to cover the 98 million miles of space, Earth would be turned into an irradiated sphere of molten matter, its atmosphere burned off, the oceans boiled off, any and all life terminated forever. Do we, ladies and gentlemen, dare anger our Sun?

We love to lay down our bodies on the world's beaches to soak up the rays of the Sun, the energy of God Himself, to luxuriate in the love it radiates down on us. But are we worthy of our Sun? Or, perhaps, we are loathsome in Its eyes? We are strong in our love, our unity and our ability to look deep into our hearts and search our souls! We all realize the world needs your Sun program, Your Majesty, if we are to find the answer to the question: in the final battle between the forces of Light and Darkness, which we call Armageddon, will it be our Sun that burns the forces of Darkness to ash with a single mighty burst, while the righteous gain eternal life in the abode of the gods that is on the Sun?"

LYBID (sitting on a throne, built especially for her, and speaking into a microphone on the podium in front):

"Neither I nor the angels of heaven know when that day will come. Only my heavenly Father knows. Paraphrasing Jesus Christ, I will say that neither I nor any other mortal on Earth has the right to speak for the Sun. Yes, you are correct in saying the Sun can make

11

Armageddon come to pass, when Its fiery light destroys the forces of Darkness manifesting themselves in material form, while the righteous ascend in their spiritual bodies into Paradise, which is to be found on the Sun planet. For me personally this is not the main issue, because in the next 100 years all those present here will have died, having gone through their life cycle, or earlier, because of illness or some other premature death.

And they will leave their mortal material bodies and in their bodies of spirit will stand before the Supreme Judgment on the Sun. And this means that the end of each individual Earthling is his personal Armageddon. But the Armageddon we speak of here is the one that determines the fate of humanity as a whole. But if within the next 100 years every last human being alive today will die, then can I not say that the human race today is living through his or her personal Armageddon?"

CHAIRMAN:

"We are in awe of your evolved personal philosophy, Your Majesty! Next to me a display showing questions from the floor. According to our tradition the question comes not from any individual delegate but from the organization he represents. So, the Masonic lodge in France, the Great Orient, asks, what is the essence of the project you announced in your previous incarnation 3000 years ago, outlining for mankind its mission – the conquest of the Promised Land by sending a manned expedition to the Sun? While we can imagine the colonization of Mars or the Moon, is it in the power of our Civilization to colonize the Sun?"

LYBID:

> "I sense that this question is a rhetorical one, that the Great Orient lodge consulted astronomers, science fiction writers and trained futurologists ahead of time and now itself in the mantle of willing advocates for the Sun..."

Members of the Great Orient lodge in the hall exchange smug glances among them- and murmur in half-whispers in French: "She is smart; her wisdom is from the, as is her beauty..."

Meanwhile, in a room in another corner of the Metropolitan opera a dozen or so Masons watch the proceedings in the main hall on a large television screen. In the middle of the room stands, lost in deep thought, an old man, a centenarian perhaps, his hair as white as the light of the moon, his face a landscape of deep furrows and wrinkles, his chest bedecked with countless medals-the Grand Master of the Masons. The powerful men in the room take flutes of champagne off a linen-covered table, clink the glasses, and listen in silence as Lybid answers a question.

GRAND MASTER (takes a sip of champagne):

> "The Sun Goddess. The most beautiful woman on Earth. What say the Prior of? Zion?"

BRENNAN:

> "I propose we give her our support and order all the lodges represented at the Congress to vote affirmative. Miguel Achoa, the Prince Apostle and Knight of the Sun, has already lobbied the lodge pontifices in her favor. He is to meet with her tomorrow morning, representing Forbes magazine."

GRAND MASTER:

"And what say the Grand Master, Keeper of the Divine Palladium?"

KEEPER:

"I have received the consent of the Grand Architect of the Universe for her to meet with the Supreme Anointed Ones. They say that an expedition to the Sun will mean a hundred-year leap in science and technology. And the application of new technologies will earn 100 trillion real dollars for the Golden Pyramid. So, it really doesn't matter what the cost of the expedition itself shall be, or whether it even reaches the Sun, but, say, is vaporized on the way..."

GRAND MASTER:

"Light is progress! Sovereign Grand Inspector Rosenthal..."

ROSENTHAL (gets up from his chair):

"I stand ready"

GRAND MASTER:

"By the powers vested in me by the Great Predicator, I have decided it is time to end the show in the hall. It is apparent to us the esteemed Daughter and wife of the Sun, Her Majesty the Empress Lybid Artemida, is worthy of undertaking the voyage to the Eternal Luminary. Go into the hall and tell the chairman of our decision. I do not want her to tire from the floodlights and the inane questions of our dear brothers, whose

14

spirituality is still evolving somewhere between Darkness and the True Light. She has to look her best for her meeting with the Supreme Sages. Inform the chairman that a jet awaits Lybid Artemida at the airport and that he is to accompany her to Eden..."

Rosenthal bows low, places his flute on the table and departs from the room...

Meanwhile, back in the main hall...

LYBID:

"...Inasmuch as the Sun contains over 99 of the matter in the entire Solar System, we must respectfully accept the truth that-as I repeat again and again in my speeches over 99% of the intelligence of the Solar System is also to be found there. Or, put another way, 99.9% of the genius of our living world. The Sun is the super intelligent and super powerful source of all life in our Solar System. One does not deal lightly with the Sun! Therefore, we must scrupulously avoid all formulations about 'colonization' or 'conquest' or 'subjugation' or 'urbanization' of the Sun, or even a technical emigration' to the Sun. We should enter into a pure friendship with our Father the Sun and establish respectful, voluntary relations with It. We will fly to the Sun in order to pay It homage, as a delegation from an Earth true to the ideals of Love, Goodness and Light..."

CHAIRMAN:

"Following up on your answer to the French Masons and the Knights of the Order Malta, the International Order of Lions asks you to explain whether the expedition to the Sun, or around the Sun, will finally provide us with an answer to the question: What was the essence of the war between the gods and the Titans?"

LYBID:

"The study of the earth's epochs lays the basis for a thesis that in the beginning the Sun and Earth were populated by demons, or Titans, and gods, and that for several generations a war raged between them. According to legend the gods defeated the Titans and expelled them. There was nothing left for the Titans to do but settle on Jupiter. One of the names the ancient Aryans had for the Sun was 'Sur'ya.' Let us together decipher the meaning of this term. First of all, let's recall the ancient Greek myth about the struggle between the gods and the Titans. Obviously, different peoples called them by different names. Among the Yakuts, or other Siberian peoples, they were referred to as the 'ay' or 'abaas.' Other peoples used still different names. The Aryans used the term 'sur' for 'gods' and 'asur' for 'non-gods' (in the Vedic Bhahavat-Giti, the 'asur' are demons). A good analogy would be such names of countries as Rusi'ya-Rus' for the Great Kyivan Rus, the land of the Rusy (today's Ukrainians); 'Angli'ya, 'the land of the Angles or Angels. 'Sur'ya' should be interpreted as 'Land of the Sur, 'or 'Homeland of the Gods.' And so, the Sun was the Land of the Gods. Along the same lines Jupiter could be called either 'Asurya' or 'Abaasstan' or 'Demonland 'or some other name like that. Therefore, we would be safe in saying that there are three forms of living beings that dominate our Solar system – gods, living on the Sun; humans, which populate Earth; and

16

demons or Titans or the Abaas or the Asuri, who settled on Jupiter. The Sun being the planet of the gods! Ladies and Gentlemen! I promise you that if the World Masonic Movement makes the decision to have all the countries on Earth fund our expedition to the Sun, the scientific knowledge gained will allow us to decipher all the mysteries surrounding the spiritual symbols and the secret doctrines, the keys to which have been lost by us in the dim past of ancient Greece, Rome, Egypt and Babylon..."

CHAIRMAN:

"The display tells me that it is the will of the majority of the delegates that we move on to the voting. Therefore, Ladies and Gentlemen! I call upon you to cast your vote, using the computer screen on the back of the chair in front of you. The matter before u is: Will the Masons support the financing of the expedition to the Sun?"

The symphony orchestra plays a brief, triumphal flourish. A moment of silence f lows, broken by the excited voice of the Congress chairman.

CHAIRMAN:

"The results of the vote: 97% are in the affirmative, that is, in favor of the Sun expedition! One percent voted nay-no doubt our frugal brethren from the Middle East trade consortiums -while 2% abstained. I would venture to guess these might be Islamist Masons, for whom the Sun is of lesser importance, the Moon being their divine symbol. Your Majesty, I congratulate you! You shall be flying to the Sun with the blessing of the International Order of Free Masons!"

The hall erupts in applause and a standing ovation. Waves of men and women bearing bouquets of flowers roll towards the stage...

CHAIRMAN:

"I announce a one-hour recess, so that our delegates, gathered here from all of the world, would have the opportunity to commune with one another in the corridor of the Metropolitan Opera. In an hour we shall all see the premier of a magnificent opera about the eternal struggle between the forces of Darkness and Light, 'Mason, Son of the Sun,' written especially for today's celebration by the authors of the famous rock-opera, 'Jesus Christ, Superstar.' Afterwards, there will be a buffet dinner and reception, lasting until dawn!"

Lybid's limousine, with an honor escort, departs from the Met. Inside are the Queen the Congress chairman and Robert Oberfell.

OBERFELL:

"A magnificent victory! Today you have conquered the world!"

CHAIRMAN:

"You have conquered more than just the world!"

On the small television screen before them pass scenes from the rather predictable "Mason, Son Sun," playing back at the Metropolitan. "Moses" sings, "Why strike you the Hebrew slave?" and with a blow with his staff kills the Egyptian overseer...

In the following scene, Hebrews, sweat pouring and bronzed by the sun, haul huge symbolic blocks of stone for the Great Egyptian Pyramid, then lay them down to form a gigantic tetrahedron. The Pharaoh sings: "Two million 300 thousand blocks, five million 750 thousand tons... Such might!"

A chorus of Hebrew women dressed in black mourning cloaks and wringing their hands sing: "One hundred thousand slaves, one hundred thousand slaves, a pyramid build!" Then, abruptly raising hands to the sky: "Be damned, O Ra!"

Lybid, Oberfell and the Chairman, ignoring the opera, continue their conversation...

CHAIRMAN:

> "The 97% of the delegates that voted for you in effect authorized you to meet immediately with the leading sages of mankind, the people who control all of the planet's media and approximately 82% of all wealth on Earth. Unfortunately, you will not be able to tell even your grandchildren that you met with these High Anointed. But know this – they approve of you and they bow low and sincerely before your intellect and beauty. You might consider this your most important achievement, Your Majesty!

Lybid closes her eyes shut. She sees herself not in a moving limousine but in a spaceship hurtling toward the Sun. G-forces pull at her body; through the flames bursting from the rocket engines, she watches Earth recede below. And what is that? Again, the fiery rocket plume? No, this light comes from up ahead-from the roiling, immortal, mighty Sun itself, dominating the vista.

Another international assembly, organized by the Avatar in honor of Lybid Artemida. As always, the indoor stadium is overflowing with people. The Avatar, dressed all in white, flies down from the golden crown topping a huge statue of Lybid, his arms spread wide, and alights onto a podium decorated, as always, with sheaf of wheat. Behind the Avatar stands a huge electronic screen showing scenes that illustrate his words. But today there is something new and awe-inspiring on the stage-Horynych, a colossal dragon breathing fire from the mouth of each of his three fearsome heads.

The steady din that hung over the stadium turns into a roar.

AVATAR:

> "I am happy to announce that the admirers of Her Majesty Lybid Artemida now number in the millions. Her popularity has reached levels unprecedented in history!"

Suddenly, a short, obese man runs up to the stage and starts to shout.

KIRSHBLATT:

> "I am Professor Kirshblatt! I protest! All of this is absolutely unscientific! What kind of Golden Tablets can there be, when there is the Bible? The Bible is the Word of God!"

Unexpectedly the Dragon Horynych lowers his heads toward the professor and with his breath of flame, chases the man away from the stage.

AVATAR:

> "This is my centurion, built with love by Fujiyama Industries of Japan in order to protect the Golden Tablets of Lybid Artemida. His supercomputer brain does not tolerate opposition! OK, Dragon, do your thing!"

The fiery dragon lowers his long neck into the crowd, the terrifying heads twisting back and forth over the fear-stricken, screaming worshippers.

AVATAR:

"Look up at the screen, everybody!"

Screams of fear turn into shouts of excitement as it becomes clear that the dragons burning eyes are really closed-circuit cameras connected with the huge screen on the stage. People in the crowd, recognizing themselves in the close-ups on the screen, start pointing and making funny-faces at the dragon-heads...

AVATAR:

"Scared, were you? it's like Goya said: The sleeping intellect gives birth to monsters. 'Seems we have quite a few brave Lancelot's down there!"

The Dragon Horynych lets out a hair-raising roar from all three of his heads, then, lifting them up high, exhales flames from his nostrils. A few dozen still-terrified people retreat, shrieking, away from the stage, while the rest of the stadium continues to buzz with excitement.

AVATAR:

"Her Majesty Queen Lybid, the goddess Arta Midia! Who were the people ruled her? All the sources available to us today say that Lybid – or Sunhilda, or Sva – over the Rus. You here in America will say – yes, the Russians, with their capital of Moscow! But in order to help you understand fully the phenomenon of Lybid Artemida, I must turn to the Holy Scriptures, the Bible..."

The Avatar opens the Bible lying on a stand before him...

AVATAR:

"I quote from the Book of Ezekiel, chapter 38, verses 2-3: 'Set your face against Cog, of the land of Magog, the prince of Rosh, Meshech and Tubal..Lybid, Ladies and Gentlemen, is the Grand Queen of the Scythians-Rus. As you just heard, a great country was divided into the Kingdoms of Rosh, Meshech and Tubal. 'Rosh' is Ros (Rus, the republic we know today as 'Ukraine.') 'Meshekh' is 'Mosokh' (Muscovy, today the

Russian Federation). The term 'Tubal' refers to 'Tobol' (lying in Western Siberia beyond the Urals, Tobol and Irtysh are even today two of the centers of the Kosaks).

The Avatar pauses and looks over the audience...

AVATAR:

"Therefore, in order to understand the origins from which Lybid has come, you should know that the Tsars of the Russian Empire, and, later, the Communists of the Soviet Union, knowingly led us into confusion by changing the names by which peoples were previously known. Thus, the Rus (the Biblical 'Rosh') were purposely renamed by the imperial Romanov dynasty, first to 'Little Russians' and later to 'Ukrainians'; what was once 'Great Rus' became 'Ukraine.' You should know that the ethnic group you call 'Russians' are not the Rus but, I repeat, the Muscovites, the Biblical Meshekh, who took for themselves the name 'Rosh.' I will demonstrate who it is that the Queen Goddess Lybid Artemida rules over and I will explain who we are, where we come from, and where we are going. In 1869 the members of the French Senate and the cabinet of ministers were issued special documentation, which read: There exists the colossal Russian Empire, which stretches over half the territory of Europe and one-third of Asia, and is made up of a mosaic of numerous enslaved peoples conquered by the Muscovites. From among these peoples, let us focus on the Ruthenians, the Lithuanians and the Poles. We in France are making an enormous mistake, a mistake compounded by its numerous consequences, by seeing the Russian Empire as a unitary entity. This "unitariness" is nothing more than a manifestation of the idea of Pan-Slavism. This "unification" is being brought about before our very eyes. For example, in academe, the names of two very distinct peoples have come to be used interchangeably. Furthermore, these are two peoples with two opposing visions of civilization and with sharply different tradition throughout their history. These two peoples are the Muscovites and the Ruten.

'The Rutens earlier had the names "Rusyns" and "Rus" and were conquered by the Muscovites in the 17th Century, after which the conquering nation took for itself the name of the conquered in order to claim for itself the nominal "right" to rule over them. What happened as a result is that the names "Rus" and "Muscovite" today are considered synonyms, even though in reality they refer to two radically different ethnic groups. This confusion also allowed the Muscovites to claim for themselves the history of the Rusyns.

'But the truth must be told: there exists in Europe a people, the Rusyns, who – with 12.5 million living under the Tsar and 2. 5 under the Austro-Hungarian monarchy – are as numerous as the population of Spain, three times as numerous as the Bohemians and equal to the subjects of the Crown of St. Stephen. This nation exists, it has its own history that is separate from that of Muscovy. It has its own traditions, its own language – distinct from Muscovite and Polish – and is fighting to hang on to its individuality.

'History must not forget that, up to the reign of Peter I, the people that we today call the "Rutens" once had the name "Rusyns" or "Rus" and their land was called "Rus" and also "Great Kyivan Rus" and the people we today call the "Russians" was once named "Muscovites" and their country "Muscovy."

'At the turn of the century most people in France and in Europe could make a distinction between "Rus" and "Muscovy." So how did the change come about? It happened only, and exclusively, because for an entire century the Muscovite government has been working to obliterate in the popular mind the true meaning of these two terms and meld them into one perception. However, let us restore the truth, which will bring light to our era and allow us to see clearly the dangers the future may bring. Let us stop arbitrarily lumping under the one name "Russians" the Rusyns – who are without doubt of Slavic stock – and the Muscovites – whose Slavic origins are very much in doubt.' (Taken from Un europeen de gulnze millions oublie devant L'Histoire, Paris, 1869, as quoted, in translation, by I. Borshchak in his Ideya sobornoyi Ukrayiny u Yeuropi v mynulomu, Ukrayinsky drukar Publishing House, Paris, 1923, pp. 22-23.)"

The Avatar closes a document folder on the stand in front of him and looks out at the audience.

AVATAR:

> "This is who we are, where we come from and where we are going. This is how we see ourselves as an independent subject of human history. We are the Rusyns, renamed by Muscovy in order to steal from us our history, culture, our very identity. We are Rusyns and they are Muscovites. And the language known today as 'Russian' is, in fact 'Muscovite,' while the language you know today as 'Ukrainian' is, in truth, the real 'Rus' language! Is it conceivable that, for example, the English would be renamed 'Germans,' the Jews as 'Arabs,' the Spanish as 'French,' the Japanese as 'Chinese' and that those peoples would hang on with pride to the false names forced upon them?"

The stadium crowd that sat mesmerized into silence by the avatar's presentation awakens in a storm of indignation...

AVATAR:

> "Ladies and Gentlemen! Know this: the true Rus nation, whose champion is Lybid Artemida, belongs to the Slavic branch of the great Indo-European family of nations, other members include the Germans, the Celts, the Lithuanians, the Latvians, the French, the Spanish, the Portuguese, the Italians, the Rumanians, the Moldovans, the Greeks, the Aryans of India, the Iranians, the Persians, the Kurds, the Tajiks, the and others. We are a great family of peoples!"

The stadium spontaneously begins to chant, "Lybid, Lybid, Lybid," which grows in its intensity and passion.

AVATAR:

> "And now I shall open the Golden Tablets of Lybid Artemida..."

The Avatar solemnly opens the book of the Golden Tablets and begins to read aloud...

AVATAR:

> "Bread and love – these are your greatest treasure, Lybid Arta Midia! Tell us, O Divine One, how true and pure is your love?"

The Sun, a grateful Golden Sun, flashes in the sky and embraces Earth in its gentle, warm radiance...

TITLE: LYBID, 3000 YEARS AGO

Scenes from the previous life of Her Majesty the Queen Lybid Artemida, the marriageable years of her youth...

The Imperial Palace on Ariana Hill in Kyiv City is covered with snow. Lybid, wearing a long fur coat, steps out of a royal winter carriage mounted on a sleigh. Accompanied, as always, by the Volkhovs Mudroslav and Liubomyr, she makes her way down a red carpet, laid down for her right up to the palace entrance. The Great King comes out to greet her. Father and daughter embrace.

KINGS OF KINGS:

"Welcome home, my child!"

LYBID:

"I am so happy to see you, Papa!"

Zlata Maya in turn walks up to Lybid and embraces her daughter.

MAYA:

"My darling, my little swan! you've flown back to us, back under your family roof my precious child!"

LYBID:

"O Mama, I missed you so much!"

The entire group walks together to the Grand Hall, where the nobles of the real await them. Lybid's beloved twin brother, Boos, warmly embraces her.

BOOS:

"Sister!"

LYBID

"Brother!"

After the joyous reunion is complete, everyone finds a place at the great table. The King directs Lybid's attention to a huge tapestry, on which in thick threads of varying colors is outlined a map of the then-known world.

KING OF KINGS:

"I have called you back to the capital, Daughter, because I need your support in a matter of great urgency! Look at this depiction of our world. Our finest masters have marked on it all the countries and all the major cities known to us from the life stories of the great leaders of years past. There we are, the country you see there. We are larger than anybody else, more numerous than anyone! We have more land and more people than any other nation on Earth. This is what makes us so strong, and there is no kingdom to whom God Almighty has given the power great enough to conquer us. But...You see here, the great swath of territory that belongs to Byzantium? We can swallow up all this land in one huge bite and not choke on it, but... If we attack Theodorex, we would frighten all of Europe and it will unite, in order to weaken us. And a Europe united with Byzantium would tear at us from two directions... To fight two such wars simultaneously just beyond Rus' power!"

LYBID:

"But Theodorex is our ally!"

KING OF KINGS:

"And so is Germanarix! Theodorex, himself a Goth, as is Germanarix, seized the throne of Byzantium and became its emperor. But he wasn't able to unite the Gothland he left with the Byzantium he conquered, which would have made him more powerful we!"

LYBID:

"But why not?"

KING OF KINGS:

"Because I gave much gold to our kinsman Germanarix, so that he would strengthen his positions and gain the throne of Gothland. Germanarix was loath to be under Byzantium, and wanted his own state."

LYBID:

"Whom would Germanarix attack first, us or Theodorex?"

KING OF KINGS:

"Your hand in marriage could decide the destiny of Great Kyivan Rus, my divine Daughter! The Byzantines have a word for this, politics. In one way or another, all of the kings of Europe are our direct kinsmen, the descendants of our divine Father Rama, who placed his children in all the major countries of the world. War and peace, good and evil, tyranny and justice-everything in Europe and across the oceans is our internal family matter. The only difference lies in who is a closer relation and who is more distant. Or, whom do we draw closer to us, and whom we push as far out of our sight as possible. Daughter, know that the essence of the Greek word 'politics' is this: to strengthen oneself by using another and then together to break a third! The only question that stands before us rulers is this: Against whom to unite? And so on to eternity! If you become the wife of Germanarix, Emperor Theodorex will be the loser. And if you become the Empress of Byzantium, then Germanarix will not risk a war with either of us, me or my son-in-law, Theodorex!"

LYBID:

"Father! I do not love either King Germanarix or Emperor Theodorex. They are both the same to me. I am obedient only to you! I have been raised by you, Father, to be willing to sacrifice my youth in a marriage with a husband I do not love, even with one odious to me, all for the sake of Holy Rus! I will enter into marriage with whatever king you shall choose for my husband!

Pleased with the response of his daughter and inspired, the Great King walks the halls of his palace. Suddenly, he is met by one of the maidens from Lybid's young entourage, the beautiful nymph Kalisto, dressed in a heavy coat of red fox furs. With a lightning-quick move she lays herself down before him, and the king, no unpleased with such boldness on the part of the young beauty, stops.

KING OF KINGS:

"Why have you thrown yourself at my feet? You have something to ask of me?"

KALISTO:

"I am Kalisto, O Great King! A nymph in service to your daughter."

KING OF KINGS

"Now I recognize you! You have grown up to be quite a beauty, little Kalisto!"

KALISTO:

"O Great King! I have a secret I must share with you!'

KING OF KING:

"Where?"

KALISTO:

"In your chambers, so that no one will hear!"

KING OF KINGS:

"Off we go, my little beauty! Ah, the sweet scent of your body! Intoxicating..."

The King and Kalisto depart. Soon thereafter, Lybid and Atalanta enter the hall. run into Tarasiy.

LYBID:

"Tarasiy, is that you?"

TARASIY:

"My Queen!"

LYBID:

"Do you recognize Atalanta, Tarasiy?"

TARASIY:

"How can I not recognize her? And there's my brother Palant!"

Tarasiy takes a few steps towards the approaching Palant, and the two close friends embrace.

TARASIY:

"I greet you!"

LYBID:

"Oh, the joy of it all!"

TARASIY:

"I must speak with you, my Queen. Face to face. Just the two of us."

LYBID:

"What is it? Has something happened? Palant, Atalanta, take these things with you. Tarasiy and I have something to discuss."

Atalanta and Palant depart.

LYBID:

"What is it you want to tell me, Tarasiy? The words I've longed to hear?"

Meanwhile, in the royal sleeping chambers, Kalisto suddenly throws off her long fur cloak and stands before the Great King. She wears nothing but the red on her bare feet and the kerchief that was wrapped around the collar of her coat.

KING OF KINGS:

"I am smitten by the arrow of Eros, Kalisto!"

KALISTO:

"I have raised myself to become a gift to you and to you alone, O Great King!"

Kalisto throws herself around the neck of the King of Rus...

In the hall, Lybid and Tarasiy continue their tete-a-tete.

TARASIY:

"I love you, O White Swan!"

LYBID:

"And I you, Tarasiy! I have loved you from the moment I saw you, a little boy!"

The same scene from the past emerges from the depths of the memory of each Lybid, preparing to lead a large party on a long journey; a young boy, dressed in golden garments, running up to her.

TARASIY:

"I am Tarasiy, son of Prince Akteon! Take me with you!"

LYBID:

"Why would you want to leave your mama's breast, Tarasiy?"

TARASIY:

"I have fallen in love with you, my Queen, and I want to see your eyes before me every moment of every day!"

LYBID:

"I don't want you to buzz around me day and night about your love, like a bee whose words would be like honey to me!"

The sweet memory passes and leaves them embracing each other. Lybid gently clings to him, but then speaks the fateful words that bury their future happiness together...

LYBID:

"I can never be yours, my beloved Tarasiy, even though you come to me in my dreams every night, as if we were husband and wife. but... this can never be. I save my maidenhood for my future husband!"

At that same moment, in the royal sleeping chambers, Lybid's father, having lost his senses to lust, relieves Kalisto of her virginity. The young nymph screams from the initial burst of pain, as her fingers dig spasmodically into the bedding.

In the hall, Lybid and Tarasiy continue their passionate exchange...

LYBID:

> "I am the gold that belongs to my beloved country! O cruel Fate! I was born to become to some king...Everything – for my father's sake! For the sake of his grand for Holy Rus!"

TARASIY:

> "And what of your own happiness? others' happiness is so abundant. And yours...?"

In his sleeping chamber the Great King emits a soft groan of sweet satisfaction, w he rolls off Kalisto. Kalisto lies on top of her first lover and murmurs sweetly.

KALISTO:

> "You have plucked the flower of my innocence, O Great King!"

KING OF KINGS:

> "I am happy that you raised your forbidden fruit as a gift to me. I feel as if I've thrown half my years! you've given me back my youth!"

KALISTO

> "I want to keep giving you this sweet delight! But I shall be riding off with Lybid to the far corners of the Earth!"

KING OF KINGS:

> "I will not allow you to leave! Stay here in the palace!"

KALISTO:

"As a wife? Or as your concubine?"

KING OF KINGS:

"As my wife!"

KALISTO:

"But what about Queen Zlata Maya?"

KING OF KINGS:

"I fell in love with you at first glance! What is your secret? What has happened to me? I don't understand myself! I want you, and no one else! I won't let you go!"

Back in the hall where Lybid and Tarasiy stand face-to-face, her hands in his...

TARASIY:

"I cannot live without you! Nor do I want to!"

LYBID:

"And neither do I want to live without you! But I will live, to save myself for my future husband. I will sacrifice myself for my father's designs. And I shall live for the sake of my Mother, whom Father loves more than life itself!

At this time in the sleeping chambers of the Great king... Kalisto is getting dressed, while the King lies naked before her...

KALISTO:

"You have planted in me the seed of a new life, O Great King!"

KING OF KINGS:

"How is that possible, my sweet dove?"

KALISTO:

"A soothsayer told me I would conceive the first time I lay with you and give a son of unparalleled beauty and wisdom!"

KING OF KINGS:

"I shall make the heavens bow before this child!"

KALISTO:

"So, you will marry me?"

KING OF KINGS:

"I will marry you! And send Zlata Maya away!"

KALISTO:

"Swear by Dazhboh, O Great King!"

KING OF KINGS:

"I swear it!"

In the hall, Lybid and Tarasiy exchange their last few words...

LYBID:

"It would be better if we never see each other again, so as not to torment one another…"

TARASIY:

"I will find a way, my beloved, to make you mine! Even if I have to give my soul to the Evil One!"

LYBID:

"Farewell, my Tarasiy, my love! Tomorrow I leave!"

Lybid rushes off. In the chambers of Queen Zlata Maya she buries her head in her mother's shoulder and gives in to her tears…

LYBID:

"Why can't I live like everybody else?"

ZLATA MAYA:

"So that your life doesn't become like everyone else's! Forget Tarasiy! He will bring you much woe! Everything you have with him is ordinary! And you, my darling daughter, are like the green stalk of wheat that, come autumn, burns like a flame of gold!"

It is the end of August and golden waves of grain cover Rus. Lybid, the Volkhovs Mudroslav and Liubomyr beside her, rides along the edge of the bountiful fields. Atalanta, Kalisto, Palant and a voivode are part of a large group riding behind them, followed by mounted soldiers. And then-several hundred young boys and nymphs, all on horseback, forming a column that winds into the distance like a huge serpent. Bringing up the rear is the young army's train. The procession, gold-and-blue and crimson banners of the royal house fluttering in the breeze, moves slowly through endless fields of ripening wheat.

MUDROSLAV:

> "Our Holy Rus! Our golden fields, blinding with their divine light, nestled in the embrace of sleepy emerald forests! When the winds sweep over and bend the gentle stalks of wheat in a playful dance, the eyes, deceived, perceive a sea of fiery waves, as if Almighty Dazhboh Himself flooded the land with liquid gold!"

LYBID:

> "The land of our fathers-it is the purest gold, Lord Mudroslav!"

Lybid drinks in the beauty of the landscape, dotted in the distance with windmills, their huge arms rotating...

MUDROSLAV:

> "I am happy you agreed to visit this village, which was built by one of my students. A blessed soul! He decided he was not made out to be a Volkhov and he came to these lands from Kyiv City to raise crops! And the land must love him, for his harvests are more bountiful than his neighbors'! The people in these parts gravitated to him, and so he built a village and named it Dazhboh's Garden. See, he sent you gifts, inviting you to be the first to cut his spring wheat crop, which he raised for tribute to your father, the Great King!"

Before Lybid and her party, stopped atop a hillock, opens a panorama of unimaginable beauty. A large village of thatch-roofed, white-washed houses lies below, surrounded on three sides by dense woods, looking out at the fields of golden wheat. Or, perhaps, kneels there in prayer for the bounty.

MUDROSLAV:

"That, my child, is Dazhboh's Garden!"

LYBID:

"I can't remember the last time I laid eyes on such godly beauty!"

The road before them starts winding down the hill.

LYBID:

"And how does this Starosta, this, talk with the land, that it loves him so and from its black belly so much living gold?"

MUDROSLAV:

"It happens because my Starosta loves his land very much and nurtures it! If the earth a living thing, then he is its protective father! that's how! For the fields to love you and to listen to your voice and your voice alone, child, the living land must not be tormented with endless plantings, but must be divided into three parts, three rotations. Sow winter wheat for the coming year, harvest it, fertilize the land again and plow it before the winter snows come. Then sow spring wheat and reap the harvest. The third year the land should be neither plowed nor seeded, but allowed to rest, steam rising. As we would let a wet-nurse, who has been feeding our children. Just as a human being tires – and has nothing more to give, no matter how much he tries-so, too, a field. And here's our, and his good people!"

The Starosta and the village's entire population come out to meet Lybid, Mudroslav and their party at the edge of the village. The Starosta stands at the front, holding the traditional symbols of welcome – salt and bread, on a cloth embroidered in a multitude of colors. Two pretty girls, dressed in holiday garments adorned richly with ornaments that glitter in the sun and wearing garlands of flowers on their heads, stand on either side of him. The rest of the villagers are assembled behind the trio, heads bobbing up and down, as they jump up to get a better glimpse of their young future queen.

STAROSTA:

"With bread and salt, we welcome you, our divine ruler, and pray Dazhboh grant you a long, long life!"

Lybid leaps from her mount; the Starosta offers her the large round palianytsia, while the two maidens bow low before her. Lybid takes the sacred bread in her hands, reverently kisses it, breaks off a piece and places it in her mouth, then passes it on to Mudroslav. He repeats the ritual, then passes the bread on to Atalanta, who does the same. By that time the rest of the column has arrived at the village's edge.

LYBID:

"Glory to Dazhboh, good people of the village

The villagers joyously shout as one, the men throwing their straw hats high into the air: "Glory forever!"

STAROSTA:

"And good health to you also, Mudroslav, my dear teacher."

MUDROSLAV:

"Good health to you, Starosta, my friend!"

Mudroslav and the Starosta embrace. Then, suddenly, the Starosta recognizes Liubomyr.

STAROSTA:

"Lo! Liubomyr! How you've aged! Soon you'll look much like me!"

LIUBOMYR:

"It's the fields that keep you looking so young!"

The Starosta and Liubomyr embrace joyously. The Starosta sees another familiar face.

STAROSTA:

"Lo! Voivode! you're alive!"

VOIVODE:

"And you thought I died in that hellish desert among the camels!"

The two old friends embrace.

VOIVODE:

"I shall send for you when I go to war at the side of the future Queen Lybid!"

STAROSTA:

> "I won't go! You'll just have to forgive me! I will stay and till the soil"

MUDROSLAV:

> "My good people! We shall now conclude the ritual of our ancestors!"

The Starosta gives a signal, and two maidens come up to Lybid. One brings up a full apron of grain, the other – a clay jar filled with water. The Starosta gives another signal – a wink of an eye – and Lybid takes a handful of grain and tosses it into the jar.

MUDROSLAV:

> "The good seeds grew, the heavy seeds, every last one of them-thank god – sank!"

Lybid joyously shouts out the proclamation for which she was invited to the exemplary village.

LYBID:

> "Tomorrow, my good and honest people, we shall together bring in the harvest of Glory to Dazhboh!"

The villagers pick up the cry and it echoes far to the horizon and into the woods "Glory to Dazhboh! Glory forever!"

LYBID:

> "Tell me, Starosta, how do you determine the crop rotation? How do you decide what and when?"

STAROSTA:

"Rye likes dry weather, so it'll grow in sand, if the season be right. We sow the spring wheat once the days are bright. When the roads turn to mud, that's when oats are king. Plant them in water, the timing's the thing. They say plant the buckwheat when the rye is fine and the grass is divine. Barley can be planted, up until trees start to bloom. Spring crops should be planted earlier in good soil, later in poor soil. But in truth, there's just too much to tell it all."

LYBID:

"And why is it important to do it this way, Starosta?"

STAROSTA:

"That is the way our grandfathers did it, and they taught us these ways. Ask the Sun Most Bright, ask the Wind on Easy Wings, ask the Cloud in the Sky. All of them help the tiller. All of them are friends of the fields!"

LYBID:

"Your answer does not fully satisfy me, good Starosta. I shall instruct our learned men, our wise, to study our customs and all the secrets the land has revealed to our ancestors -why and when to plow, what and when to plant and how, as you have said. And I will issue orders that this knowledge be written down in royal tomes, so that is preserved forever!"

Mudroslav turns to the Starosta.

MUDROSLAV:

"Lead the princess and all your guests into your village and make them welcome, as is our custom. I and Atalanta will ride around your village, to take in its beauty!"

Mudroslav and Atalanta mount their horses and gallop through a large flock of sheep up to the edge of a golden field, where men unload long tables from the wagons a woman lay out the plates for tomorrow's feast of the harvest.

MUDROSLAV:

"Glory to Dazhboh, good people!"

VILLAGERS:

"Glory forever to Dazhboh"

MUDROSLAV:

"Getting ready for tomorrow"

VILLAGERS:

"Yes, tomorrow, the feast in honor of the Princess!"

ATALANTA:

"Tell us, good people, are there any dangers hereabouts that might threaten us Princess? So, we could deal with them with nobody being the wiser?"

The men's faces reflect intense concentration, as they think of a way to help the Princess' friends.

MUDROSLA:

"Could there be an evil lurking among the furrows, of which you might not have."

VILLAGER:

"As surely as I stand here! You needn't believe me, ask any woman here. There are evil people in this world who are on good terms with the forces of darkness. And if one of them wishes you ill, he has it in his power to ruin your crops. Hell gathers stalks into a bundle, break them and twist them around into a knot. That's a bend, and there's more than one in a field: they 'll be in many different parts. The area around a bend is trampled down. If you burn a bend, your hands will ache. And if you eat bread from the grain in that field you surely will die!"

ATALANTA:

"So, what is the solution? Do you summon a Volkhovs?"

VILLAGER:

"When the harvest comes, there is no time to call a Volkhovs. We have a simpler solution. A piece of land that's cursed with a bend-we don't touch it, but harvest the surrounding areas. But if your field is dotted with bends, don't expect help from anyone; no one will go, they'll all be afraid..."

ATALANTA:

"Afraid of what?"

VILLAGERS (in chorus):

> "Him, the Evil One!"

ATALANTA:

> "I will rise at dawn and I shall walk the fields. And if I
> find bends among the crops, I shall rip them out!"

An evening feast in honor of Lybid Artemida's arrival takes place in the main square of Dazhboh's Garden, under the vast, thousand-year-old oak tree, the site of the viche, the village meeting that decides the most important issues. Princess Lybid, like an ornament, sits at the head of the main table, surrounded by her closest cohorts. The Starosta is beaming. The honest folk of the village partake of the meats and fish, nuts, milk, honey, berries, bread, meads and many other dishes, whose delicious aroma makes mouths water.

The Starosta stands up, pulls himself up to his full height, and proclaims solemnly.

STAROSTA:

> "Glory to Dazhboh! The Princess of Great Rus is with
> us!"

The villagers all rise and lift their silver goblets to quaff the heady mead.

Meanwhile, Kalisto and Palant sneak away hand-in-hand and find their way to a hayloft. Kalisto tenderly embraces Palant, arousing the passion in him...

KALISTO:

> "I love you, Palant! You, and not the King!"

PALANT:

"But it is his child you carry in your belly, not mine!"

KALISTO:

"Well, he forced himself on me, the Great King did! Raped me! We are all his servants, subject to his will! But it is you I love, and you alone. And even if the King takes me for himself and holds me in the palace, you will come to me each night and my embraces will be even more ardent, my kisses hotter! Our love will burn like an all-con- summing fire!"

Kalisto throws Palant onto the hay and greedily begins to rip off his clothes...

Back at the banquet, the Starosta, in a loud voice and pausing often for dramatic effect, tells of events long past

STAROSTA:

"I have seen how after a drenching rain the sun baked the water-logged soil and covered it with an impenetrable crust. I have seen downpours that tore the crop away by its roots. I have seen hail that broke the stalks of wheat and drove the ears into the soil, to die there!"

Mudroslav whispers in Lybid's ear.

MUDROSLAV:

"Princess, tell them something inspiring, speak to them of the principles of happiness that taught and prosperity that I taught you..."

Lybid rises from her seat and in a strong, commanding, yet gentle voice addresses the villagers.

LYBID:

> "Let us pray, brothers and sisters! Let us ask the Great Dazhboh that we may take our sickles into the fields and bring in the golden harvest before the rains come! I noticed how high the swallows fly, for the air is dry and it will be a long time before the wet season is nigh. The air is dry and warm; and so, I saw that the mosquitoes the swallows feed on fly high in the blue sky. The fish in the lake are not excited and don't leap out of the water. Geese and ducks do not run into the water, don't flap their wings, don't disturb the stillness with their loud cries. Horses don't rub themselves against fences and building walls, nor do they snort or neigh. They don't shake their heads, don't raise them high, nostrils flared, smelling the air! And you won't hear the rooster crow at night when the time's not right, nor the chickens cluck, you won't see the hen gather her chicks under her wing. The crow doesn't bathe, the magpie doesn't preen, doves don't hide and the earthworms have burrowed deep down into the soil! Milk doesn't foam at milking time!

Dogs eat a lot and sleep little, while cats lick their tails and hide not their heads, curled into a ball. spiders-with their plump, wet abdomens especially sensitive to changes in the air – are hard at work in every corner of every house; having crawled out from every crack and crevice, they spin their webs so prolifically there's no place for a fly or mosquito to escape! All of these, good people, are Dazhboh's signs of dry weather!"

In the hayloft, Kalisto moans in orgasmic rapture. Palant, breathing heavily and wet with sweat, rolls off her onto the hay

PALANT:

"I won't be able to endure it! You are mine! I'll kill them all!"

KALISTO:

"Unless you die of fright, I will be yours forever!"

Palant caresses Kalisto's extended abdomen.

PALANT:

"Your belly is so big..."

KALISTO:

"I am tired of having to hide it beneath all this clothing, like a wayward maiden..."

Palant touches a gold medallion-a five-pointed star inside a circle, hanging from a thin chain around Kalisto's neck...

PALANT:

"I have always wanted to ask you, what does this sign mean?"

KALISTO:

"You'll find out when you are worthy. And then you'll have one of your own..."

At the village square, the peasants and their guests spontaneously take to lancing...

Princess Lybid herself, lightheaded and gay from the love and joy that surround her, surrenders to the music and rhythm...

Her dance is interrupted by Kalisto and Palant.

KALISTO:

> "I beg you, O blessed one-allow us to visit my aunt and uncles, who live but an hour's gallop from here. We shall be back by morn. By your leave..."

LYBID:

> "Yes! Go! Protect her, Palant, like no merchant has ever protected a priceless pear for which he has paid an entire harvest!"

PALANT:

> "Not a hair shall fall from her head! And fear not for her maidenhood, O Goddess!"

Kalisto and Palant depart. Lybid walks up to the viche oak and embraces it.

LYBID

> "Why should I have such happiness? For what great deeds am I being rewarded with such a beautiful life? What have I done to deserve so much goodness? I thank Thee, O Great Dazhboh! How beautiful, how sweet life is!"

Sleeping in the Starosta's home, Lybid dreams a beautiful dream. She sees herself, a nymph-child, in a snow-white shirt, a wreath of wild flowers on her head, bathing in a lake. And surrounding her, waist-deep in water and also wearing white, little girls are doing a khorovod, a circle dance, moving gracefully, dreamily, to the languid rhythm of an ancient, enchanting song. The circle opens and Lybid wades to shore, met there by her mother, the Queen Zlata Maya.

LYBID:

"It's so wonderful here, Mother!"

QUEEN MAYA:

"This happy childhood of yours just doesn't want to end!"

LYBID:

"I don't want it to ever end, I want to stay a child forever! I want life to be as wonderful as a circle dance!"

Lybid sees herself wading ashore, no longer a child, but a woman, a beautiful woman at a Kupalo festival. Her long golden hair is adorned with a wreath of white-water lilies and red wild poppies. A snow-white dress that reflects the myriad brilliant colors of the starry night drapes her slim figure down to the ground. Around her waist is a belt of gold, the buckle decorated with flashes of lightning. Lybid walks in a circle of her nymphs and warriors to the Kupalo Willow, which, festooned in flowers and black cherries tied in clusters, stands in the middle of the Sacred Grove. Their senses filled with the sounds, sights and smells of the magical Kupalo's night, the maidens walk to the edge of the

Dnipro. And there each maiden takes the wreath from her head, attaches a lit candle to it and places it on the water of the sacred river. Then to each maiden a youth comes, takes her by the hand and together they run and leap through a bonfire that sends its sparks into the night sky. A handsome kosak runs up to Lybid and boldly takes her by the hand. Lybid looks at him and smiles sadly.

LYBID:

> "And who are you that dares to approach me so boldly?
> And are you not afraid of burning up in the fire?"

KOSAK:

> "I... I... I am Tarasiy..."

Before he can say anything else Lybid races to the bonfire and into the flames, the youth just behind her. She flies high, right up to the sky, the fire racing after her. She stays out of its reach, but the kosak falters and is consumed. Lybid is lifted ever higher toward the Sun. Suddenly, the night turns so bright that her eyes hurt. Lybid, looking for the source of the light, turns towards the heavens and sees the Sun, growing to an enormous size and descending into the earth's atmosphere, until it seems to stand just above her head, burning the very air and setting the surrounding woods, the wheat fields and grass meadows aflame. Only Lybid remains untouched, though the air itself glows orange all around her.

In a voice that is somehow human, yet closer to rolling thunder, the Sun speaks: "Save yourself, little Lybid, little Swan, or you shall perish in the fire!"

Lybid awakens to find Mudroslav shaking her by her shoulders, the note of urgency in his loud, stern voice chasing all drowsiness away.

MUDROSLAV:

> "Get up, child! A fiery blight has fallen upon us! The
> world around us is on fire and wants to consume us
> alive!"

Lybid sees Liubomyr, the voivode, the village Starosta and several other locals standing behind Mudroslav. The room is filled with smoke, while an eerie, flickering light comes in through the window, the air outside filled with human shouts and the cries of panicked livestock.

LYBID:

"What has happened?"

MUDROSLAV:

"Fire everywhere, child! The woods are burning, the wheat fields, even the water boils in the wells. And something else horrible has happened! Someone has tossed the decaying bodies of old dogs into the wells to poison the people and now the wells are worse than opened graves, their water viler than the slimy swamps!"

Lybid quickly and silently dresses and runs into the street, the others following. What she sees shakes her powers of imagination: a solid wall of flames encircles the village, rising to the sky, while billows of black and rust-colored smoke are whipped into wicked whirls by a whistling wind. The fiery circle tightens around the village and looms so near that it makes any thought of flight seemingly hopeless.

LYBID:

"Where did the fire start?"

VOIVODE:

"The surrounding woods and fields were set afire in such a way so as to create a burning trap from which there is no escape. Some hidden, fiendish enemy has plan planned a violent, fiery death for us all!"

Groups of villagers rush past Lybid, shouting, driving cattle, horses and sheep before them. Chickens are running around, screeching, flapping their wings. Dogs are barking and howling, running around confused, unable to decide which way to escape.

VILLAGERS:

> "Run, Princess! Save yourself! The fire! We'll all be burned alive!"

The village is invaded from the woods by its panicked denizens; deer, bears, wild boars, foxes, wolves, squirrels, rabbits, run through the village, seeking safety from the approaching flames. The sky is filled with birds on wing, large and small, until their bodies start raining to the ground as they're overcome in flight by the noxious pall.

LYBID:

> "Horror! Such horror! Too much I gloried in my wonderful life, the night descending!"

The circle of flaming pillars has entered the village and embraced some of the outlying homes; the smoke is so thick that it seems to weigh upon the ground and has turned the day into night, but for a ray of light breaking through from the solar eye in the sky.

Lybid is surrounded by her nymphs and soldiers, all looking at her with an unspoken. What do we do? Written on their worried faces.

The answer comes the next instant, as the wall of flame and the curtain of smoke eerily part, revealing a wedge of blue sky and a distant, clear horizon. Lybid seizes the moment.

LYBID:

> "There! Mount up! And all those on foot – run with all your might!"

Lybid nimbly leaps into her saddle, then turns her stallion towards the village center, the look of courage and controlled determination on her face calming the surrounding mass of humanity that was on the verge of hysteria. When others have their horses, she moves to the front and gallops off towards the opening to safety, then pulls off to the side. The other riders flash by, followed by peasants on foot, many of them pulling children by the hand, carrying infants in their arms. Scores of hunting dogs and wild animals' race past the human column, forgetting in their terror their mutual antagonisms.

As the last straggling villager passes, her, Lybid takes on last look at the village called Dazhboh's Glory and turns her horse towards the daylight that promises escape. But she sees that the living river that was rushing towards salvation has stopped, just as a patch of golden wheat was coming into view. The only road leading out of the settlement is blocked by dead trees piled high and wide; forked yellow-orange tongues rise higher and higher from among their limbs. The hayfield immediately beyond is also catching fire, but a narrow path to the right is still free from the flames and it is there that the frightened mass of people and wildlife flows.

The far side of the fields, however, is blocked off by a thick line of horsemen, all dressed in black. Spits of light escape from their midst, the flaming arrows landing in those sections of the fields that had escaped the conflagration. One of the horsemen has raised high a huge black flag affixed to his lance, mocking his trapped victims, or, perhaps, signaling a conspirator in the distance.

LYBID:

"Who are those men?"

STAROSTA:

"Probably the band of marauders that recently appeared in these lands, God knows rom where. It is they who set

57

the woods and fields on fire, to burn us all alive, the devils!"

Lybid studies the apocalyptic scene: the enemy archers let loose their flaming arrows, which fall among the wheat or reach some of the peasants who had rushed ahead into the open fields. The unfortunates shriek in pain and, engulfed in flames, run blindly about, the human torches.

LYBID:

"Damn them to hell! Whose archers, are they?"

VOIVODE:

"The devil's! Trained by the Evil One himself!"

Seeing Lybid through the smoke and fire, the strangers in black let loose a chilling chorus of war cries and let fly their arrows towards the shining figure sitting high in the saddle. But the distance is too great, and the fiery missiles fall harmlessly to the ground.

Atlanta spurs her horse and flies to her leader's side. Leaping off her mount, she takes her mighty bow in her hands, runs through the wheat to where an enemy arrow has landed and picks it up. She looks back at Lybid, who nods to her.

LYBID:

"The one with the banner..."

Atalanta draws the bowstring far back, holds it for a full breath and let's fly. The traces a low fiery arc, and two seconds later buries itself square in the abdomen of the standard bearer. His steed rears up on his hind legs, neighs in terror and bolts. The riders screams fill the air, as the rushing wind fans the flames spreading from the dark ed spot on his black tunic. His lance snagged in the bridle; the black flag drags on the behind.

The marauders quickly turn their mounts and race to safety, out of range of Atalanta's avenging arrows. A moment of shock, and then a triumphant cheer goes up from Lybid's and the villagers who witnessed the electrifying deed.

VOIVODE:

> "God bless your sharp eye and steady hand, young warrior! Among all of the countless soldiers of Rus, only two or three could match your skill with a bow!"

Lybid's gaze follows the retreating assassins, then abruptly settles on windmills scattered over the once peaceful fields, first one, then another and a third and fourth. The wind turns their huge burning arms, and it seems to Lybid that these are gentle giants dying fiery death and waving to her a last farewell.

LYBID:

> "Starosta! What can you tell me about these murderers? Where are they from?"

STAROSTA:

> "I do not know where they came from, Princess. But they have been pillaging the, countryside, raiding settlements, carrying our young women off into the woods. The people say that deep in the forest thickets they have a house on chicken legs, hidden under the cliffs, moving about... These bandits bury the treasure they've rob from rich people, and cover the site with a huge stone. And over these stones a fire burns, and twice week – so people claim-a child's agonizing cry is heard, always at midnight."

LYBID:

"I promise you, Starosta: If I survive this day, if I'm not burned alive, like a chicken on a spit, I and my warriors will find this den of thieves and burn it down. And the murderers themselves I shall turn over to you and your righteous people, to face your justice! I give you my royal word!"

MUDROSLAV:

"We must go, else we perish in the fire!"

At this time, on a distant hilltop opening up to a breathtaking vista of the Rus countryside, Kalisto and Palant stand in a tight embrace, their gaze focused on a pillar of fire in the distance, like a sorcerer rising from the primeval woods and reaching for the sky with his hand of smoke.

Dazhboh's Garden. Throngs of villagers have gathered around the viche oak with their livestock and treasured belongings. The raging fire has consumed most of the village and is advancing on the only place of refuge left, the central square. People are coughing and covering their mouths and noses with cloths, in order not to be overcome by the thick smoke. Terrified voices are heard: " We'll all be burned alive! " " There's no escape!"

Lybid and her soldiers ride into the square. Seeing them, the people run up to her and plead desperately: " Save us, Princess! Save our children from death!'

Above their cries rises a sound heard only from a fire so awesome it creates a wind and weather all its own...

LYBID:

> "Lord Mudroslav and loyal Liubomyr! Volkhuy! There is nothing left for us to do, but to call down a deluge from the heavens!"

MUDROSLA:

> " We will pray to Dazhboh Almighty for his help, and to Perun for his anger!"

Lybid, Mudroslav and Liubomyr dismount, join hands, facing each other in a triangle, and begin moving clockwise. Mudroslav's volkhvy form a circle around then, moving counterclockwise. The villagers, burned out of their homes and trying to save their lives, form their own large outer circle, and begin moving in the same direction a Lybid and the high volkhuy.

LYBID:

> "Our Father Dazhboh, and all my divine ancestors: Perun, Veles, Svaroh, Siva.   Yarylo, Khors and Koliada..."

The people pick up her passionate prayer and their voices join together and rise as one, almost drowning out Lybid's...

LYBID:

> " O heavenly children of Dazhboh! I call upon you to help us in this our hour of mortal danger! Come to me in all your glorious might!"

Suddenly, the wind picks up and brings in tall, swirling clouds, which hang like a black shroud over the village. The only light in this day-turned-night comes from the fire leaping from the buildings in the village and the woods and fields outside, bathing in eerie shades of red, orange and yellow the clouds above, the ubiquitous smoke and the entranced faces of people performing their ancient ritual for divine intercession.

LYBIID:

> "O Dazhboh! Do not allow us to perish in the flames! Come to my aid, O heavenly family of mine. Open the skies and let a mighty deluge come forth, a sea that pours down upon the Earth and quenches this infernal conflagration!"

Lightning strikes flash across the sky and the air vibrates with the deep, rumbling rolls of thunder, as if the heavens were responding in their frightening voice. The people wail in terror, bunch closer together and renew their desperate dance with a new energy.

LYBID:

> "Open, O heavenly floodgates!"

A blinding streak of lightning rends the sky, a thunderous clap assaults the senses and rivers of rain descend on the awestruck crowd. The air is filled with the hissing sound of fires doused, steam exploding and the screams of people scalded by the super-heated vapor. All that is standing, and the ground itself, are transformed, painted dark gray by one broad stroke of a gigantic brush: the torrents on their downward journey have met the ash, soot, sparks and debris filling the air and swirling up from the fires below and, like a volcano spewing ash, pour the hot ooze on the humans below.

LYBID:

> "Glory to Dazhboh!"

PEOPLE (feelings of exhilaration having numbed their pain):

> "Glory forever to our Dazhboh!"

Home of the White Volkhv in Kyiv, City of Kings. The Lord of the Temple, dressed in modest everyday clothes, is on his knees, praying to the gods of ancient Rus.

The room is illuminated by the light of several thick wax candles, while outside the night window a thunderstorm rage.

WHITE VOLKHV:

"O Great Dazhboh! Grant Holy Rus peace and prosperity and bless our King with wisdom and mercy!"

Unexpectedly, two frightened servants burst into the room.

SERVANT:

"The King is here! By himself!"

SERVANT WOMAN:

"He is here already, in the building!"

WHITE VOLKHV:

"I must get dressed!"

But before he can even get up off his knees, the Great King himself walks into the room, his royal garments dripping rainwater...

KING OF KINGS:

"Glory to Dazhboh!"

WHITE VOLKHV:

"Glory forever!"

KING OF KINGS:

"I am happy to see you, Lord!"

The King warmly embraces the high priest, taking care not to get him too wet. The Volkhov looks sternly at the servants, who stand transfixed by the sight of the Sovereign.

WHITE VOLKHV:

"Be gone!"

The servants, brought back to reality, scurry out of the room.

WHITE VOLKHV:

"I am honored by a visit from the Great King in the middle of the night! You are drenched! Why have you ventured out in such a storm, with rain pouring as from a bottomless bucket! The King has no right to risk his health, for he is responsible for the destiny and happiness of his people!"

KING OF KINGS:

"I feel as if I threw off thirty years! I must tell you, my spiritual teacher, who are like second father to me, a father sent by God!"

WHITE VOLKHV:

"Tell me!"

KING OF KINGS:

"Lord, I... I am in love!"

WHITE VOLKHV:

"What I see is that my King is acting like a boy, come to me in the middle of the with such news! This is a joke, yes?"

KING OF KINGS:

"A bit more serious than that! I am madly in love with Kalisto, a servant of my daughter, who is already pregnant with my heir! I want Kalisto to become my wife! I have come to you in the middle of the night because I need the temple's support for this marriage!"

WHITE VOLKHV:

"And what of your lawful wife, Queen Zlata Maya? I had feared that Byzantium had invaded us, or perhaps the Goths, but this is something even more terrible and dangerous!"

KING OF KINGS:

"I am happy!"

WHITE VOLKHV:

"And I? I am frightened to death by this news! New changes will again sweep over Rus... We just got the people of Rus, the nation's we conquered and all of the kings of the world – the ones that all our allies, as well as our enemies -accustomed to..."

KING OF KINGS:

"To what?"

WHITE VOLKHV:

"To the pantheon of the living gods Rus worships, the gods you are now trying to replace! And this means that we will have to teach all these peoples all over again. Get them accustomed to the new names! This will take years! I may not live that long! And to cast away one set of your children, in order to elevate those yet to be born..."

KING OF KINGS:

"So, the Temple is against?..."

WHITE VOLKHV:

"The Temple cannot be against its beloved King. Nor can it even be in disagreement with him. It always agrees, if there is something you need... But that is not how thing are done, Great King... You amuse yourself in debauchery with a mere child, and I must summon the Volkhovs from all the corners of the empire to decide how the Temple of Dazhboh will respond to this sordid affair!"

KING OF KINGS:

"Then decide in my favor!"

WHITE VOLKHV:

"You have my word! I will convene our council immediately!"

The King impulsively embraces the high priest.

KING OF KINGS:

"I am grateful to you, O Lord of human souls!"

WHIITE VOLKHL:

"I will come to you myself with my advice on what is to be done."

KING OF KINGS:

"Good night to you, my spiritual teacher! Glory to Dazhboh!"

WHITE VOLKHV:

"Glory forever!"

The King leaves the room. The high priest calls his secretary.

WHIITE VOLKHV:

" Dionisiy!"

The secretary enters the room with a quill, a small jar of ink and a paper scroll in his hands.

WHITE VOLKHV:

"You heard our conversation?"

DIONISIY:

"A great misfortune awaits Rus! Our King has completely lost his head over the young body of this damned Kalisto! And we can't refuse the King, lest the country be split in two!"

WHITE VOLKHV:

"Dionisiy, this is what you must do: go inform the spiritual teachers of Princess Lybid Artemida, the honorable Mudroslay and his son Liubomyr, about all this. They must reach an agreement with the Princess, in the event we're not able to rein in the King. Where are they now?"

DIONISIY:

"A carrier pigeon will find them!"

WHITE VOLKHV:

"Yes! Praise be to God! Send the feathered messenger at once!"

Lybid, covered from head to foot in ash and soot, sits tall in the saddle, surveying the burning hideout of the marauders. The fort, hidden deep in a forest ravine, consists of a score or so of tall, impressive structures built of heavy oak, with steep roofs – buildings that could easily pass for a noble's manor-all surrounded by a wall of tall, spiked timbers and a wide moat filled with fetid swamp water. The spikes above the gate were adorned with the heads of hostages slaughtered when their families failed to pay the ransom, as well as the skulls of horses, cattle and goats. A flock of cawing crows circles above the fortress, suggesting a sort of kinship with the raiders. Inside the walls a life- and-death battle rages between Lybid' s warriors and the marauders, resounding with the of swords, the cries of the wounded, the groans of the dying.

Suddenly, the gates of the fort open and a group of raiders -some on horseback, others on foot – break out in a desperate bid to escape.

LYBID (shouting):

"Glory to Dazhboh!"

The princess spurs her steed and, drawing her sword, races after the fleeing bandits. a dozen of her warriors hot on her heels. Moments later the hacked bodies of the horse lest fugitives lie scattered over the ravine floor, while the swift arrows from Atalanta's bow bring down the hapless riders one by one.

Lybid turns her mount and rushes through the open gate into the murderers' den, only to see her soldiers finishing off the last of the few still standing.

The voivode rides up to her side.

LYBID:

"You fought with great courage and skill!"

VOIVODE:

"For you, Divine Lady, I would conquer the world!"

LYBID:

"There had to be at least a hundred of them here!"

Riding with Lybid through the piles of dead and dying marauders and their abandoned weapons, the voivode excitedly describes the winning battle.

VOIVODE:

"I believe I've solved the puzzle! They built this stronghold and launched their raids from here, often on the holy days. When our people gathered in the Sacred

Groves and temples to pray to Dazhboh, these murderers would raid the local markets, take everything of value and torch the village. The people could stand no more and started to organize a resistance. Three counties had already agreed to unite their forces and were ready to march against this stronghold. But you got here first, Princess! As soon as they saw us outside their walls, the bandits started to bury all of their hordes of stolen treasure in the ground. And not simply to bury but to put a curse on it, so that it would never fall into the hands of anyone else... And their ataman was ready to fall to the ground, in order to turn into a black crow and fly away. But your devoted warrior Atalanta put an arrow through his leg, and we were able to capture him and several dozen of his bloodthirsty killers!"

LYBID:

"Bravo, Atalanta!"

ATALANTA:

"Forever with you, Princess!"

The Ataman and the rest of the captured raiders sit on the ground in gloomy silence, except for the moans of the wounded.

LYBID:

"Pans, are they?"

Lybid points out that every one of the captives wears a helmet topped with a goat's horns and goatskin, in the manner of Germanarix, king of the Goths.

VOIVODE:

"Pans! The scum! it's the peasants that named them 'Pan'!"

Mudroslav rides up to Lybid.

MUDROSLAV:

"Pans. Strange how Germanarix is so popular among these cutthroats that they emulate him in most everything they do! they're all dressed like him! Like the god Pan!

So that in the night they would look like devils with goat's legs and horns!"

Lybid leaps from her horse and walks up to the captives.

LYBID:

"Why did you come to pillage the land of Holy Rus? You set the woods and fields on fire; you poisoned the wells. You thought I would die in the flames, together with my nymphs, my warriors and all the good people of the village. And then you would come and through the burned-out ruins, searching for gold and silver and precious stones..."

Women's hysterical screams are heard coming from inside a burning stable. Lybid's soldiers lift the timber barring the doors and out into the yard rush ten sobbing, half-naked young women, who had been kidnapped by the marauders from nearby Rus villages.

Lybid walks into the raiders' massive temple, built of rough-hewn, heavy logs. A wounded priest, his Gothic ceremonial robes splattered with his own blood, throws him- at her feet.

GOTH PRIEST:

"Mercy, Princess! I beg you! Spare my life! I am not to blame!"

The voivode's swift kick in the rump sends the holy man sprawling.

VOIVODE:

"Take him away!"

Two soldiers grab the priest by the arms and drag him away screaming in terror. Meanwhile, Lybid is staring at a life-size wooden figure standing in the center of the temple, obviously the object of the bandits' veneration. Carved masterfully from a single block of oak, the idol is not a representation but an astonishingly true likeness of King Germanarix. His bulging eyes of emerald shine with an imbecilic malevolence.

LYBID (gasps):

"It's Germanarix, King of the Goths! My odious suitor! Reaching with his hairy paws deep into Holy Rus! Let's go!"

Flushed with fury, Lybid walks up to the marauders sitting tied up on the floor.

LYBID:

"This is who you worship here? King Germanarix, who plunders all over Europe?"

ATAMAN:

"The god Pan is our god!"

MUDROSLAV:

"Fool!"

Mudroslav turns to the village Starosta, who has just appeared with the local. The villagers, burned out of their homes and hungry, rush over to a large kettle hanging the fireplace and help themselves to the fragrant, hot borsch.

MUDROSLAV:

"Starosta! Burn down this bordello and put a curse on this place of misery!"

The smoking ruins of the village. A roar rises from the peasants, as Lybid Artemida and her warriors enter, bringing the captured thieves for trial before the people. Curses are hurdled at the prisoners; a few women have broken through the circle of guards and pummel the captives with their fists.

The throng makes its way to the village square and stops under the ancient oak, its mighty trunk and limbs ravaged by fire. As the trial begins, charges fly at the prisoners - of husbands, sons and brothers killed, daughters and wives carried off...

STAROSTA:

"Ataman! And all you other accursed, whose names we shall not mention so that the sooner you and the evil you did be forgotten! You are guilty of violating our girls and women, of murder and pillage, arson, poisoning wells, burning crops and forests and our dwellings! Your punishment is death!"

The mob goes berserk, turning into a savage animal ready to pounce and tear the bandits to pieces. They stop in their tracks at the ataman's desperate cry, sharp as the crack of a whip.

The mob goes berserk, turning into a savage animal ready to pounce and tear the bandits to pieces. They stop in their tracks at the ataman's desperate cry, sharp as the crack of a whip.

ATAMAN:

"People, stop! I will give you all my hidden treasure, if you let us live! Gold and silver and bronze, enough so that your children, your grandchildren and your descendants will not have to work for 300 years! You'll live like that nobles at the royal court! No, better, much better, if only you spare our lives!"

LYBID:

"And what is this treasure you propose to trade for your life, from these people who have lost everything?"

ATAMAN:

"I have gold and silver beyond counting! All my life I have hoarded treasure, more than you can imagine!"

LYBID:

"Speak!"

ATAMAN:

"I have buried treasure everywhere, O Divine Lybid! Know this, good Princess! There is a boat loaded with silver that I had buried in the sands, but it can only be reached if the river is drained. And hidden in secret hollow trees deep in the forest are chests full of luxurious robes spun of gold and silver and encrusted with precious gems, and icons of Dazhboh, burning with pure gold! But all of this is protected by a curse for 300 years!"

LYBID:

"Absolute nonsense!"

Lybid's words break the spell the ataman's tale had cast over the mob, which roars anew and surges towards the captives. The ataman's screams grow louder.

ATAMAN:

"Stop, all your poor people! I also have hidden under the banks of the mighty Dnipro-Slavuta twelve sacks full of gold and silver, so heavy that only a barge hauler can lift them!

VOIVODE:

"Don't listen to this cutthroat!"

ATAMAN:

"Let me live, good people! I haven't told you everything! There is a wondrous cave in Obolon on the Dnipro-Slavuta, with four barrels full of gold suspended on chains, and guarded by a monstrous bear!"

VOIVODE:

> "Lies, all of it! Good people, these are old tales told by robbers into order to delay their hour of violent death! A condemned bandit will stay the hand of justice for years by promising mounds of non-existent treasure. And, shackled in chains, he'll lead the king' men around for years, their shovels digging up the forest in a search for treasure that isn't there. He plays them for fools, saying he has forgotten where the treasure lies buried, but he'll recall where under torture or in his sleep, and so on!

The Starosta grabs the ataman by the scruff of the neck.

STAROSTA:

> "Uproot this devil! Now!"

LYBID:

> "What does that mean, Lord Mudroslav!"

MUDROSLAV

> "It's an ancient form of punishment reserved for bandits, Princess! The Rusychi use it to this day. So that the body of the robber would be forever held down by the crushing weight of a mighty oak tree, never to rise from under the earth, his soul never to return in a different body!"

Lybid looks on with interest as the peasants cut the roots on one side of the viche oak.

Meanwhile, Mudroslav and others tell her some folk tales

MUDROSLAV:

"The locals here like to tell each other tales about the proper way of securing a robber's treasure. If the treasure that is unearthed turns into a wild animal or even a person, one must strike it backhanded with the left hand, saying, 'Glory to Dazhboh! Spill it!' Without this it is not possible to possess the treasure. They say there was an old beggar woman from Pochayiv, who was wandering all around a village, and a rooster stuck to her, tugged at the hem of her skirt, threw himself at her feet and when she finally struck with her cane, he disintegrated into a pile of gold coins!"

STAROSTA:

"One evening an old man happened to be walking from his village into town., Suddenly, there's a loud noise in the middle of the field and he sees a barrel rolling towards him and he hears a loud voice: 'Call out the devil!' The frightened old man stepped aside and as the barrel rolled past him, he heard the distinct ring of coins!"

MUDROSLAV:

"He should have called on Dazhboh to break the barrel open with a thunderbolt. It would have spilled gold or silver coins and the old man would have had two thirds, giving one third to Dazhboh's temple!"

VOIVODE:

"Some time ago some of my lads, having applied burning coals to the feet of captured robbers in. order to loosen their tongues, went out to search for their buried treasure. And along the way they urged an old man, who lived by himself at the edge of the village, to help them find the treasure. But the old man refused, saying, If Dazhboh wills it, he'll even toss the treasure through the window. On the way back my soldiers saw a dead ram lying under a bush and decided to throw it through the old man's window. Upon rising in the morning, the old man sees a dead ram lying in the middle of his modest home. He prays, then takes the ram by the feet in order to toss it outside and the ram bursts open, spilling royal gold hryvnias. that's what happened!"

MUDROSLAV

"Now it is you who is lying! What no doubt happened was that the robbers themselves sewed the hryvnias inside the ram and when they were being pursued by your fierce boys, they dropped it! But what people tell about us, the, servants of God, is honest truth! There was a young Volkhov and every day a stranger with a beard and unkempt hair and dressed in a torn blue shirt would appear to him. He would appear and then run into the pigsty and disappear, and always in the same place. Our young Volkhov figured out what this was all about and started digging in that spot. He dug a deep hole and came upon a beer kettle covered with a skillet. He was about to pull it out when he heard a loud, deep voice saying, 'And what are you doing here, good man? What the devil do you want?' And this young Volkhov had the sense to go summon his old Volkhov master and they decided to pull up the kettle together, just as it was about to sink deep into the earth. And both off them became very rich men!"

LYBID:

> "These are all tall tales, told to simpletons, Lord
> Mudroslav! I think that your Volkhov, the young one
> and the old, are both thieves! What probably happened
> is that a wealthy man, confessing to them on his
> deathbed, told them the secret of gold he had stolen and
> buried. And they, in order to avoid paying taxes to the
> king and explaining their sudden riches to the people,
> lied. They told the simple folks the tall tale of how the
> gold, through a miracle of God, came to them itself
> from under the earth! Just wait till the White Volkhv
> gets a hold of them! He'll grab them by the throat with
> his bony fingers and shake them by their shameless
> beards!"

The peasants, using long poles for leverage, have lifted up the long roots
on one side of the oak, creating enough space to slide a human body
underneath.

The ataman is screaming and cursing, as if possessed.

LYBID:

> "I will no doubt never see anything like this in Kyiv!"

The villagers, with the help of a few of the soldiers, push the bound
Ataman under the oak's tentacles.

ATAMAN:

> "Princess! I will give you and you alone my greatest
> treasure hoard, which I hid in the Devil's Grove! Ten
> barrels of royal gold hryvnias of last year's mintage All
> for you, if you spare my life!"

LYBID:

> "That will be the last lie you ever tell! The gold hryvnias
> – the entire ten barrels my father had minted last year –
> were distributed to merchants, secured by their goods,
> and today the gold is again in the royal treasury, repaid
> as taxes!"

MUDROSLAV:

> "Farewell, cutthroat!"

The Ataman struggles with his last surge of strength, his shrieks filling the air. But as the villagers quickly pull out the long poles that held the oak tilted, the mighty tree returns to its place, crushing the ataman. The shrieking stops abruptly, as if a stone lid had been placed over a coffin.

MUDROSLAN:

> "'Under rooted,' he is! The customs of Rus are
> sometimes very harsh! The ataman was to blame. And
> for this he has paid with his life!"

Lybid now turns her eyes to the great throng of people who lost everything in the fire and who now gaze with hope at her. What will their future queen tell them? How are they to begin their lives anew?

LYBID:

> "Good people! Your Dazhboh's Grove, your paradise,
> has been burned to the ground! The wells have been
> poisoned and the surrounding woods burned. The life
> that you have known here is no more! You have no
> water. Your crops have been destroyed. Soon you will
> begin to die from thirst and disease, if you stay here."

VILLAGERS (shouting):

"Where are we to go"

LYBID:

"Go and bury your dead! And then. I shall lead you to water! To the river! You will save yourselves and begin a new life! The fish in the river will save you from hunger, while you build your new homes and sow your crops!"

Lybid leads the way on her charger, followed by her soldiers, then the nymphs, and finally the great mass of villagers, driving what is left of their livestock, as the princess' yelping hunting dogs rush up and down the flanks. Setting out in search of a new life, they look back one last time at the smoking ruins of their homes, over which towers the ancient oak, the bodies of several score marauders swinging from its mighty limbs.

The Palace of Volkhv Councils in Kyiv, the City of Kings. The White Volkhv, grim and anxious, strides purposefully into the main hall.

WHITE VOLKHV:

"I have gathered you here, my brothers, in response to a grave danger that looms over Rus. A danger that can lead to a breakdown in authority and law and order! What I am about to tell you must die together with us!"

VOLKHVY:

"The secrets you tell us will never pass our lips! This is not the first time..."

WHITE VOLKHV:

"The Great King has lain with Kalisto, one's of the Divine Lybid's nymphs! She is carrying the king's new successor!"

VOLKHVY:

"Horrors! What horror!"

WHITE VOLKHV:

"The King has lost his head over Kalisto! He wants to take her for a wife and make her his queen!"

VOLKHVY:

"It cannot be! The shame of it! Instead of Queen Zlata Maya?"

WHITE VOLKHV:

"I must know who is responsible for this hideous plan! Who orchestrated this? Who instructed Kalisto? The Byzantines, perhaps? Whose spies are behind this new attempt to divide up power in Rus? Who put the serpent into the king's bed?"

VOLKHVY:

"We will get to the bottom of this! We will sort it out!"

WHITE VOLKHV:

"I order you to get on with this task immediately! The Temple commands it! We are a thousand pair of eyes watching what happens in this, god's world! We are in all the states on Earth and in the chambers of every king! I ask you to use all your powers, your every influence, to find the culprit and to see he is punished, thus destroying this conspiracy!"

The White Volkhv pauses, looking around at the gathered spiritual leaders of Rus.

VOLKHV:

"Let us pray, O brothers, that Almighty God enlightens our wise Lybid as to how she must act, so that this danger is averted through peaceful means and with no harm befalling Holy Rus!"

The White Volkhov raise his arms high, as the assembled priests pray together.

Lybid, her face and clothes covered with soot and ash and surrounded by warriors likewise smeared, sits on her stallion high on a hilltop. Her eyes take in the blue width of a river meandering below, then stop on a wide brush-covered sandy spit of land surrounded on three sides by a watery loop. The banks are overgrown with thick groves and – a beautiful place, a paradise on Earth!

Thousands of people, weary from the long journey, let loose a joyful shout and rush in the river, along with horses, livestock and hunting dogs, all driven by a fierce thirst. Nymphs, boys, soldiers and peasants, men and women, plunge run into the water, drink the water, bathe, wash the clothes they are wearing.

After a while the people begin to take their garments off and the river bank is soon turned into a realm of the nude.

LYBID:

"I want soldiers standing guard here day and night; the river to the left of the cape is for men, to the right – for women!"

MUDROSLAV:

"Well done!"

VOIVODE:

"I have given the orders, Princess!"

LYBID:

"The people are not to mingle!

LIUBOMYR:

"I have found a place, O Divine One, where you may bathe far from human eyed There no one will disturb your."

LYBID:

"I can wash up and change into royal wear, thank God!"

Suddenly, a dove appears out of nowhere and hovers wearily over Lybid and he entourage.

MUDROSLAV:

"A feathered messenger has arrived, Princess!"

Mudroslay extends his arm and the dove sets down on his hand.

MUDROSLAV:

> "We welcome you, little one! What news do you bring us from Kyiv City?"

Mudroslay takes the bird to his bosom, pets it and expertly retrieves a tiny scroll tied to a tiny leg. He walks up to Liubomyr and together they read the message sent by the White Volkhv in coded script.

VOIVODE:

> "The best kind of messenger! he'll never reveal his secrets, because he doesn't speak human and Dazhboh for the time being has not deemed us worthy of understanding the language of our feathered friends!"

The two Volkhovs finish reading the note.

MUDROSLAV:

> "Princess, we have to talk, just the three of us. In your tent, so that no one can hear. Voivode! Set out guards around the princess' tent and order them to be vigilant, so that nothing is overheard!"

Lybid Artemida's tent. Lybid sits in her traveling throne, while the two are nervously pacing back and forth.

MUDROSLAV:

> "I just received some news, Princess! News that are quite insane! It seems that you nymph, Kalisto, has lain with your father and is in the seventh month with his child. She has been hiding her protruding belly under a pile of skirts and coats!"

LYBID:

"I do not believe what I hear!"

MUDROSLAV:

"Nevertheless, it is true! And your father has decided to make Kalisto his wife! Which means that your mother will be pushed aside, in order to allow Kalisto to become queen, in her stead! And, obviously, the newborn will be become the king or queen after the death of your father, may God give him health and long life!"

LYBID:

"I am thunderstruck!"

MUDROSLAV:

"Your father has sent priestesses trained as midwives, along with a company of cavalry to escort Kalisto to Kyiv as the queen! They will be here within three days. The priestesses will assist with the delivery, if need be..."

LYBID:

"What shocking news! I'll lose the throne! What will happen to Boos? And to all my kin on mother's side? Kalisto will triumph! My father will distance himself from us, to the delight of all our enemies and even my loathsome suitors!"

MUDROSLAV:

"This is someone's revenge, Princess! Kalisto is but a puppet, through whose loins a dark someone is manipulating your father. The White Volkhov has begun investigating this entire affair. He has sent secret agents far and wide! His spies are everywhere! Sooner or later, we will find out who is behind this!'

LYBID:

"Later? Or sooner? Right now, I am covered in mud... Oh, if only I could wash off the filth that has been poured over my soul! Order the nymphs to accompany me to the river!

And then I will decide what must be done... Kalisto is here and she is not going anywhere! I will deal with her! I will be by the river, cleansing myself."

Lybid and a large group of nymphs, escorted by Liubomyr and two dozen other Volkhovs, walk along the sandy beach, past hundreds of nude bathers, male and female, of all ages. The people shout to her: "Hail, Princess! But Lybid is so distraught, so lost in the woe that has befallen her, that she neither hears nor sees them.

Suddenly, Lybid's gaze falls on a female figure that stands out among the hundreds of naked female bodies. it's Kalisto, dressed from head to toe and filthy as Death itself.

Lybid heads toward her, smiling sweetly.

LYBID:

"Ah, my dearest friend! Why aren't you bathing, like all the others?"

KALISTO:

> "it's cold. And I'm shivering. I'll bathe later. At night, by the light of the moon!"

LYBID:

> "Well, do as you wish. But at least wash your face!"

Suddenly, Kalisto gasps as a wave of nausea hits her and she runs to the bushes to vomit.

LYBID:

> "Why, you're quite ill, Kalisto! Atalanta!"

The young woman appears by Lybid's side.

LYBID:

> "Atalanta, you and I will go bathe. Then you will return here for Kalisto and take the poor maiden to my tent! It seems that Father Sun has made her sick! See, He has cast His heavenly light upon poor Kalisto and she's feeling nauseous, as if she were pregnant!"

Kalisto visibly blanches, as Lybid reaches over to kiss her on her cheek, before leading her nymphs away. A short distance later, Lybid whispers to Atalanta...

LYBID:

> "Kalisto vomited because she is pregnant. That is why she declines to bathe, because she is ashamed to show her big belly. She bathes by herself, and only by moon light, in order not to get caught!"

ATALANTA:

"If you wish it, Princess, I will drown her at night..."

LYBID:

"With a child in her womb? I feel so betrayed! By my own father! And the great shame that awaits me! O Great Dazhboh! Give me strength!"

Lybid and the nymphs are bathing nude in the river. The maidens, singing and holding hands, dance in a circle around her. But their beloved princess is inconsolable, and gazes sadly at her own reflection in the water.

Meanwhile, the betrayal reaches a new stage... Palant leads Kalisto beyond the royal camp, splendid with the brilliant colors of the tents and banners, and into the deep woods. There, in a meadow, waits a company of young horsemen, eager to drink of the love of Lybid Artemida's young nymphs. They are led by Tarasiy.

KALISTO:

"It is time to put an end to the divine innocence of Lybid Artemida! I have grown tired of waiting. Why do you hesitate, bridegrooms? A bit terrified, are we?"

TARASIY:

"Her Majesty's Lybid Artemida's protective detail is off on patrol in different directions. We would have never been able to sneak in so close to the camp if it hadn't been Palant's turn to command the Princess' guard for these twenty-four hours. It was he who sent the mounted patrols off in the opposite direction, so that we could safely gather here."

PALANT:

"I will be relieved at sunrise tomorrow. So, we only have this day! And if the new patrol finds you here, they'll give you a good licking and chase you off!"

TARASIY:

"Let's go over our plan one more time..."

PALANT:

"As we agreed, I will lead you all to the isolated place on the river where Lybid is bathing with her nymphs. The place is quite a distance from the camp and unguarded. After all, they're all naked, and who would dare gaze at a goddess in the nude?"

TARASIY:

"And what about the Volkhovs...?"

PALANT:

"The Volkhovs will go into the forest to pray, so as not to be tempted by the nude maidens. You will scatter them all throughout the woods, like rabbits! And if they dare to resist, tie them up like children! These are priests, innocents!"

TARASIY:

"I'll take the princess by force, and you, lads, round up the nymphs..."

The young horsemen, their hormones raging, laugh lustily...

TARASIY:

"Virgins, my lads! Immaculate maids, all of them! As if selected for the temple!"

KALISTO:

"Their fathers, in order to avoid the shame to the family name, will be forced to give them to you as wives, and you will rise to the ranks of the celebrated!"

PALANT:

"As easy as that!"

The "suitors" exchange lascivious looks and remarks...

KALISTO:

"And you, Tarasiy, rejoice! Very soon you shall lay down with Lybid Arntemida herself, and she will conceive your child. After that, who among the rulers of Europe will want her for his bride? It is you who will become the King's son-in-law!"

TARASIY:

"And you, Kalisto, should likewise rejoice! The great King has sent a large detachment of knights to escort you back to Kyiv City as his future queen! We were able to outride them by one day only! We are here today and tomorrow they shall be in this place... And you will be our queen!"

Kalisto beams and claps her hands with joy, while Palant turns glum.

91

KALISTO (turning to Palant):

> "I will keep my promise, my beloved! The time will come when I will be your wife!"

TARASIY:

> "Lead us, Palant, my brother!"

Lybid is bathing in the river. The nymphs are lying on the sand, joking and laughing, while their princess is standing knee-deep in the water, looking down sadly and absentmindedly making circles in the water with her hands, moving the yellow water lilies around.

Behind the near-by bushes, Tarasiy is watching Lybid.

PALANT:

> "We go. God speed, Tarasiy!"

TARASIY:

> "Go!"

Palant and Kalisto depart.

TARASIY (whispering to his cohorts):

> "Here it is, lads! The prey is before you! Off with your clothes! To battle!"

The "bridegrooms," following Tarasiy's lead, tear off their clothing in a lustful frenzy.

Meanwhile, a Volkhov has crept close to Tarasiy and his band behind a camouflage of bushes and leaves...

And, nearby, the Volkhvs are standing over several of the youths, who lay bound on the ground.

LIUBOMYR:

> "I won't even bother to send for the soldiers in the camp, you miserable heathens! I shall deal with all of you myself!"

One of the captives unexpectedly frees himself and grabs a sword that was lying on the ground. As he lunges at Liubomyr, the Volkhv feints and sends him sprawling with a hooking kick to the ankles. The boy is soon sitting bound on the grass again.

LIUBOMYR:

> "Foo! We are more than Volkhvs! When the White Volkhv cannot trust the military, we become warriors-Volkhvs! The finest young beauties of Holy Rus are there, alone! And I have orders from the Lord of the Temple to put to the sword anyone who would dare lust after these sacred virgins!"

The eyes of the prisoners bulge out of their sockets in fear, as the volkhvy cast off their white robes to reveal suits of mail and swords hanging at their sides.

The Volkhv scout appears.

VOLKHV:

> "I found them, Lord Liubomyr! The 'suitors' are getting naked and ready in the bushes."

LIUBOMYR:

> "Volkhvs, follow me! Radomyr, show us the way! Glory to Dazhboh!"

At the beach, the bushes part and Tarasiy's youths, laughing and whooping, rush at the nymphs, who scream in fright and surprise. The boys are upon them before they can run.

TARASIY:

> "Take these Amazons!"

The amorous attackers throw themselves at their naked prey, grabbing their arms and trying to pin them down in the sand. The girls, still screaming, try to fight back, biting and scratching. But only one, Atalanta, is able to free herself and break away. Six naked "suitors" rush after her, but are quickly left behind, as Atalanta proves true to her reputation of being able to best any man in a race.

Tarasiy stands naked and grinning before a mortified Lybid Artemida, who has knelt down in the water and crossed her arms in front to hide her nudity. Her beautiful face burns with anger.

TARASIY:

> "I shall possess you, my world divine! You will be my wife and I your husband! And now I will pleasure you..."

LYBID:

> "I will die before I allow this shame! I'll swim out and drown myself!"

Tarasiy throws his head back and roars with triumphant laughter.

Atalanta races through the forest to the military corner of the royal encampment, where the soldiers are gathering after their swim, and screams in a voice loud enough to raise the dead from their graves.

ATALANTA:

"Trouble!"

The Sun hangs low in the western sky as Atalanta, wrapped in a soldier's cloak, races down a forest path, a mounted Kosak detachment straining to keep up. As she rushes out of the bushes onto the beach, she sees something other than the scene of mass rape she expected. The maidens and their princess, all dressed, stand in a group off to one side, while their would-be rapists are kneeling, naked and bound, on the sand, while the warrior Volkhvs stand grimly over them, their swords drawn.

The soldiers burst through to the beach and rein in their steaming mounts at the water's edge, then lead them to where the prisoners await their fate. Liubomyr is visibly displeased at the cavalry's arrival.

LIUBOMYR:

"Voivode! Why are you here?"

VOIVODE:

"The maidens! The Princess! We heard there was trouble!"

LIUBOMYR:

"You are not needed here! We ourselves did what had to be done!"

The voivode is taken aback, embarrassed.

MUDROSLAV:

"Daughters! Who here succeeded in ridding herself of her innocence?"

LYBID:

"No one! Lord Liubomyr was able to save us in time!"

LIUBOMYR:

"I had the clothing of these serpents collected here and I would venture to guess a wagon would be necessary to have it all hauled away. Or, perhaps, we could burn it all right here and send them home naked?"

Lybid walks up to the bound Tarasiy.

LYBID:

"So, you wanted to defile me, my beloved Tarasiy? Tried to sully my maidenhood, in me?"

TARASIY:

"I love you madly, my golden-haired doe!"

LYBID:

"Oh, so you hunted me down as if I were a deer? Very well, then, I shall turn into a deer and I shall myself hunt you!"

Lybid walks up to Mudroslav and delivers her decision, in a loud voice, a shout almost, so that all can hear.

LYBID:

> "What happened here will be impossible to conceal. All of Rus and all of Europe will learn of this! I do not want there to be any talk about how the "suitors" got what they came for! I will drown them all in their own blood!"

The "bridegrooms" chime in with fearful protests, but Lybid, ignoring them, continues with her harsh verdict.

LYBID:

> "I will turn Tarasiy into a deer. Sew him up inside the skin of a buck with heavy antlers and set my dogs on him!"

VOIVODE:

> "It shall be done, Princess!"

ATALANTA:

> "O goddess of justice, I beg you for the right to vengeance on those who tried to shame me!"

LYBID:

> "Point them out to me and you may have your revenge!"

The sun is about to set beyond the forest, while in the East the sky is already dark. Soldiers are sewing Tarasiy inside a buckskin with a majestic set of antlers. The hunting dogs, brought from the royal camp by Atalanta, are barking furiously, their blood lust anticipating the imminent hunt.

LYBID:

"Atalanta, you begin!"

The Volkhv prod six of the prisoners towards Atalanta, who just a short while before had to flee from them to save herself.

ATALANTA:

"I will untie you and give you the chance to run to save your lives. Just like I had to run from you. I will then pursue you and whomever I run down I will kill!"

Atalanta uses a knife to cut the ropes binding the wrists of each of the captives. One tries to resist...

"SUITOR":

"And what if we refuse to run?'

ATALANTA:

"From the hunting dogs? Hey! Sic! Sic!"

The animals lurch at the prisoners, but are restrained by the chains that Atalanta hold together in her hands. The terrified youths' flight mechanism kicks in and they flee in the only direction open to them – down the path that stretches along the edge of the water. Atalanta waits until they disappear around the bend, then unsheathes her sword tears after them.

VOIVODE:

"That's the end of them! Death on the wing!"

Atalanta runs effortlessly like a deer and just beyond the bend falls upon the nearest victim. Her sword descends and the boy tumbles into the river, his head split open.

The fleet avenger continues on without breaking stride and soon the second would be rapist feels the burn of steel going through his heart. Atalanta catches up with each of fugitives, strung out along the path according to his running prowess. Except for one, who seeks refuge in the river by diving in and swimming furiously toward the far side. Atlanta takes her bow off her back and, on the run, lets loose an arrow, which a second later implants itself in the back of the swimmer's head. Motion ceases, as his lifeless body slips below the surface, the arrow alone indicating the beginning of his long journey to the Sea.

The Avatar's voice is heard reading the Golden Tablets of Lybid Artemida.

AVATAR:

> "There was another story about Atalanta, which circulated at the royal court, as well as among the commoners. It was said that a group of suitors came to seek her hand in marriage and demanded that she pick from among them. And she purportedly replied that she would enter into a running contest with them, they being free to dispense with weaponry, while she would carry a sword. And whomever she should catch she would kill, and whoever escaped would become her husband. But because she was swifter than any man, she always emerged victorious in these contests, never had to marry, and rejoiced in remaining a chaste maid. And thus, it was!"

The solar disc touches the tops of the trees on the western horizon. Lybid walks up to Tarasiy, bound up inside the freshly dressed skin of a large buck.

LYUBOMYR:

"It is done!"

The Volkhv turns to Lybid, as the soldiers step away from their handiwork – a deer, seemingly alive and standing on its hind legs, but with a human face showing from beneath its antlered head. The face is breathing heavily.

LYBID:

"I love you and it pains me greatly to see you die."

TARASIY:

"I... Forgive me! And spare my life! My love, my only love!"

LYBID

"You have taken from me the innocence of youth and trampled on my heart! In front of others! For the first time in my life, my eyes have seen the naked body of a man standing before me. And you laughed the laugh of a victor over me. For this you must die!"

Atalanta has returned and tosses a bloody leather sack at Lybid's feet.

ATALANTA:

"Five heads, from five scoundrels that no longer have any use for them! And a somewhere out there feeding the fish!"

Lybid abruptly turns to the voivode.

LYBID:

"The deer is ready! Loose the dogs!

ATALANTA:

"Sic! Sic! Get him!"

With a hunter's instinct bred over a hundred generations and already in a frenzy from the smell of deer blood the dogs throw themselves at Tarasiy, who lets out a bloodcurdling shriek and begins the last, desperate run of his young life. Atalanta holds the chains tight, allowing Tarasiy at least a hundred strides towards an impossible escape.

Tarasiy races along the river's edge, first passing the first headless corpse left by Atalanta, then the second and third. Sweat and tears mix on his unhappy face, as his lips whisper a final prayer.

TARASIY:

"Dazhboh! Perun and Veles! I want to live! Save me, O Dazhboh!"

But Lybid's dogs quickly close in on their prey and bring down the man-deer with the magnificent antlers. Their teeth rip first the animal hide, then the human flesh inside and finally, the throat emitting the last horrible screams of the youth who would possess the divine Lybid.

The last rays of the Sun spill over the outline of the black forest, as a palpable sadness settles over the landscape along with the darkness. A large group of nymphs and soldiers on horseback follow Lybid back to the royal camp. They are met at its edge by a throng of excited peasants, who hail their princess.

MUDROSLAV:

> "I love our common people! Whatever the princess does, be it good or bad, the people rejoice. Her presence is always cause for celebration!"

Reaching her tent, Lybid dismounts and walks inside. There sits Kalisto on a chest, while Liubomyr, holding a handful of gold necklaces and bracelets up to her face, interrogates her.

LIUBOMYR:

> "Where did you get these? Who gave them to you?"

KALISTO:

> "The Great King!"

LIUBOMYR:

> "You are lying! These are the work of Persian hands, not Rus artisans! And these Chinese pearls? The King gave them to you?"

Kalisto despairingly tosses her head side to side, trying to escape Liubomyr's burning stare.

Lybid walks up to the young woman.

LYBID:

> "Who gave you this jewelry?"

KALISTO:

> "I did! I gave it to myself! I am now your queen! I shall become the wife of the King!

Yes, I carry your father's child. Which means that I, as his future wife, am even now your step-mother! And you must learn to be the compliant daughter and obey me in everything, else I will have to send you into exile far beyond the Urals!"

LYBID:

"Cunning, scheming, little Kalisto! You think you have fooled us all? Spun your web of deceit around everybody? I shall find out who sent you to seduce my father!"

Into the tent walks the voivode, shoving the bloodied priest of the marauders before him.

VOIVODE:

"The raiders 'priest has admitted everything, Princess! Laid out for us the entire web of this plot, which includes Germanarix! And the Byzantines! They all schemed to tear you away for themselves! I have sent Palant with a mounted patrol to bring back their messenger! It seems this band of cutthroats arrived in these parts a half-year ago, knowing that you would be here in the early autumn."

Lybid turns to the priest.

LYBID

"Where did you get that information? Who gave it to you?"

He silently nods at Kalisto. The pregnant nymph suddenly bolts for the tent opening, only to be stopped, kicking and fighting, by the voivode.

LYBID:

> "Sew this viper inside a bearskin and feed her to the dogs!"

In the fast-fading twilight a throng of people – soldiers, nymphs, peasants- stands at the edge of the royal camp. They are watching a dark, hulking figure – re-resembling - a human only in the strides it takes that are unlike those of any other species on Earth – struggle towards the supposed safety of the woods, pursued by a pack of barking dogs. At the edge of the forest the chase is up, as fangs sink into ankles, legs, arms and throat. As the echoes of Kalisto's death scream fade away the only sound heard are the of the dogs tearing away at her still- warm flesh.

Mudroslav, Liubomyr and two other Volkhvs ride up to the ravaged corpse, past pack of dogs that have left their prey, responding to the command of the voivode's whistle. A soft sound emerges from the pile of flesh, the cry of a baby miraculously brought into the world from a womb ripped open.

MUDROSLAV:

> "A miracle! A miracle from Dazhboh! A child born
> from dying! A boy! Life is mightier than death!"

Lubomyr takes a careful look around. There is no one nearby; off in the distance, by the royal camp, the crowd of silhouettes is quietly dispersing.

LIUBOMYR:

> "The people are leaving. No one knows."

Liubomyr climbs down from his horse and picks the child up from the bloody remains of its mother.

MUDROSLAV:

"Gave birth to a prince, the viper did!"

Liubomyr carefully cradles the baby in his arms.

LIUBOMYR:

"The dogs ripped free the umbilical cord!"

MUDROSLAV:

"I shall order the child to be taken to northern Hellas, to Pausaniy. He will never learn of his real father. His name shall be Arkad, and from his line will come the people that will be known in history as the Arcadians!"

Atalanta, all smeared with dried and drying blood, wanders aimlessly and joylessly among the crowd that witnessed the end of Kalisto. She sees Lybid Artemida ride up to her tent, escorted by her nymphs and soldiers. The voivode is leading away the hunting dogs, who pull in different directions, still excited and agitated by the blood orgy.

She hears the peasants talking among themselves on their way to the river.

FIRST PEASANT:

"The horror! Lybid Artemida used her magic powers to turn Kalisto into a bear!"

SECOND PEASANT (reverently):

"The powers of a goddess!"

THIRD PEASANT:

"If she wanted to, she could turn us all into swine with one flick of her finger – into boars and sows and piglets, to be eaten by her Kosaks for dinner! Or into anything at all! Myron, you, for example, she'd immediately turn into a gander!"

MYRON:

"And you into a rat, you idiot!"

Atalanta walks through the peasants' camp on her way to the river to wash away the filth and stench of the tragic day. Here and there bonfires send sparks up to an ink-black sky and light up the faces of people sitting round. At one, the Starosta is telling a large crowd of peasants the terrible truth about the day's events, in actuality a tale he has already spun, which will astonishingly quickly reach all the corners of Rus and settle in the imagination of her people as something as powerful and as permanent as any truth.

STAROSTA

"And the corpses there – headless torsos and bodies lacerated – all along the river' banks! A scene from hell! it's their rich clothing that was distributed to those of us who lost everything in the fire."

STAROSTA'S WIFE:

"it's the truth my husband speaks! there's more of them lying dead and naked in the river than one can count! that's the truth!"

PEASANT WOMAN:

"But did they let any of them live?"

STAROSTA'S WIFE:

"The old gave orders to release all of the rest of the young men – naked, mind you – so that they would frighten all of Holy Rus with tales of the horrible fate that befell who dared to see the nymph's nude!"

BTAROSTA:

"Our Princess, Lybid Arte-Midia, used her magical powers to turn her nymph Kalisto into a she-bear and sicked her dogs on her. And, my dear people, I saw with my own eyes how Princess Lybid turned Prince Tarasiy Akteon into a stag!"

PEASANT WOMAN:

"Tarasiy?"

STAROSTA:

"I myself saw the antlers growing out of his head and branching out and his arms and legs into a deer's legs. His neck became elongated, his ears pointed, and a hairy hide covered his entire body. He began running around frantically, like a frightened deer. He finally saw his reflection in the river and he tried to cry out, but couldn't. And tears flowed from his eyes, but they were the eyes of a deer. Yet his mind remained that of a human. What was he to do? Where was he to run? The hunting dogs picked up the scent of a deer – they didn't recognize their own master – and they tore after him in a frenzy..."

PEASANT WOMAN:

"What do you mean master'? Whose dogs, were they?"

STAROSTA'S WIFE:

"His, dearies!"

STAROSTA

"His, every last one! The magnificent buck sped away like the wind, his splendorous antlers thrown back, the dog pack in hot pursuit! Slowly they narrow the gap to their pray, till finally their fangs sink deep into the flesh of the woeful Tarasiy. He despairs to cry out: Spare me! It is I, Tarasiy, your master! But the only sound that tears forth from the buck's breast is an agonizing cry that carries at once the pain of utmost regret, loss and misery known only to humans. The stag Tarasiy falls to his knees, his eyes filled with terror, desperation and pleading. But death is imminent, as the maddened dogs tear his flesh to pieces..."

One of the village women, overcome by the harrowing narrative, cries out, "O god of mercy! "and collapses on the ground.

STAROSTA (a note of satisfaction in his voice):

"And thus, died this stage, Tarasiy Akteoniv, who dared to violate the peace of the goddess Artemida, the only mortal who cast his eyes on the divine beauty of the daughter of the King of Kings and Queen Zlata Maya!"

Meanwhile, Atalanta, hidden by the darkness from human eyes, disrobes on the river's edge and slowly walks into the water. Starlight dances upon the gentle swells, as the warrior maiden luxuriates in the warm current. Suddenly, she spies a yellow light slowly moving in the distance until finally it stops.

"Lybid, a torch in her hand, stands alone over the torn body of Tarasiy, which lies at water's edge, his once proud head in the water, with but the stag's bloodied antlers breaking the surface. The tormented cry of a loving woman's soul forever wounded rend her bosom: Why, O Dazhboh? Why?"

[Subtitle:] "LYBID, 3000 YEARS HENCE"

Close-up of the face of Lybid Artemida against a backdrop of the American flag. A solemn ceremony at Arlington National Cemetery across the Potomac River from

Washington, DC. An Army bugle plays "Taps," as the Queen places a wreath before the Tomb of the Unknowns, then pays silent tribute to the fallen American heroes.

September 1, 2000, a fateful day. veteran's Hall in Manhattan.

The sun shines bright, as car after luxury car drives away from the curb in front of the building, carrying high-ranking military officers in ceremonial uniforms and their civilian masters. Uniformed police and security agents in civilian hold back excited crowds of celebrity worshippers, while allowing journalists, photographers and video cameras access to the anointed. Antenna-sprouting television news vans beam live reports to millions of homes around the globe. Close-up of a TV screen with the CNN logo dissolves into a shot of Betsy Rosenberg standing in front of Veteran's Hall, as delegates and guests walk in, out and about.

BETSY ROSENBERG:

> "Good afternoon! This is Betsy Rosenberg, CNN! I am happy to bring you this report about the apparent success Her Majesty Queen Lybid Artemida has had at this World Congress to Ban War. The audience again and again interrupted her address enthusiastic applause. Senior officers of all the branches of the U.S. Armed Forces, senior Pentagon officials and high representatives of NATO countries, whom you see having Veteran's Hall, are heading back to their headquarters convinced – as many of have assured me –

that Lybid Artemida is the person to bring everlasting peace planet... And where is the Queen at this moment? Her Majesty is still in the hall, by military veterans from countries all over the globe and answering their questions..."

The CNN picture, which intermittently cuts away from Betsy Rosenberg to scenes the building then back to the reporter, goes inside the hall and pushes in from a wide shot to a large group of military and civilian officials encircling Lybid. The Queen is wearing the battle armor of Artemida, the Sword of Ariy at her side. Instead of her crown a gleaming open-faced helmet covers her head; a long scarlet cape falls from her shoulders.

The U.S. secretary of defense steps out of the surrounding circle, within which Robert Oberfell, utterly unsuccessful in his attempt to hide his anxiety, surreptitiously at his wristwatch.

SECRETARY OF DEFENSE:

> "In the name of the Armed Forces of the United States
> I have the honor of assuring you that you can count on
> the full support of the Department of Defense in your
> noble quest for a lasting peace in the world!"

Members of the American delegation bow respectfully before the Queen and depart. Their places are taken by a group of European officials, headed by the Secretary General of NATO.

SECRETARY GENERAL:

> "The North Atlantic Alliance is with you, Your
> Majesty! We look forward to your visit to Brussels!"

The NATO delegates bow before Lybid Artemida and depart. Finally, a crowd of veteran old-timers of all races and nationalities, some dressed in military uniforms in varying degrees of outlandishness and bedecked with medals, others in civilian clothes but all of them full of unbridled enthusiasm and energy, surges forward. First to stand before the Queen are two ancient U.S. officers.

ADMIRAL JOHNSON, U.S. NAVY(RET.):

> "We have decided, all of us, to escort you to your limousine, Your Majesty! But first as the honorary Chairman of the World Congress to Ban War, I ask you to stay a few minutes longer for a photo together, one which we will treasure forever!"

LYBID ARTEMIDA:

> "It will be my great pleasure!"

GENERAL SMITH, U.S. ARMY(RET.) (to the assembled veterans):

> "Gentlemen, I ask that we all gather around Her Majesty for a photograph!"

The veterans quickly and in a disciplined fashion spread out behind and to the side of Lybid Artemida. A disabled veteran in a wheelchair, making his way past gives the Admiral a salute.

ADM. JOHNSON:

> "Mancuso, is that you?!"

MANCUSO:

> "Aye, aye, Sir!"

ADM. JOHNSON:

> "Your Majesty! The man before you is a legend, a hero of the landing at Normand and one of our finest

sharpshooters. An Italian-American, John Mancuso! Would it be all right if we put Ensign Mancuso right here in front of you? And maybe you could your hand on his shoulder?"

LYBID ARTEMIDA:

"I will be pleased to do so, Admiral! Ensign Mancuso, please do me the honor..."

MANCUSO:

"If I had known at Normandy that my picking off the SS would one day allow me to meet Queen Lybid Artemida and get my picture taken with Her Majesty, Admiral, Sir, I would have sacrificed not just my legs but my arms as well for the liberation of Europe!"

GEN. SMITH:

"McKenzie! McKenzie! Over here!"

Smith takes another veteran by the sleeve and pulls him over to stand before the Queen.

GEN. SMITH:

"Your Majesty, this is Gen. Eisenhower's renowned flag bearer from World War III" himself the center of attention, the old vet looks down, embarrassed, then confidence, as Lybid looks at him, smiling..."

MEKENZIE:

"My claim to fame is the result of a bit of luck... Remember the famous meeting on April 25, 1945, when we and the Soviets defeated the Nazis and shook hands on the Elbe River? The meeting between your Marshall Zhukov and our Gen. Eisenhower at Torgau? Well, the young G.I. with the flag in all of those news reels from that day... That was me!"

Several photographers gesture for the veterans at the sides to tighten up the formation, then raise their Canons, Nikons and Minoltas up to their eyes.

PHOTOGRAPHER:

"Here we go! Cheeeeese!"

Cameras flash and click, as the photographers snap one shot after another with the necklace of cameras hanging around their necks. The veterans pose proudly, as a meeting that will forever remain in their memories and on film comes to a close.

Somewhere in Manhattan. A key turns a lock and Sievers walks into an apartment. He quickly closes the door behind him and emerges in a large room brimming with video monitors and other electronic equipment that could grace a space mission control center, Ekkart sits in front of a row of video monitors, while a dozen technicians calibrate ad tune assorted hi-tech apparatuses.

EKKART:

"I was getting a bit nervous. You showed up exactly one minute to launch."

SIEVERS:

"I told you I would be here at the last moment. I had to take my granddaughter with me, I left her at the children's playground. My friend Valentina is watching her...So, what is the situation?"

EKKART:

"The snipers, machine guns and AA batteries are positioned on the rooftops of nine skyscrapers. You and I can monitor the effectiveness of the fire live on these screens, or even direct missiles at targets in Brooklyn or further out on Long Island!"

SIEVERS:

"How much firepower do we have?"

EKKART:

"As much as a NATO infantry battalion. But the most important thing we have is that our communications signal is protected by a digital anti-detection system, code named 'Chinese Swindler.' The Americans don't have it, they don't even know about it. And this means that no one – not the police, not the CIA, not even the National Security Agency – can intercept or disrupt our satellite telecommunications. It's something the Red Chinese developed in secret, a marvel of the Twenty-first Century, really!"

SIEVERS:

"How many men do we have in position?"

EKKART:

"Of the ones we picked, not a one has backed out. And they know they will die every last one of them!"

SIEVERS:

"Then let's begin!"

At Manhattan police headquarters computer screens suddenly go blank. The lights go out on the large electronic map of the borough covering much of one of the walks of the operations room. A low buzz of surprised voices quickly grows into angry shouts and streams of profanities. The captain in charge of the shift shouts into a telephone receiver.

CAPTAIN:

"Communications and power are down!"

The only reply he gets is the rising din in the darkened room.

CAPTAIN:

"Why isn't the emergency power on? It's supposed to kick in automatically! Listen up, everyone: Let's get terrorist response teams set up and going!"

At Veterans Hall, the old soldiers escort Lybid Artemida, flanked on either side by Admiral Johnson and Gen. Smith, to the door. Lybid, outwardly continuing to exude delight at the warm and heartfelt reception, lets a furled brow betray an inner sense of foreboding. The veterans continue to revel in the delight of the moment.

Robert Oberfell bends down to whisper something in Lybid's ear...

OBERFELL:

"Everything is going so well... But for some reason, I feel like something's not right. I suggest you allow me to drive you away from here..."

LYBID:

> "I feel it, too – a veil of deep sadness over something about to happen, something deadly and evil. Like what Caesar must have felt as he walked into the Senate for the last time, or Lincoln on his way to his box in ford's theatre, or Kennedy just before the shots in Dallas. I have this sense that all these wonderful people here are about to die..."

The large group approaches the main exit.

OBERFELL:

> "I can't shake the feeling that something horrific awaits us the other side of that door...

Secret Service agent John Kramer appears from the side with the rest of Lybid's security detail, which, politely but firmly, separates her from the veterans.

KRAMER:

> "Thank you, Gentlemen!"

The agent steps in between Lybid and Oberfell and ushers her towards the door...

KRAMER:

> "There is a throng waiting for you just beyond that door..."

LYBID:

> "And you have suddenly become my producer?"

As Lybid Artemida walks through the door, held open for her by Kramer, and steps onto a red carpet, the crowd of several thousand filling the street behind a double police line, erupts in a storm of excited cheers and shouts.

At the terrorist command center, Gerhard Sievers and Hermann Ekkart stand before a row of TV monitors, watching Lybid emerge from Veterans Hall. Kramer is close by her side, as she raises both arms in acknowledgment of the tribute.

EKKART:

"Hold fire until I give the command!"

The screens in the room show the scene in front of Veterans Hall as relayed from TV cameras at different positions and angles. Red dots of laser beams play on Lybid Artemida's shining armor, as the Nazi assassins sight their weapons on their distant prey.

SIEVERS:

"Well, then, let's get on with it!"

EKKART (with supreme confidence):

"This will be the grandest killing in all of history!"

Betsy Rosenberg continues her report, the CNN director appropriately switching from camera to camera.

ROSENBERG:

"There she is, the woman of the hour, Lybid Artemida..."

Abruptly, Lybid waves a final good-bye with her hands, turns on her heels and disappears inside the building she just left. Her breathing is labored, her face flushed from a strange emotion.

LYBID:

"I won't go!"

KRAMER:

"What happened, Majesty? The people are waiting for you!"

LYBID

"Why aren't the people allowed to come up to me? Why are they being held being held back by the police, behind barricades?"

OBERFELL:

"I'll take care of this right now!"

Robert Oberfell runs out the doors and shouts at the police captain in charge.

OBERFELL:

"Let the people through, immediately!"

KRAMER:

"Oberfell, what are you doing?"

OBERFELL:

"Who authorized you to keep the people from Her Majesty? they've been waiting for her since 9 this morning!"

KRAMER:

"But they'll make a mess of the red carpet!"

OBERFELL:

"That's not your problem!"

The police captain, recognizing Oberfell, gives his officers the signal to take down the yellow tape and move the barricades aside. Thousands of people rush towards the building's entrance.

At their command center, Sievers and Ekkart see Lybid again emerge from the Hall, A thousands of hands reach out to touch her; however, the Queen suddenly turns around and again disappears inside.

EKKART (agitated):

"What the devil is going on?"

SIEVERS (calmly):

"Obviously, she has a sixth sense, like a sacred cow being led to a ritual slaughter."

EKKART (in Arabic, into a radio transmitter) (English subtitles appear at the of the screen):

"Shooters, listen carefully! It seems she's not Kennedy and she's not Martin Luther and will not cooperate in her own destruction. Get ready for the alternate plan!"

...Back to CNN's coverage...

BETSY ROSENBERG:

"I cannot explain what is happening here at Veterans Hall. According to protocol, Her Majesty was to have left the building at the head of her group and walked to a waiting limousine, which was to take her directly to Washington. For some reason protocol has twice been interrupted and at present I have no information as to why this has happened..."

Looking up at the screens before them, Sievers and Ekkart wait anxiously I for Lybid to appear again at the entrance to meet her fate. A human sea has run up to the front doors of Veterans Hall, roaring with a thousand voices. When the Queen does not emerge, the crowd takes up a swelling chant: "Lybid! Lybid! Lybid!"

SIEVERS:

"She's not coming out!"

EKKART:

"Damn! Damn it all! what's our next move? You give the order, Gerhard!"

Sievers takes the microphone in his hand and speaks in Arabic.

SIEVERS:

"Attention, everybody! We have a change. We are now going with Plan 'B'! Tease 'Sinai'! Your orders are to make your way inside the Hall and kill Lybid Artemida and everyone that's with her. More blood! Allah will be pleased!"

Looking intently at the TV monitors showing the throng outside the Hall, Sievers and Ekkart see first one, then two, three... ten terrorist commandos grimly make the way towards the entrance. The crowd continues its chant: "Lybid! Lybid! Lybid!.."

Inside the building Adm. Johnson and Gen. Smith deferentially address Lybid Artemida. The nearest veterans have also picked up her anxiety.

ADM. JOHNSON:

"You're not feeling well, Your Majesty?"

LYBID:

"There is no way to explain this, Admiral..."

OBERFELL:

"The Queen has a foreboding of something evil about to happen. And I share it..."

GEN. SMITH:

"I felt it in combat, more than once..."

KRAMER:

"The people are calling for you, Your Majesty!"

LYBID (angrily):

"I will not go!"

Desperate, Kramer, co-conspirator of the Nazi terrorists, rushes to the nearest fire box, breaks the glass and sets off the alarm.

KRAMER:

"Everyone evacuates the building! Fire!"

The veterans, shouting and screaming, instinctively rush for the doors; the human wave carries Lybid and Oberfell out onto the sidewalk, where they are pushed about helplessly, like in a storm-tossed sea.

Betsy Rosenberg, off to one side of the front entrance, clutches her microphone...

ROSENBERG:

"Something terrible is happening here! This is, if. Like..., a scene from Sodom and Gomorrah!"

At the terrorist command central, Sievers and Ekkart feel their nerves at the breaking point. The crowd pouring out of Veterans Hall has carried Lybid right up in her armored limousine.

SIEVERS:

"Don't let her get in that vehicle! Open fire!"

In an instant, the sidewalk and street in front of the building turns into a scene from hell, bursts of automatic gunfire mixing with cries of pain and terror, shouts of desperate men, sounds of breaking glass. Pieces of human flesh and a rain of blood splatter those left standing and those already writhing on the ground... The commandos, kept away from Lybid by the surging masses, have fired point-blank in an attempt to cut through the human wall that shields their prey... But the wall stands, as scores of bystanders climb over the piles of bodies of the dead and dying for the supposed safety of the street, only to be cut down in turn by the merciless gunfire.

Sievers and Ekkart feel the tension leave their bodies, as they allow themselves to breathe easily. They watch the veterans scurry back inside the Hall, leaving many their comrades lying on the sidewalk...

EKKART:

"Now things are moving!"

SIEVERS (into the microphone):

"What are you shooting at, you blind idiots! don't let her get into the limo! Kill her!"

The monitors show how well the shooters have carried out their crude, grotesque plan. Only a minute has gone by and Lybid stands alone amidst the carnage. Robert Oberfell rushes up to her, grabs her by the shoulders and tries to push her into the limousine. But it is too late. Eight commandos -two of their number having been eliminated by "friendly fire" – have surrounded the Queen and raise their assault weapons for one last lethal burst...

EKKART:

"That's it! The end of her, at last!"

But no! The two old Nazis watch on the screens as a line of police from Lybid's motorcycle honor escort, in helmets and black leather jackets, guns drawn, silently materializes behind the backs of the assassins. With not a sound of warning, the cops open fire and don't stop until the last terrorist lies still in a pool of blood.

SIEVERS:

"Damnation!"

Oberfell, shielding Lybid with his body, pushes her into the limo.

OBERFELL:

"Inside! Get inside!"

Lybid's security detail has broken out of Veterans Hall and rushes to surround her. Among them is Kramer, gun in hand. Calmly walking right up to the Queen, he raises the automatic and empties the cartridge into her chest. The 9-mm rounds have as much effect as buckshot against an elephant's hide.

KRAMER:

"What the hell?!"

LYBID:

"Fool! You thought my armor is like a tin can?!"

Before anybody can bat an eye, Lybid's mailed fist connects with Kramer's jaw and the Nazi henchman collapses on the blood-smeared sidewalk.

Betsy Rosenberg rushes up to the group, trailed by a cameraman with a rolling betacam on his shoulder. She looks down at the fallen thug, then up at Lybid, and punches the air with her fist.

ROSENBERG (excitedly, into the microphone):

"You go, girl!"

On tries Kramer tries to get up, but can't focus his eyes. He manages to stand up on wobbly legs, staggers, then falls down again.

Tension at the terrorist command center mounts; Sievers is biting his lower lip, at his hair.

EKKART:

"Kramer has given himself away!"

On the screen, Kramer, now on all fours, is surrounded by Lybid's security people. The microphone hidden under Kramer's lapel transmits every word spoken around him to the terrorist lair.

BECURITY AGENT:

"Kramer! What is this? you've turned?"

The agents surround Lybid, shielding her with their bodies.

LYBID:

"Arrest him!"

The security men level their automatics at the traitor.

A grim-faced Ekkart turns towards Sievers.

EKKART:

"Under interrogation, and drugged, he'll give up everything."

SIEVERS (into the radio microphone):

"Kill him!"

Lybid looks with bitterness down at the man crawling towards her, the man who betrayed her. Abruptly, Kramer rises to his knees, straightens up his back, throws his head back, spreads his arms wide and lets out a long, savage scream.

Somewhere, an anti-tank missile is launched...

The explosion tears Kramer to pieces, his blood splattering the security agents. Seconds later, German-made MG machine guns mounted on surrounding skyscrapers send a heavy caliber rain down on the group surrounding Lybid. Betsy Rosenberg screams and collapses on the ground; one by one the security agents are cut down with multiple mortal wounds. Lybid, Oberfell and several of the motorcycle policemen make it to the limousine's door. machine-gun rounds ricochet off the vehicle's heavy armor plating.

LYBID (turning toward the fallen journalist):

"Betsy!"

POLICEMAN (pushing Lybid into the car):

"Save yourself!"

LYBID:

"I won't leave her!"

Lybid frees herself from her protector's grasp and runs towards the journalist. The impact of several rounds knocks her off-stride, but she keeps her feet, picks the woman up and carries her to the limousine.

LYBID:

"Help me!"

Oberfell slips his arms under Rosenberg's body and places the CNN reports on the back seat beside Lybid. The driver looks back, awaiting the order to take off Oberfell slams the door shut behind the two women and the awful squall of death sounds instantly mutes.

LYBID:

"There, Betsy, we're safe!"

The motorcycle policemen take cover and instinctively fire at the shooters positioned high above them and out of range of their automatics. Through the limo's windshield Lybid sees the lead squad car turn on its flashing light. She sees Robert Oberfell run up the driver's side, pound on the roof top and shout something into the window.

OBERFELL:

"Go! Go!"

Oberfell turns around and runs back to the armored Town Car, opens the door and jumps inside, letting in, for a moment, the thunderous sounds of the gun fight raging around them. The police cruiser, its siren wailing at 120 dbs., its lights flashing, tears away from the curb, followed an instant later by Lybid Artemida's limousine.

OBERFELL (calmly, hopefully):

"We're on our way."

Machine gun rounds continue to hit the vehicle from all sides, but bounce off harmlessly, Betsy Rosenberg opens her eyes and moans.

BETSY ROSENBERG:

"I know I'm dying..."

LYBID (to the driver):

"Straight to a hospital, Rolf! Now!"

DRIVER:

"Yes, ma'am!"

LYBID:

"Betsy, you just hang in there! Your wound is serious, but it's not fatal! Stay with me!"

BETSY ROSENBERG:

"I'm dying. I know it!"

LYBID:

"You're going to live!

Coughing spasmodically, tears of pain and sadness in her eyes, but hope in her voice,

Betsy Rosenberg whispers her final words.

BETSY ROSENBERG:

"Save the world..."

Her fingers reflexively dig into Lybid's forearm, as her eyes are still and her head falls to the side.

An RPG round launched from a rooftop chases down the limousine and explodes in a rear wheel well. A thousand sparks fly, the driver fights to regain control over the lurching vehicle and finally brings it to a stop a block away. The lead car makes an abrupt turn-around and races back, screeching to a halt at the side of the disabled limo. Before the security agents can open their doors, a second round, headed towards the side where Lybid sits, slams into the squad car.

Inside the limo's passengers' compartment Oberfell, instinctively reacting as if the fiery burst could penetrate the bullet-proof window, raises his arm to shield his head and face.

OBERFELL:

"Outside! Quickly!"

He throws open the door opposite the side of the attack and pulls Lybid by the hand.

LYBID:

"What about Betsy?"

OBERFELL (quietly, but firmly):

"She's dead. I'll have somebody come back for her body. Quickly!"

Another RPG round rips apart the driver's compartment and sends his head and other body parts flying in the flaming burst.

Lybid takes one last look at Betsy Rosenberg's pale face, before being pulled under the car by Oberfell. A moment later the vehicle is swiped by a city bus, which, having taken an RPG hit, comes to a stop alongside. The driver is slumped, dead, over the steering wheel, as the few surviving passengers attempt to crawl out through the windows. Machinegun fire continues to rip apart its interior and the bodies therein.

OBERFELL

"The barricade is up, Your Majesty! I'm going to try to get through to the White House..."

Oberfell quickly takes out his cell phone and hits a speed dialing button.

OBERFELL:

"Cornwell? Robert Oberfell..."

From under the cover of the heavy vehicle Lybid takes in the hellish street scene. Several cars, hit by terrorist rounds, are on fire. Others are trying to maneuver to safety around the burning hulks and corpses strewn all around. machine-gun fire continues to rain down, pitting the Veterans Hall facade, shredding cars, cutting down panic-stricken, safety-seeking bystanders. Some of them, along with a few remaining veterans, cheat death by reaching the building.

At their command post Sievers and Ekkart watch the winding down of the phase of the first phase of their terrorist extravaganza.

EKKART (into the radio mike, in Arabic):

> "The woman has taken cover under her vehicle. Grey Wolves! Grey Wolves! Commence your attack!

SIEVERS:

> "Grey Wolves! Close in!"

Down at the end of the block and around the corner the doors swing open on eight parked nondescript vans and men in black police uniforms, helmets and goggles pour out onto the asphalt. They rush towards Lybid's limousine, covered from above by machine-gun fire.

Oberfell screams into his cell phone.

OBERFELL:

> "Inform the president immediately! He needs to know this!"

Oberfell starts to slam his phone into the sidewalk, but stops himself.

OBERFELL:

> "The bastard hung up!"

LYBID

"They don't want the president to know. it's part of the conspiracy!"

OBERFELL:

"If it is, it sure beats the JFK killing!"

The area is lit up with flashing red, blue and white lights and the sound of sirens mixers with gunfire bursts, as a dozen police squad cars race in from the opposite end of the block. They screech to a stop about thirty yards from Lybid and Oberfell, their further progress blocked by a line of burning and otherwise disabled cars. As New York's fines jump from their cruisers, they are met with a hail of lead coming from the rooftops above.

Taking cover, they return the fire. A few of the policemen have reached the limousine.

POLICE LIEUTENANT:

"Thank God, you're alive!"

The officer speaks into his two-way radio.

POLICE LIEUTENANT:

"Her Majesty is alive! I've got about forty men here, including two SWAT teams!

Positioning them around the limo!"

The van-based terrorists swarm in, their assault weapons blazing. A battle at close quarters erupts.

Inside Veterans Hall, bullets fly in through the windows and ricochet off the walls. Adm. Johnson, Gen. Smith and the rest of the surviving veterans have taken refuge in one of the corridors out of the line of fire.

ADM. JOHNSON:

> "Queen Lybid Artemida is in mortal danger! We must save her!"

GEN. SMITH

> "Admiral! The oath we swore as American soldiers is still binding, and will be for the rest of our lives! As the president of the Veterans Congress, you are our commands here! Give your orders."

The two flag officers salute one another.

ADM. JOHNSON:

> "OK, listen up! Marines, Airborne, Navy, everybody! Line up to my right!"

The veterans jump to attention and quickly form a line. The Admiral addresses his troops...

ADM. JOHNSON:

> "Men, consider yourselves activated! I'm placing you under the command of Gen. Smith! we'll use cells phones as our means of communications..."

Out on the street, wailing sirens announce the arrival of new police units. The right side of the block has turned into a parking lot of vehicles, from behind which police officer fire upon the advancing terrorists.

Down at the opposite end of the block, a dozen or so police units arrive on the scene and attack them from the rear. The terrorists are forced to temporarily halt their assault on Lybid Artemida's position and concentrate their fire on the police lines on either side. The law enforcement ranks thin, as the terrorists' superior firepower takes its toll.

On the rooftop of one of the surrounding skyscrapers a terrorist squad deploys a multiple rocket launcher, aiming it at the police massed on the right side of the block.

At the terrorist command center, Gerhard Sievers and Hermann Ekkart watch the second phase of the assault reach its culmination.

SIEVERS:

"The missile launcher is ready!"

EKKART (in Arabic):

"Fire!"

The launcher sends a deadly stream of rockets down on the police position. One vehicle after another explodes, secondary explosions following a split second later as fuel tanks ignite. Every last one of the police officers lies dead or dying, as a black cloud of acid smoke covers the scene.

Pressed against the side of the limousine, Lybid, Oberfell and the police lieutenant watch with horror.

LIEUTENANT:

"Any second now they'll turn their fire on us..."

OBERFELL:

> "And unless something happens, there'll be nothing left
> for us to do but say our last prayers..."

At the opposite end of the block several police officers are pointing up at one of the rooftops. A group of them rushes the building's front entrance. As they open the front door a fierce explosion cuts them down to a man.

A second team of fifteen fights their way to Veterans Hall, takes up positions inside and opens fire on the terrorist attackers. Adm. Johnson runs up to the group.

ADM. JOHNSON:

> "Who's in charge?"

The policemen for a second or two gape at the rows of medals on the old man's chest.

Then one of them gives a quick salute.

LIEUTENANT EDWARDS:

> "I am! Lt. Edwards, Sir!"

ADM. JOHNSON (returning salute):

> "Admiral Johnson!"

LT. JOHNSON:

> "Are there any terrorists inside the building."

ADM. JOHNSON:

> "No. But we want to help. Give us weapons. we're professional soldiers!"

Police Lt. Edwards gives the admiral an incredulous stare and, putting his hands on both his shoulders, begins to turn him away from the coming firefight.

LT. EDWARDS:

> "Excuse me, Sir, but the only thing you are right now are professional old farts, Sir!
>
> Old age is hard work, Sir, and it would be injurious to your health to wear yourself out with warfare! Leave the fighting to us young warriors! [to the rest of the veterans] You are not to interfere with the police officers. Everyone who is not an active-duty law enforcement officer must leave the foyer now!"

An RPG round streaks in and explodes on a wall, killing or wounding a dozen men. A terrorist team is forcing its way through the Hall's front entrance. Johnson and Edwards scramble in opposite directions.

Johnson and a few of the veterans pick up the weapons of the dead policemen. Johnson tosses an automatic to Smith, and the group disappears down a side corridor.

From behind the armored limousine Lybid and Oberfell watch as a terrorist team rushes through the Veterans Hall entrance. A firefight ensues and the police are quickly wiped out by the heavily armed attackers. Lt. Edwards, his body riddled with bullets, falls to his knees, tries to get up, but finally crumples to the floor at the feet of a terrorist.

The attackers are looking over their handiwork when, suddenly, Johnson, Smith and the rest of the retired commandos spring from behind a corner and open fire. Before the terrorists can get off more than a few shots they are cut down where they stand. The marble floor of the foyer is slick with the blood of policemen, veterans and terrorists.

Johnson and Smith run up to the dying police lieutenant and raise him up off the floor.

JOHNSON:

"We would have been proud to fight alongside you and your men."

EDWARDS:

"Yes, Sir. I'm sorry. Go and finish the job we couldn't!"

The police lieutenant gives the vets a feeble salute. The veterans lay his lifeless body down on the floor.

JOHNSON:

"Pick up all the weapons!"

The old troopers run around gathering the automatics and assault rifles.

High above on a rooftop the commander of the terrorist unit watches through binoculars, then gives the command to put the RPG's into action once again. The first three episode on the sidewalk outside Veterans Hall, one rips the main doors to pieces, three more explode inside. The corridors fill with heavy smoke.

Mancuso rolls up to Johnson on his wheelchair and screams above the din

MANCUSO:

"Admiral! Get me a sniper's rifle!"

JOHNSON:

"Hell, yes! For the best goddammed sniper in the history
of the Marine Corps!"

A police sniper's rifle, wet with the blood of its previous owner, now deceased, is bended o Mancuso. He wipes it with his necktie and sleeve, rolls up to the window and sets his optical sight on a figure on the rooftop above.

MANCUSO:

"Learn from the best, while I'm still alive!"

The terrorist commander, looking through his binoculars, can't make out what is happening inside the Hall. As the smoke clears, he sees a veteran in a wheelchair aiming his rifle upward, right at him...

Mancuso slowly pulls the trigger and the bullet goes through the binoculars. The head of the terrorist leader explodes. The rifle cracks twice more and the bodies of two more terrorist shooters tumble off the roof. A hundred pairs of eyes follow them down on their graceful flight to their demise on the street asphalt.

Mancuso, turning his head back to the admiral, grins widely and lets out the excited laugh of one revisiting past victories and another job well done.

On another rooftop an anti-tank weapon stares down at the celebrating sniper. A trigger is pulled and a moment later an explosion sends flying parts of his body and his wheelchair.

Adm. Johnson shakes off a temporary state of shock and embraces Smith.

JOHNSON:

"Defend Veterans Hall with your life, Larry! And above all, don't let them violate our battle flags!"

SMITH:

"You can count on me, Sir!"

Meanwhile, the terrorists have turned their fire on Lybid and her defenders crouched behind the armored limousine. The Queen momentarily loses consciousness. Coming to, she sees the terrorists stepping over the bodies of policemen who was ready to take a bullet, and did, in order to save her. Oberfell writhes on the sidewalk, holding his belly with both hands. a dark red stain spreads on his shirt. The terrorists slowly and deliberately walk towards Lybid, their assault rifles held level. One of them releases a burst and the others follow. Bullets ping off her armor and helmet, as she turns her head away and down.

Oberfell, lying behind the backs of the terrorists, fighting off the pain and the coming unconsciousness, picks an Uzi off the sidewalk and with one sweep dispatches the assassins.

Lybid runs to him. At that moment three more terrorists leap onto the hood and roof of the limo. Oberfell covers Lybid with his body and takes the hail of lead headed her way.

Unexpectedly, Johnson and his veterans appear out of nowhere and in a short firefight cut down the last of the Grey Wolves.

LYBID: (holding the dying Oberfell in her arms):

"Robert! Robert!"

Oberfell opens his eyes and looks into hers...

OBERFELL:

"My Queen..."

LYBID:

"Why did you shield me with your body? My armor was my protection..."

OBERFELL:

"A young man's foolishness. I forgot...' trickles from the corner of his mouth..."

LYBID:

"Robert! don't leave me..."

OBERFELL:

"I'll call you later, ma'am..."

LYBID:

"Why are you joking? I won't let you die! Robert..."

OBERFELL:

"I will wait for you on the Sun! Remember me forever in your Kingdom!"

Lybid lowers her head down to his, and her tears wash over his lifeless face. Adm. standing over her, puts his hand gently on her shoulder.

JOHNSON:

"Now is not the time to mourn, Your Majesty. I'm leaving you twelve of the finest Airborne troopers and

Marines for your protection, all over 65. I'll be giving the police a band. Here's a cell phone and my number. we'll need to stay in touch. On their TV monitors, Sievers and Ekkart watch the third phase of the Lybid assassination attempt also end in failure.

EKKART (into a radio microphone, in Arabic):

"Jihad shame! The Grey wolves-all cut down by a bunch of retirees!"

SIEVERS (into a radio microphone, in Arabic):

"Adm. Johnson and about three dozen aggressive old farts are marching down the street. Concentrate your fire on them!"

Ekkart grabs Sievers roughly by the shoulder.

EKKART:

"Lybid Artemida is still alive!"

SIEVERS:

"Damn that Johnson! Stubborn old fool! I've had constant run-ins with him at the U.S. Veterans Council!"

A police helicopter appears in the sky and swoops down into the canyon between the skyscrapers.

PILOT (into his radio):

"I see lots of fires down on the street. Seems like all the squad cars are burning Every last one!"

Down on the ground people turn hopeful faces up at the aircraft, waving their hands.

VETERAN:

"He'll call for reinforcements! The cavalry's a-coming!"

The pilot skillfully maneuvers between the buildings, then rapidly gains altitude.

PILOT (into his radio):

"All birds listen up. Get over here, on the double. We've got ourselves a battle down there!"

The pilot's face freezes as his eyes focus on a figure standing on a near-by rooftop the mouth of a missile launcher gaping right at him. Another terrorist standing a few feet away is working a video camera, recording the scene. The pilot impulsively screams he pulls the stick in, like a rider reining in his mount. The helicopter's nose lifts up, like a rearing stallion, and hangs in the air for a second, before the missile hits it just behind the pilot's seat. The explosion sends chunks of metal and plastic, bits of flesh and bone, flying in all directions. The helicopter dips its nose and plummets down onto the street, exploding over the police units gathered at the far end of the block. An expanding fireball engulfs the SWAT teams, just as they were readying an assault on the terrorists' rooftop positions.

At Manhattan police headquarters, the power has come back on. Computer screen flicker back to life, the borough map lights up. Cheers go up, as detectives, uninformed officers and staff release pent-up tension and refocus on what they were doing when interrupted. The borough commander grabs a phone.

COMMANDER (shouting into the receiver):

> "Emergency powers kicked in; communications are back on line!"

The room is a-buzz, as everyone weighs in with his version of what happened.

COMMANDER:

> "Gentlemen, get back to work! I need to know what our SWAT teams are doing!"

Two police helicopters with elite teams on board are streaking towards the columns of smoke rising between skyscrapers in the distance, like ancient volcanoes come to life.

PILOT (into his radio):

> "I see the smoke! we're going in!"

The navigator, pointing to a spot on a map, yells to the pilot and team leader.

NAVIGATOR:

> "A helicopter was brought down as it entered a street from the southwest. We should approach from the south, going low between the buildings and set it down behind smoke cover, you all get out and cover us while we high-tail it out of there, going low!"

TEAM LEADER (into radio):

> "OK, listen up! This is your fearless leader! we're about to pay a visit to hell! Let's kick ass! I'm first on the ground! Whatever I do, you do!"

At the terrorist command center, Sievers and Ekkart are listening in...

EKKART (into the radio, in Arabic):

> "The team leader will go first, out of helicopter No. 1. I want all fire concentrated on him!"

SIEVERS (interrupting loudly):

> "No! Hit them while they're still in the air! don't let them land! I order you to bring both copters down!"

RADIOED REPLY (in Arabic):

> "Both orders acknowledged!"

The helicopters descend, sending oily, black smoke spilling out and up in hellish vortexes. One lands, while the other hovers low over the street. A panorama of broke machines and broken human bodies unfolds around them.

PILOT:

> "This is scarier than the Gulf War!"

The team leader leaps from one of the choppers, followed by one group of commandoes.

Meanwhile, a group of veterans has taken cover behind the bullet-ridden, over turned bus.

VETERAN NO. 1:

> "What the hell are they doing? The fools are going to get themselves killed!"

VETERAN NO.2:

"They think this is like the movies!"

Back at the limousine...

LYBID:

"That's it! they're finished!"

The police commando leader runs from the helicopter and into the crosshairs of two rifle scopes. One trigger is pulled and his helmeted head is separated from his body, which runs a few more steps before tumbling down and rolling to a stop.

RADIO VOICE (in Arabic):

"One shot!"

A salvo of RPG's explodes around and amidst the rest of the commandos before they can react to the death of their leader. Arms, legs and other assorted body parts fly out the circle of death.

The pilot of the landed chopper panics...

PILOT (screaming):

"We're out of here! Airborne! Airborne!"

EKKART:

"Kill him!"

The helicopter rises only a few feet and explodes, as an RPG round and a SAM slam into it a split-second apart.

Demonic, sadistic laugher cracks over the terrorists' radio channel.

Panic sweeps the second helicopter...

SQUAD LEADER:

> "Abort landing! Abort landing! let's get the hell out of here!"

At the limousine...

LYBID:

> "O God! No! you've got to land and ..."

The second helicopter gets hit while rising between the buildings. Its flaming hulk falls on a movie theatre marquee and explodes...

LYBID:

> "What horror! All these lives lost, protecting mine..."

The White House. A military aide rushes into the Oval Office...

MILITARY AIDE (out of breath):

> "Mr. President! What is described as the beginning of World War III has broken out in New York!"

PRESIDENT CLINTON:

> "Captain, World War III can break out only in the Middle East and never in New York!"

AIDE:

> "There are reports of attacks by Arab and Nazi commandos in Manhattan! It seems their target is Lybid

Artemida! More than a thousand police have been killed!"

PRESIDENT CLINTON:

"Get me the Marine air base commandant!"

Marine Corps air base staff room. Flight controllers stare intently at radar screens.

COLONEL:

"Attention, all officers! Listen carefully! Some kind of high-intensity fighting is going on in New York. The police chief there just called. Said 90% of his men in Manhattan are either dead or wounded. We need to be ready for when the President decides he wants us to jump into that fight."

The phone rings. The duty officer picks up the receiver...

DUTY OFFICER:

"Marine air base staff. This is Staff Sergeant Polanski speaking! How may I help you?... [straightens up] Yes, sir! [to the colonel, as he hands over the receiver] Sir, it's the President of the United States..."

COLONEL:

"Mr. President, this is Col. Masters... [listens for about 15 seconds] Yes, away, Sir!"

The colonel hands the receiver over to Polanski and turns to his staff, who have been going about their duties.

COLONEL:

"OK, listen carefully! That was President Clinton! I want two of the Harriers now up on patrol to head over to mid-town Manhattan! Now! Exact coordinates will be given on the way! Queen Lybid Artemida is under attack by terrorists and could use some help! And the President has called out the Marines!"

Two Harrier jump jets flying north over the Atlantic veer left and ten minutes later streak low over Staten Island... the Statue of Liberty, Battery Park and down into a skyscraper canyon.

PILOT OF FIRST PLANE:

"I see their positions, down on those rooftops! Get ready to fire cannons!"

PILOT OF SECOND PLANE:

"Let's splatter them and go!"

The pilots see a quick flash at each terrorist positions and two SAM streaking towards them. An alarm sounds in their earphones, as radar picks up the missiles.

PILOT #2:

"Coming at us, six o'clock!"

At the Marine base, the Colonel shouts into a radio microphone...

COLONEL:

"Evasive maneuver!"

PILOT #1:

"No room!"

He goes into a sharp climb, but too late; the missile explodes near the tail, riddling the fuselage with shrapnel. The plane stays on its upward flight for another second before the jet fuel in its tanks ignites and turns it into a fireball just above the tallest of the surrounding buildings. Flaming debris rains down on the nearest rooftops and the street below; the fuselage crashes into a police cruiser, about a hundred feet away from the veteran's detachment.

Meanwhile, the second Marine jet has evaded the other missile, which goes just under him and slams into one of the upper floors of a skyscraper. Its radar screen shows another SAM honing in; the pilot's reflexes fail him and he screams as he sees a building looming just ahead. The terrorists on the rooftop watch, frozen in place, as the plane heads right at them, then disappears below the edge. The Harrier crashes through the ceiling-to-floor glass exterior; the wings shorn off, the fuselage continues on through the furniture, equipment, cubicles and inner walls and into an elevator shaft. An instant later the pilot's ejection seat is triggered and rockets up the shaft. The pursuing missile follows the plane through the gaping hole and the two explode a second apart. The force of the blast accelerates the ejection seat's tumbling flight up the shaft, towards an elevator car stuck just below the top floor and shaking violently from the force released below. The four women and two men inside, screaming hysterically, try to hang on to the walls. The ejection seat – now upside down, the unconscious, strapped-in pilot hanging – crashes into the elevator car, crushing the passengers and carrying it along upward...

Standing on the rooftop, which is shaking violently as if in an earthquake, the terrorists see the elevator car blast through the top of the shaft, followed by the ejection seat and a roaring, expanding volcanic eruption. The elevator car disintegrates in the air, splattering the terrorists with human blood and pieces of flesh and bone.

TERRORIST (shouting, in Arabic):

"Damn! Never in my life..."

The pilot's parachute deploys and is carried a hundred feet upward by the force of the blast. The terrorists on the rooftops and people below watch the unconscious pilot dangling helplessly in the air.

At the command center...

SIEVERS:

"Kill him!"

EKKART:

"No! I forbid it!"

SIEVERS:

"OK, let him live!"

The parachute floats down toward the street.

The terrorists on the rooftop exchange anxious glances...

TERRORIST No. 1:

"The building's turning into a torch! we'll be roasted!"

TERRORIST No.2:

"Let's get down from here...?"

The terrorists rush through a doorway leading to the stairwell and fly down the stairs. A closed door they just passed blasts open, followed by a fireball that fills the stairwell and heads upward...

TERRORIST No. 1:

"Made it..."

The terrorists, giddy with laughter over their good fortune, continue downward...

Meanwhile, the pilot, having regained consciousness, lands hard on the asphalt near Lybid Shielded from the snipers' view by the billowing chute, she rushes to the pilot and drags him to the safety of the limousine.

A veteran runs up to her and helps take off the pilot's helmet.

PILOT:

"Am I alive? Tell me I'm alive!"

VETERAN:

"Yeah, you're alive and you shitted in your flight suit..."

PILOT:

"I think I broke my back! No, my legs! The pain is excruciating!"

LYBID:

"You look unscratched! Your flight suit is undamaged..."

The pilot, juiced up by adrenalin, gets up, looks himself over, then looks up at the rooftop from which he just escaped, and shakes his fist...

PILOT (angrily):

> "I've survived! And now I'll get every one of you mothers..."

VETERAN:

> "Get down, you idiot!"

Ekkart watches on his monitor...

EKKART:

> "There are no miracles! Open fire!"

A short burst from a machinegun on a nearby rooftop and the pilot's body is ripped apart by .50-caliber bullets, splattering Lybid and the veteran with his blood. They run to opposite directions. Lybid gets tangled up in the parachute; the vet is caught in a hail of lead and is dead before his body hits the sidewalk.

Lybid drags the chute back to her safe position beside the limo, as bullets blue chunks of concrete from the sidewalk around her. Her cell phone rings and she get from under her chain mail armor. The man on the other end of the line is the preside of the United States...

In the Oval Office, an anxious Bill Clinton stares at the speaker phone and gets out from behind his desk. The room is filled with U.S. government officials and White House aides...

BILL CLINTON:

"Halia, you're alive?"

LYBID:

"I'm alive, but there's not a living soul by me, just piles of corpses! I'm pinned down by fire from all sides!"

BILL CLINTON:

"I've sent a detachment of Marines to get you out of there! Hang on for another time minutes and there'll be about thirty Cobras and Apaches arriving soon! I'll be taking off for New York in the next few minutes. Do you have a weapon with you?"

LYBID:

"There are every imaginable automatics and assault rifles scattered all around!"

BILL CLINTON:

"Good! Grab one and hold off those bastards!"

The Nazis' scanners have intercepted the conversation between the U.S President and Queen Lybid Artemida; Sievers and Ekkart listen in...

EKKART (speaking into a radio microphone):

"Gunter, turn on voice masking equipment and get me on that line."

GUNTER:

"Done, sir!"

EKKART (into the microphone, in an electronic voice):

"Greetings, Mr. Bill Clinton, President of the United States! Pity that you're in Washington and beyond my reach for the moment! Otherwise, I would personally rip your throat out!"

BILL CLINTON:

"Who's this on the line?"

EKKART:

"Chief of staff of the Army of the anti-Christ, Angel of Death Hermann Ekkart. Faithful son of the teacher of the Fuhrer of the German Nation, Adolf Hitler! And Arab sheik Abu Bekaar Saladin! You have never seen my face! I have launched a war, the final war in the history of mankind, to cut a swath through piles of your corpses for the coming of our Fuhrer, Adolf Hitler, who has been born anew and will soon appear, the ultimate anti-Christ!"

CLINTON:

"I assume it is you who have perpetrated this horrific, senseless slaughter in Manhattan! What do you hope to gain by it?"

EKKART:

"The target is Lybid Artemida! Her death is imminent!"

BILL CLINTON:

"But why?!"

EKKART:

"To make the way for Adolf Hitler!"

CLINTON:

"You understand that you have launched a war against the United States of America?"

EKKART:

"Yes! Precisely! And you will die, Mr. President!"

CLINTON:

"No, it is you who will be brought to justice for these crimes!"

The line is disconnected and the President of the United States is led out to the South Lawn, where Marine 1 is waiting for him. Clinton climbs on board, followed by a dozen civilian and military aides. The last to board are six Marine guards. The huge helicopter takes off, quickly gains altitude and heads northeast, flanked on both sides by a squadron of military assault helicopters. Four Air Force F-15's patrol the air space from a height of 10,000 feet...

Still holding her cell phone to her ear, Lybid hears nothing but short, urge bursts. She anxiously looks skyward, then around her, and sees nothing but corpses. She realizes the loneliness of her situation...

At the command center, Hermann Ekkart barks at his communications officer...

EKKART:

"Why was I cut off? Get me on that line again!"

Lybid's cell phone rings again and she lifts it to her ear...

EKKART:

> "Lybid! Come on out in the open! I swear to you – you will die a quick death and then we will withdraw our forces! Otherwise, thousands will die, along with you!"

LYBID:

> "If you kill me now Hitler will gain dominion over the Earth and then two or three billon innocents will die! I must live!"

EKKART:

> "You have no conscience, you cold-hearted bitch!"

LYBID:

> "Why do you fear me so?"

EKKART:

> "Fifty-five years ago, I was a young officer in the SS. I now deeply regret obeying Hitler's orders not to harm your mother and father, whom we had in our hands. A mistake of historic proportions!

The conversation is monitored at police headquarters and at a military listening post. A pall of smoke hangs over the Manhattan street and envelops the surrounding buildings...

EKKART:

> "I could have killed your father and raped your mother! Then you would have been my daughter. And the course of history would have been altered in quite a different direction!"

LYBID:

"What did you say, your hideous pervert?!"

EKKART:

"I said I regret not raping your mother!"

LYBID:

"I shall destroy you, Nazi swine! You and all your demented cohorts!"

Lybid quickly looks up and down the sidewalk and, crouching low, runs from behind her disabled limousine. She quickly gathers an m-16, an Uzi and a Beretta automatic from among the many that lie next to the dead and the dying, who no longer have any use for them. She carries them back to the vehicle that has kept her alive...

EKKART:

"Attention, the Adolf Hitler Arab SS company! You have three minutes to kill Lybid Artemida! There are no police left alive! In seven or eight minutes the U.S. Marines will be here! Your orders are to kill Lybid Artemida or die! Kill her! Kill her now!"

A large group of terrorist elite commandos immediately advance from their covert, positions, darting like roaches from one burning or overturned car to another. A storm of automatic gunfire hits the limousine, the ground around Lybid and the facade of Veterans Hall opposite her...

General Smith and a score of veterans, some of them wounded, surrounded by the bodies of their comrades in arms, watch through the demolished doorway.

SMITH:

"They're keeping her pinned down so they can take her alive, or, if not, kill her! We can't let that happen! We have to save her, at the cost of our old lives, if that's what it takes! We'll attack their flank, split them and destroy! OK, line up!"

The old vets quickly line up smartly in the corridor, standing at attention, their faces and determined...

SMITH:

"It seems we have once more been called to duty, no doubt for the last time. An Almighty and just God has allowed us again to stand together as soldiers for a just cause, and, if that be His will, to die in battle for that cause. We have long ago been replaced by men much younger than we. I don't know about you, but I live in fear of the possibility of wasting away from the diseases that come with age – cancer, heart failure, stroke... Many of us have gone under the surgeon's knife and will no doubt be there again. It is just a matter of time before we lie bedridden or bound to a wheelchair in some nursing home... But what is most painful for an old trooper who has felt the intensity of battle, who has stoically faced death and delivered it, is to surrender to dementia, to be so helpless as to lose control of his natural functions. I for one want to die as a soldier, without fear and infirmities, to burn up like a shooting star over my final battlefield! Whoever wants to join me in facing death one more time in battle, rather than dying in a sickbed, step forward!"

The veterans, to a man aroused yet focused, all take a step forward...

SMITH:

> "Now, many of us no longer have the eyesight we used to. So, we'll try to get as close as possible before opening fire. If your buddy next to you has taken a hit and goes down, grab his weapon and keep moving! And don't waste ammunition! Let's get ready to attack!"

The veterans quickly take positions at the blown-out windows facing the street and wait for Smith's command. The general hits a button on his cell phone...

SMITH:

> "Admiral Johnson?"

Johnson and his veterans are crouching behind several overturned cars, pinned down by heavy machine-gun and automatic fire.

JOHNSON:

> "Yes, Larry! We've got heavy fire all around us! If we raise our heads, were liable to get them shot off!"

SMITH:

> "The Nazi bastards are moving in on Lybid Artemida, moving in for the kill!
>
> We're going to outflank them and attack from behind! When they turn their fire on us, you hit them from your positions!"

JOHNSON:

> "You got it! Let's see if we can get them in a crossfire!"

The terrorists rush out from their cover for a final assault on Lybid, automatic weapons spitting out hot lead.

JOHNSON:

"Larry! they've begun their final push! This is it!"

SMITH:

"We see it! it's time!"

From Smith's position it's clear that the commandos, advancing rapidly down the street, have left their rear unprotected. Smith switches off his cell phone and places it in a shirt pocket.

SMITH:

"Move out! Flanking assault from the rear! Death to the Nazi dogs!"

Maj. Gen. Larry Smith, U.S. Army (retired), rushes out through a demolished window frame and, followed by his men, runs crouching toward the nearest police cars that stand burning to the left of the building's entrance. Machine-gun fire continues to rain down from the surrounding rooftops. One veteran fall, then another and a third, but the rest reach the spot where a detachment of police had made a stand and take the weapons from their dead hands.

One of the old-timers, clutching his chest, begins to stagger and falls at the feet of leader.

GEN. SMITH:

"Sam, what's happening to you?"

The old veteran gasps for air, manages to let out a raspy "My heart! "and lies still.

SMITH:

> "His heart gave out, in his last battle. He gave his last. A hero's death..."

Bullets are flying about, like swarms of lethal wasps...

SMITH (into his cell phone):

> "Johnson, Larry here! we're armed and attacking! Use your cell to coordinate our moves!"

JOHNSON (heard in the phone's receiver):

> "Right! Let's sweep them up! Like at Monte Cassino!"

SMITH (as he puts his phone away):

> "OK, men! As the kids say these days, let's rock! Death to the Nazis!"

Lybid sees a group of veterans, in the uniforms of different countries, appear out of nowhere and rush towards her. Three are cut down and tumble to the sidewalk, but ten make it safely to her side. The vets surround her and open fire on the advancing terrorists.

Lybid's cell phone rings...

LYBID (shouting into the phone):

> "Yes, General Smith! We see you on their flank! Courage!"

She folds her phone...

LYBID:

> "Gen. Smith and his men are counterattacking! let's keep the enemy busy!"

Smith's veterans sweep in from the side, cutting off the terrorists' escape route. Up on the rooftops, the machine guns, one by one, fall silent, the ammunitions belts dropping empty at the feet of the gunners.

At the command center...

EKKART (shouting angrily into a phone receiver):

> "Out of ammunition! Leave the machine guns, get down to street level with whatever you can carry and cover your comrades!"

Through the windows Ekkart and Sievers see an armada of assault helicopters and air support jets approaching over the New York skyline like a threatening cloud...

SIEVERS (sarcastically):

> "The 'cavalry' has arrived. Time to depart."

EKKART:

> "To fight again another day!"

Sievers walks to the kitchen, opens the refrigerator and sweeps a few handfuls of chocolate candies into a small leather bag.

SIEVERS (jovially):

> "Mustn't forget the sweets for my sweet granddaughter!"

The two old Nazis walk out of the apartment. Ekkart goes to call up the freight elevator, while Sievers stands in the doorway, as their young aides turn off the electronics, stuff what they can into huge athletic equipment bags and walk out. Sievers locks the door and the entire group gets into the waiting elevator. Ekkart presses the button for the ground floor, On the way down, there is only silence, as the men wearily glance at one another. The young Nazis look intently at their leaders, their eyes full of questions that need no voicing.

EKKART:

> "I've decided that tomorrow will be a day off! Sleep late, stuff yourselves, find some women. And next week, we'll launch our operation to buy up Microsoft shares!"

SIEVERS:

> "We have had one hell of a day!"

The group walks out of the building and stops at the entrance to look up at the aircraft that, for a good thirty seconds, roar across the swath of blue high above.

EKKART (sarcastically):

> "Look – a fly-by, just like on the Fourth of July!"

The conspirators quickly separate. Ekkart and two aides disappear down the street, the rest of the young Nazis pile into waiting vans and drive away. Sievers heads for a children's playground around the corner.

From the playground – filled with joyous laughter and kids running up, over and slides, swings, monkey bars and sand boxes – the Manhattan skyline looms in the distance. A thick plume of black smoke that rises from the top of a skyscraper and a gray cloud that hangs low over the immediate surrounding area are the only blots on an otherwise clear blue sky. Several of the mothers and grandmothers of the children have come together and are chattering anxiously, their glances alternately fixed on the distant ominous sign and searching for their little charges.

One of the older women runs up to Sievers as he approaches.

VALENTINA:

> "Did you hear, Mr. Sievers, what they are saying? That Hitler is alive and has attacked New York with a new Nazi army?"

SIEVERS:

> "What is this nonsense, Valentina? We stopped Nazism over fifty years ago! And Hitler went kaput!"

VALENTINA:

> "But what about the explosions in Manhattan?"

SIEVERS:

> "I imagine they're shooting a very expensive Hollywood film. But, after all, life is one big movie, Valentina. A film production!"

Sievers walks up to a swing. His granddaughter jumps off and wraps her arms around his waist. He pulls her in tighter with one arm; with the other he pulls a box of chocolate candies from behind his back and offers it to her.

SIEVERS:

> "Sweets for my Barbie!"

Meanwhile, the battle in front of Veterans Hall is reaching its climax...

Streams of lethal fire cut down one fighter after another on -both sides. The exchanges soon begin to subside, however, as veterans and terrorists both begin to run of ammunition.

VETERANS:

"I need ammo! who's got ammo?"

LYBID:

"Take it off the dead! Pick it up wherever you can!"

The furious blaze that began on the rooftop of the nearest skyscraper is moving down, consuming floor after floor. One of the veterans taps Lybid on the shoulder and points up. Lybid looks upward and sees people hanging out the windows and, in a despairing and mindless attempt to escape the pressing flames, dive into the void. The bodies, some of them on fire, tumble gracelessly downward, ending their flight, and their life's journey, in heaps of biomass on the pavement and asphalt below.

LYBID:

"The horror..."

She stops in midsentence, refocusing on the life-and-death struggle directly around her. The terrorists, reeling from the vets' strike at their flank, have abandoned their assault on Lybid's position and direct their weakened fire against smith's troops. Running between and around vehicles, some of them get close enough to lob grenades at their, attackers, thinning their ranks.

LYBID:

"Let's lend Gen. Smith a hand! Get ready to attack!"

Lybid tears off her crimson coat, which falls at her feet, and puts on a blood-smeared bulletproof vest taken off one of the police dead. She holds an automatic in her left hand and an assault rifle in the other...

MEKENZIE:

"Hold it a second! We need a banner!"

McKenzie, the World War II standard bearer, U.S. Army, picks up a rifle from the pavement and attaches Lybid's cloak to the barrel. He raises it high, to the cheers and shouts of a visibly inspired group of vets: "Atta boy, McKenzie!" "Way to go, McKenzie!"

LYBID:

"Forward! In the name of Life on Earth!"

Lybid stands up and, ignoring several hits to her Kevlar vest, leads the veterans in a fierce charge against the remaining terrorists. Rolling over hoods and leaping from behind cars, she pours fire from the automatic in one hand and the assault rifle in the other. of the terrorists, who had the misfortune of being nearest to the avenging queen, soon lie in their own blood on the street.

McKenzie runs just behind her, holding high her standard, until a bullet pierces his battle ribbons and plunges into his heart.

LYBID:

"The banner!"

A decorated Afro-American veteran grabs the flag from the hands of the fallen McKenzie, but takes only a few steps before he also is cut down.

A Chinese veteran, one of the last of the defenders of Nanking, keeps the standard from hitting the ground and with a battle cry carries it forward. A moment or two later he also falls, his body riddled by bullets.

The flag is picked up off the ground by an old Jewish soldier.

JEWISH VET:

> "Death to terrorism!"

Dressed in the uniform of the Israel Defense Forces of the 1950's, the Jewish veteran holds the colors above the proud heads of the advancing old-timers.

The terrorists have decimated smith's unit with the grenade attack and are concentrating their fire on the last few veterans still standing. The general has taken several but let's in the stomach. Two veterans, one black, the other white, drag him behind a vehicle. Barely conscious and coughing up blood, he takes out his cell phone and hits a number.

SMITH:

> "Forgot to call the wife... Emily? I won't be home for dinner tonight; sweetheart Don't be cross with me... No, I'm not drunk... I'm sorry, but you're about to widow... Love of my life..."

Three huge men, dressed in black from head to toe, with full helmets on their heads appear before the fallen American officer. The two vets lunge at them with bare hands, but are sent reeling by several point-blank .45 rounds.

Two of the Ninjas grab Smith by the arms, while the third takes out a knife and with a few swift practiced strokes separates his head from the body. The killer then sticks the head onto the end of a rifle barrel and raises the grisly trophy high, as the three let cries of blood-frenzy.

Their celebration is cut short by the surprise appearance of the veterans of Admiral Johnson, who dispatch them with extreme prejudice. Johnson's troops are joined by Lybid and her cohorts and the combined force takes the fight to the terrorists.

Behind an overturned bus a terrorist stomps on a wounded old-timer lying in the street, but pays for his sadistic delights with a chest full of lead from Lybid's automatic.

JOHNSON:

"Hand-to-hand combat!"

The veterans, cursing and yelling in between wheezes and coughs, throw themselves on their surrounded foe, two and three on each terrorist.

Four U.S. Army helicopters appear in the sky and swoop down towards a terrorist unit on the street, rockets firing, gunners in the open doors spraying the group with light machine gun fire.

JOHNSON:

"The air cavalry has arrived!"

But somewhere towards the end of the block terrorist launchers fire and the choppers are set ablaze by round after round of RPGS. Secondary explosions send chunks of metal, human parts and burning fuel flying.

A dozen terrorists regroup and counterattack. Lybid, finding herself in their midst, keeps shooting until hearing empty clicks in both her firearms, then carries on the fight with lethal blows and kicks, part of a martial arts system passed on from the distant past of Kyivan Rus. Three graying and balding Japanese veterans fight alongside her, using methods handed down to them from the times of the samurai.

Between two burning police vehicles the counterattacking terrorists are pushing back Johnson's vets. Three fighters descend on the admiral, who fights them off until knocked off his feet. He gets up onto his knees, but no further, as a terrorist bullet to the head brings an end to a life lived gallantly and courageously. With a cry of vengeance Lybid attack one of the killers, grabbing and twisting his right arm, so that the pistol in his hand discharges, wounding one of his buddies. Lybid takes away the weapon and empties the cartridge into the two.

Lybid sees the advancing main group of terrorists, led by Smith's killer, who carries the general's bloody head stuck on a rifle barrel.

A stark contrast: Lybid's banner -her crimson cloak, held high as a symbol of honor and courage-and the terrorists' grisly totem.

Cries of anger and hatred rise through the ranks of the veterans. Lybid, like an avenging angel of three thousand years ago, draws the shining Sword of Ariy from its scabbard and throws herself into the final fight.

She is immediately hit by a score of bullets, which whine and zing and spark as they bounce of her helmet and armor. The Queen keeps her head low, so as to expose as little of her unprotected face as possible, while her sword flashes in her hand.

One of the terrorists directs his machine gun at her, but Lybid is upon him before he can fire off a round. He raises the weapon over his head to fend of the descending avenging sword. The Sword of Ariy slices the heavy assault weapon in two, then cleaves the terrorist's helmet, head and torso down to the waist...

The fear-stricken terrorists turn to flee from Lybid. She remains in pursuit, smiting the laggards with her terrible sword. One of the fighters, crouching behind a huge riot police shield that he has set on the pavement, opens fire on Lybid with an assault rifle. He gets one burst off before her wonder-sword slices the bullet-proof shield as if through plywood. The

170

terrorist lets loose an unearthly scream, as his severed hand falls to the ground, still holding on to one half of the shield. Lybid pivots and with a lightning-quick side-sweep of her sword through his neck ends his pain.

Marine Harriers jump jets streak towards Manhattan. Crossing the southern shore of Long Island, the pilots see two skyscrapers burning like candles, sending columns of smoke skyward.

VOICE OVER RADIO:

"Wingman! I need you to recon the AA capabilities of the bad guys! 'eagle' and 'fox' squadrons-stand by just outside the Manhattan perimeter, ready to go in!"

The three groups disperse to begin their holding patterns, while a lone reconnaissance jet heads towards the towering columns of smoke. Flying over the East River radios back:

PILOT #1:

"This is Harper! I'm over the Brooklyn Bridge and heading west. Quite a scene ahead – vehicles overturned and burning, bodies everywhere. Traffic over the blocked completely by cars and pedestrians!

The Harrier swoops down towards the battle area...

PILOT#1:

"Passing the burning buildings. People jumping out of windows... Going in for another pass..."

The Marine jet makes a curving turn and again drops low, one hundred feet above the skyscrapers...

PILOT#1:

"Looks like all our choppers have crashed and burned!
The bad guys seem to have potent AA capabilities!"

At that moment, in confirmation of his words, a SAM leaves its shoulder-held and streaks after the Harrier, striking one of the engines. The explosion rends the aircraft, sending the flaming fuselage and pieces down to the street, where they rain upon veteran and terrorist alike.

LYBID:

"Death to terrorists!"

With several quick strokes the Queen finishes off two of the terrorists she had backed against a disabled school bus. The others run, but are soon overtaken among the overturned vehicles by Lybid and the remaining veterans. Lybid pauses briefly, as three terrorists fall down on their knees before her. Out of nowhere the trio of smith's killers rise behind them and shoot their kneeling comrades in the back, punishing the deserters and clearing the way for themselves.

The Ninja leader flings smith's head at Lybid, then takes off his own helmet, revealing a hate-filled, hideous face marked with recently healed burn scars.

TERRORIST LEADER (pointing at Lybid):

"Kill"

His underlings rush at Lybid, their AK-47s blazing. Lybid, however, leaps up and, with a graceful flip other their heads, lands behind them. The three Japanese veterans who were standing behind Lybid, though mortally wounded, throw themselves at the attackers and wring their necks, then themselves fall dead on the pavement.

The battle's climax. The Ninja leader, screaming like a madman, pulls the pin on a grenade in his hand and rushes at Lybid. The grenade explodes and conceals him, Lybid and the nearby combatants in its fireball.

In her mind's eye Lybid sees herself on the roiling surface of the Sun, walking among long tongues of flame that reach out to the blackness of the Cosmos beyond.

The scene fades and Lybid sees herself at a podium in the White House...

LYBID:

> "I exhort humanity to a new way of thinking about the
> Sun. The Sun is a Planet a Planet-God of our material
> world. Think: if 99.866% of all the matter in our Solar
> System is found in the Sun, then it seems, clearly and
> simply, that 99.866% of the intellect in our Solar system
> is also concentrated there!
>
> Lybid sees her birth, her father's caring hands lifting her
> high and toward the Sun. She hears his voice: "O Great
> Yarylo! I consecrate your daughter, born for the glory of
> the peoples of the Earth, to You! O Queen! It is your
> destiny to return to the Sun, not as Spirit but as Body,
> to be alive, yet not consumed!"

The newborn shines like an angel in the rays of the Sun.

The Sun radiates with all the colors of the Cosmic flame, like a Father rejoicing...

Scenes from Lybid's life pass before her eyes as in a kaleidoscope: there she is, a child drinking milk from an earthen jug and spilling some all over herself and laughing her mother and father laughing with her; there she is, fighting school bullies, standing up for her brother; addressing the world's religious leaders; at the White House, telling President Bill Clinton, "The

173

world's moral community must condemn the killing of a human being as an indelible mark of shame for the killer... We shall put an end to war!"

...As Lybid regains consciousness she sees Marine 1 descending slowly from the sky its downward draft clearing the area of the smoke and dust that have enveloped it over the past few hours. Looking down through a window Bill Clinton sees Lybid Artemida, lying amidst the corpses, yet somehow shining with the divine light of the victorious in battle Lybid, alive and unharmed, pulls herself out from a pile of bodies, sits on the concrete with her head between her knees and begins to weep... The helicopter lands, Clinton gets out, crouches down beside her and puts his arm around her shoulders... Lybid buries her face in his chest...

CLINTON:

"You're alive! Alive! And you've won your final battle!"

The site of the battle just ended is a bedlam of fire engines, emergency response vehicles, military people, journalists and law enforcement personnel. Lybid and the President of the United States walk among the dead. They see the face of Gen. Smith as latex-gloved hands return his severed head to the rest of him in a body bag and zip it closed... There's Adm. Johnson being placed in a body bag... An ERT medic zips up a bag containing the remains of Betsy Rosenberg... Another carries away the body of Robert Oberfell... Lybid looks upon his face for the last time...

LYBID:

"The UN should declare Ekkart's Neo-Nazis outlaws. The peoples of the world unite in hunting them down and bringing them to justice!"

BILL CLINTON:

"The United States will leave no stone unturned to find them, wherever they may hide! America shall put all of its might to bear in order to destroy this army of the new Hitler!"

The American president's words are broadcast live over all the major channels.

In the living room of a large building Sievers sits in a rocking chair, his lap covered with a thick plaid blanket, and watches CNN with numerous relatives and guests. His gaze fixed on the screen, he stretches lazily and reaches down for another potato chip from the bag on his lap...

SIEVERS:

"There is a God in heaven! she's alive! How fortunate for the United States of America!"

All those present express agreement with Sievers' sentiments, especially his sixteen-year-old grandson.

GRANDSON:

"We avoided embarrassment before the international community, right Granddad?"

SIEVERS:

"By surviving that terrible ordeal, this great woman saved us from the horrors of the possible revival of Nazism. Remember, my boy-the greatest evil in the history of mankind was Adolf Hitler. Over 50 years ago, we Americans of the Greatest Generation bought against Hitler and emerged victorious in that life-and-death struggle, thus enabling the United States to become the super power it is today."

ELDER GUEST:

"Right on, Brother Dalem! We broke Nazism's back!"

MALE ANNOUNCER (on the TV set):

"It is with great sorrow we announce that among the dead outside Veterans Hall was the veteran CNN correspondent Betsy Rosenberg, who headed the coverage of events surrounding Queen Lybid Artemida. Our sadness is deeper still because the entire CNN crew also perished, among them..."

While the television screens show photos of the deceased camera operators, sound men and other personnel, Sievers' daughter-in-law gives voice to her agitation.

DAUGHTER-IN-LAW:

"Who is this Ekkart person? The one who threatened President Clinton and Mrs. Lybid over the phone?"

SIEVERS:

"Ekkart Jr. is the blood-thirsty nephew of Adolf Hitler's teacher, my dear. He is a horrible person, a real monster! He personally conducted experiments on inmates of Nazi concentration camps in Germany and in occupied Poland... Roosevelt, and Stalin all put a price on his head! But there was a Nazi war criminal who was even more despicable than Ekkart!"

SEVERAL GUESTS: " SIEVERS:

"Gerhard Gottlieb Sievers! The nephew of an SS colonel, Wolfram Sievers!"

176

GRANDSON:

"And who was he?"

SIEVERS:

"Why...But, of course, how are your young people supposed to know this? History is not fair, children! Only the elder Sievers gained any renown -or, more properly, notoriety – as the commandant of a system of the SS Anenerbe Institutes of the Occult! Under his command over 750,000 European Gypsies were killed! Col. Wolfram Sievers was tried and found guilty by the victorious Allies at the Nuremberg trials and hanged as an especially murderous Nazi war criminal! But history is silent about the unreachable Sievers Jr., the shadow of SS Reichsfuhrer Heinrich Himmler himself. Silent, obviously, out of fear. The ace of Nazi occult studies, mysticism and the black arts, SS Major Sievers escaped, to the sorrow e of the entire world. Even the terrible Ekkart the Grat trembles at the very mention of the name Gerhard Gottlieb Sievers!"

Sievers scans the room, a smug and self-satisfied look on his face. But one of his guests, CIA veteran Alexander Hardale, unexpectedly bursts out in jealous anger.

HARDALE:

"Enough, Sam! Enough of poisoning young minds with this nonsense! Who was the one who survived? Did Sievers the Younger survive? It sounds as though you've been reading Prof. blooming's pseudo-history babble! The old rat who never got anywhere near the front. But that didn't prevent him from selling himself as an eyewitness and lying in the tabloid press about how Gerhard Sievers sold his soul to the devil, and the devil brought him back to life and pulled him out of the execution pit!"

SIEVERS:

"What's eating you, Hardale?"

HARDALE:

" Because I'm one of the very few people alive today that actually saw Gerhard Sievers my own eyes.!"

SIEVERS'SON (with sincere naivete'):

"I didn't know you were a real war hero, Mr. Hardale!"

HARDALE:

"Allen Dulles himself ordered me dropped into Nazi Germany on a mission to assassinate Sievers. I hunted this viper over all of Europe! Three months! On April 12, 1945, with this very hand I sent a bullet right into his heart. And then I personally pushed him into the execution pit! After the war I was secretly awarded the Congressional Medal of Honor for this one mission!"

The assembled guests have gathered around Hardale and Sievers.

SIEVERS:

"I had no inkling that all these years I've been in the presence of such a heroic figure. How long has it been – ten years, right? – that we've been drinking from the same whiskey bottle and going boar hunting?"

Hardale stands there in silence, not sure where Sievers is going with the remark. His vanity, the vanity of an old war veteran who is sure he didn't get all the praise his exploits merited, convinces him it was meant as a compliment.

HARDALE:

> "Yes, Dalem! Unlike you, I was a real hero! If you had met Sievers the Younger face to face, you would have been paralyzed with fear and you would have dropped a load down your trousers!"

SIEVERS' SON:

> "I can't believe what I'm hearing! Thousands of people were killed in Manhattan today - Americans, veterans of various foreign wars, dedicated men and women of law enforcement - and you bicker about events that took place over 50 years ago! Both of you should be ashamed!"

A woman appears on the television screen...

TV ANNOUNCER:

> "Excalibur! That was the name of the sword of the legendary King Arthur of the Round Table! As some Americans might remember, former president Ronald Reagan was said to have been descended from King Arthur! We have been inundated with telephone calls - thousands of them - asking whether the gleaming sword with which Queen Lybid Artemida today dispatched dozens of terrorists is in fact that same legendary Excalibur of King Arthur fame. Let's get the view on this of an expert on heraldry, Prof. Katz."

Dr. Katz appears on the screen, standing in a room filled with coats-of-arms, shields, swords and other medieval weapons.

KATZ:

> "According to legend, the sword with which Lybid Artemida killed the terrorists today once belonged to the god of war, Ariy, and was bequeathed to the Queen by herself several millennia back in time! This terrible sword was forged from a wondrous meteorite that fell from the heavens about three thousand years ago in the land of the Rus.
>
> The metal is said to be super-hard and stronger than any other metal in human history. Legend has it that Ariy himself forged the sword using a heavy stone hammer when the metal was still superheated from its fall through the Earth's atmosphere!

The screen shows a rapid sequence of close-ups from the battle around Veterans Hall. In one scene Lybid brings her sword down on a helmeted terrorist head and cleaves it in two.

KATZ:

> "The Sword of Ariy slices through even today's super-hard composite helmets as through a watermelon! It's really a marvel of ancient technology! If one was to accept the legend's claim that the metal used to make the Sword of Ariy was sent to Earth by the gods themselves, the next question would be whether its ability to cut through any modern material is at the molecular level or comes from some kind of Divine energy!"

The screen shows a scene in which a heavy-caliber bullet ricochets off Lybid's helmet in a spray of sparks. The women before the TV set gasp, while the men silently flinch.

MOTHER-IN-LAW:

"My Lord! Right in the head!"

Sievers, shaken, turns to one of the older men in the room.

SIEVERS:

"CNN estimates that Lybid was hit by almost a hundred bullets. How was she able to survive that?"

The TV audience sees the inside of a police station, where a group of experts are examining Lybid Artemida's battle armor and helmet under strong lights.

POLICE WEAPONS EXPERT:

"Astounding! Just some scratches and minor dents, from around sixty handgun and rifle bullets! The armor is made from a metal that doesn't appear to be of an Earthly origin. The helmet shows evidence of nine direct hits. And this dark mark in this deeper dent seems to have been made by a Teflon-covered .45 caliber bullet that can penetrate a standard-issue police vest. The design of Lybid's helmet protects the wearer from her or his neck being broken due to the shock of a bullet's impact. The Queen's armor – in actuality a robe made of metal - is designed in such a way as to disperse the energy of a high-velocity bullet over the entire body. The robe is said to have been 'sewn' almost three thousand years ago of a metal that came from a meteorite and is not in the periodic table. According to our preliminary analysis the metal outperforms any type of steel by at least a factor of three in all the known parameters. This is truly a garment meant for a god!"

One of Sievers' grandsons switches the channel to a CNN live report from the scene of the battle.

FEMALE REPORTER:

"A lot of blood was spilled here in this section of Manhattan in the past few hours. The fire on the top floors of the skyscraper looming off to my right is still raging, despite the efforts of a dozen companies of firefighters. But we no longer see people throwing themselves out the windows..."

The screen shows New York's fire chief standing against the background of the skyscraper.

FIRE CHIEF:

"Obviously, anyone caught on the upper floors of the building has either burned to death or suffocated. The blaze is so powerful that we may not be able to put it out even in a week..."

FEMALE REPORTER:

"What are the chances that it will burn itself out?"

FIRE CHIEF:

"That would happen only when the fire has consumed everything inside the structure, and that would likely take several weeks. But on behalf of the Fire Department of our great city I pledge that, through the courage and dedication of our firefighters, the blaze will be brought under control within 48 hours!"

There is a shot change to show the building from a distance.

FEMALE REPORTER:

"The towering skyscraper burns tonight like a torch set down among the buildings of Manhattan. To many it seems like the huge smokestack of a crematorium, in which thousands were burned alive. This is a frightful night. The police and the National Guard, armed to the teeth, are conducting mopping-up operations on foot and in armored vehicles, block by block, building by building. The subway system, underground garages and the sewer system are among the facilities being checked. Anyone acting even the least bit suspicious is being arrested."

At the Sievers residence the guests and family members watch in stunned silence, as the realization sets in that the streets of their city have been taken over by the armed forces and law enforcement agencies. To some it appears that the peace in their lives is now a thing of the past.

HARDALE:

"Who is behind all this?"

SIEVERS (sarcastically):

"Only the Powers of Darkness are capable of bringing something like this about!

The Anti-Christ, the son of the Virgin Mary and the Prince of Darkness, Satan himself!

Eh, Brother Hardale?"

HARDALE (angrily leaping up from a couch):

"If I were you, I wouldn't goad me, Brother Dalem! Unlike you, who knows combat only from books and movies, I didn't sit out the entire Second World War in a warehouse in Honolulu! I don't receive $1000 a month for a fake 'disability suffered at the front, but in reality, in a barroom brawl over some whores in Macao! Maj. Abraham Goldberg was right in wanting to file a request for an inquiry into how you managed to work your way into our Normandy Invasion Veterans Association! And Maj. Goldberg is not one to mess around with! That tongue of yours will get you in hot water yet!"

Sievers' large family stands in embarrassed silence over his war "record."

SIEVERS:

"I don't pretend to be a Normandy landing hero, Brother Hardale! But thanks to books and movies, especially 'Saving Private Ryan,' I've turned into a sort of aficionado of that chapter of history. So, maybe, sometimes my imagination gets the better of me and I start seeing myself as a Normandy warrior! But, Heavens no! I didn't mean to make fun of you. I just wanted your opinion, as a man who knows a lot about these things, as to who might have been the perpetrator of the bloody events in Manhattan."

HARDALE (trying to sort out his emotions):

"The author of this slaughter, Brother Dalem, is, obviously, a Hitler fanatic, somebody of the caliber of

Otto Scorceny or perhaps Gerhard Sievers himself. You, a mere mortal, would just crap in your pants if you ever came face to face with that devil"

SIEVERS' SON (with disgust):

"Are you two at it again?"

A second reporter appears on the screen.

MALE REPORTER:

"The battle of Manhattan is still not over! There are reports of localized skirmishes. The toll of the fighting up to now is quite shocking. It is our sad duty to report that almost all of the veterans who came from many countries to take part in the International Congress to Ban War have been killed while putting up a heroic resistance to the terrorists. The police force has suffered terrible losses. All told, over eighteen hundred bodies have been found and the count continues. New York has not known devastation on this scale! The President of the United States has proclaimed a national day of mourning!"

The grandson switches the channel again and the guests see a video replay from the scene of the tragedy, where President Clinton and Lybid Artemida vow to make the terrorists pay for their crime...

LYBID:

"The UN should declare Ekkart's Neo-Nazis outlaws. The peoples of the world should unite in hunting them down and bringing them to justice!"

BILL CLINTON:

> "The United States will leave no stone unturned to find them, wherever they may hide! America shall put all of its might to bear in order to destroy this army of the new Hitler!"

Sievers nods his head in agreement...

SIEVERS:

> "We Americans will exact vengeance on the Arabs for this attack upon our soil!"

High in the sky the Sun seems to erupt in anger at Sievers' blasphemy, shooting flares from its Corona...

New York. September 7, 2000, National Day of Mourning in the U.S.

A large grandstand has been set up in Times Square for a ceremony honoring the victims of the September 11th Battle of Manhattan. President Bill Clinton stands with his wife, Hillary, on his right and Queen Lybid on his left, and further flanked by Secretary of State Albright and members of the Cabinet and Congress.

A funeral procession goes slowly up Broadway and past the grandstand. In the lead is a Bradley Fighting Vehicle carrying a large bronze vase with a burning Eternal Flame of remembrance. It is followed by row upon row of a police escort on Harley Davidsons, U.S. flags flying high off the back. Next, army gun carriages carrying coffins draped with the Stars and Stripes, six abreast, are drawn by pairs of black stallions. Behind each row families of the dead walk over the flower-strewn asphalt, carrying portraits of their loved ones. U.S. military jets streak overhead, paying homage to the victims of the terrorist attack. President Clinton steps up to the rostrum...

CLINTON:

"Distinguished guests to our shores, friends, my fellow Americans! The terrible tragedy that took place here several days ago has united all of us, has brought us closer together. On September 11th, Hitlerism, which is the enemy of all mankind, again did the Devil's work, emerging from its defeat of a half-century ago, to reap its bloody harvest, this time in Manhattan..."

To the side of the presidential grandstand, U.S. war veterans, holding back tears, decoration ribbons on their chests, silently watch the mournful procession. The war hero Hardale and the pseudo veteran Gerhard Sievers are among them...

SIEVERS:

"Brother Hardale! We should be the ones lying in those coffins up there. I can't take this! I can't stand the pain!"

Sievers wipes his moist eyes with a handkerchief.

HARDALE:

"I will never forgive myself..."

SIEVERS:

"We were supposed to be there in Veterans Hall on September 11th, another day of infamy! You and I should have been up there in the presidium, which means that we probably would have died together in the final battle of our lives..."

HARDALE:

> "I don't understand how we are still alive. What was it you served me on that day That I literally got sick to the stomach and spent almost the entire day on a toilet seat?"

SIEVERS:

> "Obviously, it was the will of God that you be spared!"

Sievers, pretending to be deeply religious, nods his head and raises his hand to the sky, as if asking the Almighty to be his witness.

SIEVERS:

> "It was the Lord's will!"

In the middle of his speech President Clinton chokes up and fights to regain his self-control.

CLINTON:

> "My fellow Americans! We shall never forget those members of the Greatest Generation, who, having gone through all of the trials and tribulations of World War II, heroically gave their lives on this, their final battlefield. We mourn today with their loved ones, we share the pain of all those whose hearts will never again be warmed by their loving smiles, who will never again be taken back to their sweet childhoods by their loving voices..."

Listening to the words of the American president, Lybid suddenly remembers the day when she and her mother stood weeping over a grave in an old cemetery in Podillia. Standing over a grave, looking at an enameled photo on the gravestone and remembering the handsome, serious face with the high forehead and bright sparkling eyes, the face of a great man of modesty, her father, Vasyl Kovhanych. Her thoughts take her fifteen years back in time...

August 1985. Soviet Ukraine. The Podillia region. As her father continues his narrative Lybid sees people and events from the past vividly drawn up to her consciousness. She feels herself an active, though invisible, participant in the unfolding drama...

LYBID:

"Daddy, please tell me how you met Mother."

VASYL:

"I remember the date and time, down to the very minute. I have never forgotten that day, because at the moment I saw your mother I knew my life had changed forever and the Sun has since then shined on me in a very different, special way..."

The last days of August 1941. Hitler's hide-away, "Wolfsschanze" in East Prussia. An open passenger car drives up to a large building and three men get out - Hermann Ekkart and Gerhard Sievers on either side of a young captured Ukrainian partisan, Vasyl. Near the entrance to the building, which houses an assembly hall, SS and Wehrmacht officers, along with several civilians, are taking a smoke break. A stocky powerful-looking man with a round face, dressed in the uniform of an SS captain, hurries up to the vehicle. Sievers is the first to address him.

SIEVERS:

"Captain Beck, is it not?"

BECK:

> "Yes. Sir! No need to identify yourselves. Both of you, Gentlemen, are legends among the SS!"

Sievers, Ekkart and Beck exchange greetings and head for the building, the first two leading Vasyl by his arms.

EKKART:

> "We are handing over a prisoner to your care, Captain Beck."

BECK:

> "SS Reichsfuhrer Himmler himself signed today the orders assigning me to head the program..."

SIEVERS:

> "You are to be congratulated! It is quite an honor!"

The four men walk into the assembly hall, a spacious room with walls of polished mahogany. Among the groups of uniformed men and civilians mingling about they recognize Himmler, propaganda Reich minister Goebbels and several SS general officers.

Burning floodlights light up the room, as if in preparation for a filming session. Movie cameras on dollies stand in the four corners.

EKKART:

> "The Reichsfuhrer is here..."

SIEVERS:

> "And so is Dr. Goebbels..."

BECK:

> "The very flower of the Third Reich is here, Gentlemen!
> Bormann, Rosenberg, Albert Speer... And Goering will
> arrive by evening. The main thing for us is not to fall flat
> on our faces in the mud!"

Vasyl does not understand anything of what passes among Sievers, Ekkart
and Beck, but the presence of so many luminaries of the Nazi movement
send a chill down his spine...

Sievers, Ekkart and Beck lead Vasyl around a large group officers to an area
of the room which is sectioned off by a wooden barrier, as in a courtroom.
Vasyl looks and is struck dumb by a vision of blinding beauty. On the
other side of the partition Hanna Vitranenko is drawn up off her stool, as
she feels her heart gripped in a vise at the sight of the young man staring at
her. For the two of them time has slowed down to the speed of
enchantment and they see no one but each other...

SIEVERS:

> "Cupid's arrow, right on target!"

EKKART:

> "Amazing! And at first glance... Just as forecast in Prof.
> Fleischmann's reincarnation tables... I even find it a bit
> frightening..."

BECK:

> "A perfect match!"

Sievers swings open a small gate in the partition and pushes Vasyl through
to a stool next to the young woman. Beck, in broken Russian, utters the
information that both captives have been longing to hear...

BECK:

"Hanna, this is Vasyl. Vasyl- Hanna!"

The two young Ukrainians say nothing, just keep staring in each other's eyes. Sievers calls two SS junior officers over to the partition.

SIEVERS:

"Guard them!"

As the two lieutenants click their heels, Sievers, Ekkart and Beck turn and walk away to take seats in the first row in front of the stage.

Hanna is the first to break out of the trance.

HANNA:

"I saw you in a dream..."

VASYL:

"I seem to have lost the gift of speech..."

Vasyl massages his throat, as if to soothe a soreness. For some reason, though they have already been introduced...

VASYL:

"Vasya..."

HANNA:

"Hanya..."

BOTH (together):

"I am very pleased to meet you!"

VASYL:

"What are the two of us doing here? Maybe there will be some kind of National Socialist show trial, with us as the defendants?"

HANNA:

*"We are being shown too much respect for that. This is a party scientific conference, where you and I will be examined under a microscope, like patients by doctors. Like some spoiled children, these dark characters will be rudely pointing their fingers at us, as if we were animals in a zoo. I know this, they have already told me."

VASYL:

"But what are we to them?"

HANNA:

"You'll find out in a short while..."

Hanna and Vasyl do not know German, so their interest in the Nazi chieftains and the delegates to the conference soon wanes. They focus on a short, fat man with a roll of poster paper in his hand, who is making his way across the room. As he squeezes past the high echelon Nazis, they nod to recognize his presence, not bothering to conceal their disdain.

VASYL:

"And who is that strange fellow?"

HANNA:

"We are about to find out."

The energetic fat man swings open the gate to the enclosure and sits down on a third stool, set up for him next to the two young Ukrainians. He addresses them in perfect Russian.

FLEISCHMANN:

"Warmest greetings to you, dear friends! At last! I am Prof. Fleischmann and I am delighted to make your personal acquaintance! It was I who picked you out! Without me you would not have met. Although, it is karma: your meeting was foreordained, thanks to my scientific discovery and the personal orders of Adolf Hitler!"

HANNA:

"You mean this game..."

FLEISCHMANN:

"This can hardly be a game, when Hitler himself will very soon appear here and when all these arrogant, smug Nazi bosses have gathered here at this secret conference in order to personally look you over! You have no idea of the grand destiny, in a historic sense, that lies in store for you!"

VASYL:

"And you, you are an enthusiast..."

FLEISCHMANN:

"I am merely a dedicated scientist!

HANNA:

"How is it that you know Russian so well?"

FLEISCHMANN:

"Actually, I have equal command of thirty different languages, including three that are considered dead - ancient Persian, Akkadian and ancient Hebrew. And Russian was spoken in our home every Saturday, when the entire family gathered for the Sabbath.

My dear grandparents were from Russia."

VASYL (unenthusiastically):

"It's all clear now."

FLEISCHMANN:

"What's clear to you? You will be together for a very long lifetime, and you will have two children, a son and a daughter. And the girl will grow up to be the most famous woman in the history of mankind!"

HANNA (distracted by other concerns):

"But what will happen to us today?"

FLEISCHMANN:

"I only know what will happen to me. I was informed by an SS colonel and an official of the National Socialist Party's secretariat, who personally are responsible for preparing every appearance of Hitler, down to every last detail, like, for example, where on his table a pitcher of water is to stand. And I know that today I will be demonstratively treated like a doormat. These humiliations are very painful to me, as they would be for any highly intelligent person. Unfortunately, the acts of humiliating me, from a scientific and a racial point of view, are very much a part of the agenda of this miserable conference. I've been given – dictated - a few phrases, which I will be allowed to offer at today's proceedings.

To mumble a few pathetic words in my own defense, to prove that I have the freedom of having and expressing an opinion of my own in the presence of the Fuhrer. Hitler, in his usual manner, will then accuse me of something and order me to be silent, publicly humiliating me as a human monkey. I will be presented here not as a scientist of world renown, but as a crude exhibit for the study of a lower species and baseness, supposedly personified by me as a brilliant representative of the repulsive, from their point of view, Jewish people."

HANNA:

"As an internationalist, I truly am at a loss to understand what difference it makes to them whether or not you are Jewish."

FLEISCHMANN:

"Hitler will explain it to you today, in vivid detail. I am but a small, insignificant victim of their totalitarian racial doctrine. And in return they will allow me to live. They have even given me my own laboratory in the bowels of an SS facility! The Germans are, if nothing else, supremely practical!"

Vasyl, Hanna and Fleischmann abruptly cut their conversation short, as Himmler looks at his wristwatch and the din in the hall immediately subsides, as on command.

HIMMLER:

"Perhaps it is time to begin..."

It immediately becomes clear that this was, in fact, a prearranged signal; from loud-speakers suspended from the ceiling in all four corners of the hall the Nazi anthem blares forth, performed by a first-rate choir. All the participants of the conference on the occult leap to their feet and fervently sing along with the recording. The two lieutenants guarding Hanna, Vasyl and Fleischmann nod at them, and they get up, as commanded When the anthem is over, Himmler, Goebbels and other top SS make their way to the stage. There, Himmler, as head of the presidium, walks up to a lectern and gives a command.

HIMMLER:

"Please be seated!"

The entire auditorium sits down.

HIMMLER:

"I give the floor for a word of introduction to the Reich minister of Propaganda, Dr. Goebbels!"

Joseph Goebbels, with obvious delight, springs up from his chair, approaches the lectern and launches into a trademark oratorical flourish.

GOEBBELS:

"I wish to inform you of an unbelievable sensation in our victorious National Socialist movement! The mystery of reincarnation has been solved! We have smashed the thousand-year riddle that human religions have wrestled with, trying to reconnect with the reincarnated souls of their gods, their kings, their heroes..."

FLEISCHMANN (out of earshot of the audience, mockingly):

"We..."

GOEBBELS:

"We and you, gentlemen, have a purely scientific method at our disposal. Thanks to the successful practical application of this new direction, we can, with guaranteed accuracy, predict the future birth of potential gods and heroes of our sworn enemies. We will be able either to destroy certain reincarnated families or take newborns from the breasts of their mothers to be nursed by our women with the mother's milk of German nationalism. We will turn them into our sons and daughters. We shall scientifically and systematically Germanize Slavic, Anglo-Saxon and other heroes, we will have them raised by fanatical Germans and National Socialists. We shall turn them into the sworn enemies of their own people!"

Goebbels returns to his seat to a storm of applause and Himmler steps up to the lectern again.

HIMMLER:

"I now give the floor to the head of the National Socialist reincarnation project, SS Colonel Walter Heneke!"

Heneke walks over to the enclosure holding Vasyl, Hanna and Fleischmann.

COL. HENEKE:

> "I wish to report, Gentlemen, on the phenomenal success of the SS occult unit in Ukraine. The Slavic man and woman you see here are the future parents of the legendary Lybid, Queen of the Rus and Scythians and venerated by other ancient peoples as the goddess Artemida, Athena, Danu, Diana, the Queen of the Masageths Tamilis and the Georgian Queen Tamara. Today the SS knows her other names and reincarnations. The woman here- the future mother of the fiercest enemy of the Goth state headed by King Germanarix - was captured after a one-day battle in Ukraine by a special unit of the SS. This was a special reconnaissance commando operation, code name 'Doctor Faust,' boldly and expertly executed under the leadership of SS Captain Beck, who is present here among us. I ask him to stand!"

Beck stands up and bows in all directions, getting his reward as Himmler and the rest of the audience applauds.

HENEKE:

> "This was a very complex airborne operation and was supported by Panzer units from Gen. Guderian's tank army..."

Fleischmann on his own initiative interprets Heneke's presentation for Vasyl and Hanna.

HENEKE:

"I will not be using the phrase 'thanks to,' because Prof. Fleischmann, who is present here among us, is a miserable Jew. I will instead use a phrase more appropriate in a racial context - 'with the aid of.' So, with the aid of the reincarnation tables of Prof. Fleischmann...'

HIMMLER:

"I will interrupt you here, my dear Colonel Heneke! I am stunned, both as the Reichsfuhrer of the SS and as a sincere German! Why are we true Aryans and National Socialists - using the term 'Reincarnation tables of Prof. Fleischmann, a term coined by a self-serving Jew? This insults me as a German! First, we Germans prayed to their Jewish Bible, and now we'll pray to, or meditate on, some Jewish reincarnation tables? We should give them an appropriate name! 1 ask you, honorable Dr. Goebbel as the genius of our national propaganda, to find for these tables a worthy national name or, better yet, a National Socialist reference!"

GOEBBELS:

"I am completely in accord with the Reichsfuhrer's wise proposal. The Ministry of Propaganda will immediately get to work on this issue!"

Fleischmann lets out a quiet groan of despair and pronounces his own verdict on the proceedings, heard only by Vasyl and Hanna.

FLEISCHMANN:

"What an abomination..."

While Fleischmann is genuinely distressed over what is going on in the hall, Vasyl and Hanna can only guess at what is being said in a language so strange to them.

HIMMLER:

"From where did Prof. Fleischmann take his, take the reincarnation tables? Probably stole them from some German archives, or an ancient library. If we, with the aid of these reincarnation tables, can peer into the future, practically as deep as we want, then think what an awesome weapon these tables could be in the hands of world Jewry, as it is, the Jews already have at their disposal various occult mechanisms - which we have yet to research fully- and they have made them the foundation of their Masonic organizational pyramids of a hundred levels, which they have built throughout the world through their banks and their synagogues.

"I think that it would be better to have Dr. Goebbels, as the minister of propaganda, quote what our Fuhrer has said about this!"

GOEBBELS:

"The Fuhrer teaches us that the various trappings the Masons use in their rituals - the skeletons, skulls, coffins and other paraphernalia - are but children's games. There is in them, at the same time, a dangerous element which must be taken into account! The Masons have created a kind of priesthood; they have developed an esoteric doctrine which is tied - by symbols and mysteries - to the different ranks of the consecrated. A hierarchical organization and consecration with the use of symbolic rituals that magically play on the imagination are a potent and dangerous element. And for this reason, our National Socialist Party should and will also make use of this force. An order, a hierarchical order of a secular priesthood. We, the Masons, the Church - there is only room for one of these three forces at the top. We are the strongest and therefore we shall move aside the other two!"

HIMMLER:

"The Fuhrer has gathered us here to have us develop new approaches to using occult institutions in the service of the German nation. Our policy must include the destruction of all forces, with the exception of those which promote our one constructive idea. This means that we must have a monopoly on all scientific knowledge like that of which that prime specimen from our scientific zoo, the Jewish astrologer Fleischmann, who sits here among us, might have boasted in peaceful times. In the Third Reich we shall ultimately root out astrology! We cannot allow astrologers to pursue their calling, except, of course, those that are working for us! In a National Socialist state astrology should be elevated to a lofty position! Astrology is not for the masses. In its essence and mission astrology is a mystery and should be kept hidden from outsiders. It should only be a disciplined servant of the National Socialist Workers Party of Germany!"

FLEISCHMANN:

"Reichsfuhrer, Sir! Minister of propaganda, Sir! But I am not an astrologer, nor am I a Mason. I was never a Mason! I am simply a scientist, a student of karma!"

GOEBBELS:

"You are a Jew! You are guilty of being a Jew! If you were a Nordic scholar and not

a Jew, the entire German people would be singing your praises and you would have great honors bestowed on you!"

An adjutant walks up to Himmler and whispers something in his ear. Himmler immediately snaps to attention and loudly and solemnly announces to the audience...

HIMMLER:

> "Gentlemen! The Fuhrer of the German people, Adolf Hitler!"

An officer standing at the door opens it, and the staccato sound of boots marching echoes in from the corridor. Four of Hitler's aides, golden braids on their chests, march through the door two-by-two. Behind them the Fuhrer himself walks briskly into the hall.

Goebbels is the first to raise his arm in the Nazi salute, as he begins to shout in leading the welcome for Hitler...

GOEBBELS:

> "Sieg!"

DELEGATES:

> "Heil!"

GOEBBELS:

> "Sieg!"

DELEGATES:

"Heil!"

GOEBBELS:

"Sieg!"

DELEGATES:

"Heil! Heil! Heil!"

Fleischmann, taking advantage of the fact that the guards' attention is focused on Hitler, whispers to Vasyl and Hanna.

FLEISCHMANN:

"Hitler just adores these kinds of theatrics."

Hiler returns a lackadaisical salute, barely raising his arm, and heads for the enclosure where Fleischmann, Vasyl and Hanna sit. The Fuhrer stares in silence, especially at Hanna, then lets out a shout of satisfaction.

HITLER:

"Wonderful!"

The hall erupts in applause. Hitler signals the assemblage to stop the ovation and, in the abruptly silent hall, pronounces his verdict.

HITLER:

"I think it would be appropriate to honor the courageous Captain Beck of the occult unit of the SS for capturing this Rus queen in the heat of battle! Capt. Beck has earned the highest award the German nation can bestow, the Iron Cross, First Class!"

CAPT. BECK:

"Thank you, my Fuhrer! Heil, Hitler!"

Hitler again turns his attention to Vasyl and Hanna.

HITLER:

"Gentlemen, observe these perfect specimens of the Slavic race. Their outward features themselves give eloquent testimony to their German roots. There is no doubt they have German blood flowing in their veins, as, for example, in the Volga Germans of Czarist Russia!"

The hall buzzes in appreciation of the great man's perceptiveness. Then the Fuhrer, no doubt seeing himself as Zeus wielding a thunderbolt, whips out his right hand, index finger pointing at Dr. Fleischmann.

HITLER:

"And now, Gentlemen, look at the titled Prof. Fleischmann, the Satanic manifestation of the Jewish element in Germany! Look at this portrait of a subhuman who dared to feed on the body of Aryan science!"

FLEISCHMANN:

"Fuhrer! I am not a plagiarist! I am the one who discovered the reincarnation table!

I alone, working by myself! They appeared to me in a dream, my Fuhrer, just as the periodic tables appeared to Mendeleev. I never appropriated anybody else's work!"

HITLER:

"That was quite a monologue! And I approve! Jews are not only able to take from us Germans the riches of our lives! Using their Satanic kabalistic science, they can also steal our dreams! I keep such Fleischmann's in special laboratories, so that they return our scientific breakthroughs to us! In protecting the German nation from the Jews, I am also doing God's work! The Jewization of our spiritual life would have sooner or later led to our complete destruction! We do not at present know which souls in the Aryan racial component the Jews use in their despicable kabalistic schemes, nor do we know the means by which they do it!"

GOEBBELS:

"Your every word about the Jews should be inscribed in gold on marble tablets, to be displayed in the central squares of the world's capitals, my Fuhrer!"

Hitler nods approvingly in Goebbel's direction, then turns towards Hanna.

HITLER:

"Jews... Yes, the Jews... I look at this beautiful, obviously German, woman and I think with horror of the Satanic satisfaction on the faces of dark-haired Jewish youths, as they steal unsuspecting gold-tressed virgins and desecrated them with their blood, forever taking them away from their own people. The Jews use every means possible to undermine the racial foundation of the nation they want to subdue. The Jews will do anything not only to systematically deflower maidens and women, but also to contaminate the blood of a nation in general. It was they who brought Negroes into the Rhine valley in order to carry out their goal of destroying the white race they hate with their entire being, to bring it down off its cultural and political pedestal and become the rulers of the world!"

Captain Beck, in an uncontrollable fit of blind fanaticism, leaps from his seat and, throwing out his arm in a Nazi salute, screams...

CAPT. BECK:

"Heil Hitler!"

His shout serves as a signal for the rest of the Nazi audience; the SS occultists and civilian pseudoscientists also leap as one from their chairs, extend their right arms and yell: "Heil! Heil! Heil!"

Capt. Beck, aroused by the success of his initiative and breathing hard, stares entranced at Hitler.

HANNA'S COMMENTARY:

"In two years', time, Capt. Beck, this fanatical SS officer, will become completely disenchanted with Nazism and will come to see it as a criminal and misanthropic ideology and, already as a Lt. Colonel of the SS, will become an active participant of the German officers' conspiracy against Hitler."

As Hitler walks up to Hanna and Vasyl, one of the SS officers guarding them prompts them to stand up. Hitler then launches into his new monologue.

HITLER:

"I want to conduct a grand occult experiment on this young pair! I have already determined their destiny and will personally issue instructions necessary to see it fulfilled!"

September 13, 2000. Washington. The Oval Office of the White House.

U.S. President Bill Clinton leads Sol Liebermann up to Lybid Artemida...

BILL CLINTON:

"Today I signed an executive order naming Sol Liebermann your personal secretary, replacing the late heroic Robert Oberfell."

LIEBERMANN:

"It's an honor!"

LYBID:

"Mr. Liebermann, I have not forgotten how at the first 'Hitler' readings on June 11 of this year you cast doubt on the sincerity of my parents..."

LIEBERMANN:

"I did not mean to cast doubt: I did not understand correctly the context and circumstances..."

LYBID:

"Sol! My mother has landed at the airport and the president's helicopter will shortly bring her here. I sincerely doubt that you will show any embarrassment when you look her in the eyes."

CLINTON:

"I really had no one else to assign to you. So, I'm asking you, Your Majesty, and you, Sol, to try and forget any misunderstandings from the past. Please, for the sake of Robert's memory...

A concerned Hillary Clinton walks up to the trio...

HILLARY CLINTON:

"Marine One, with Mrs. Hanna Vitranenko-Kovhanych on board, is about to land.

Perhaps we should all move out to the South Lawn...

Accompanied by Secret Service agents and Marine Corps guards, the party walks from the Oval Office to the helicopter pad, where the presidential aircraft is in the process of landing. The door opens and a Marine guard steps out onto the stairs and stands to the side, giving a smart salute. Hanna appears in the doorway, looks up and waves, smiling. As the president and his party waves back, Hanna takes the guard's extended hand, walks down the stairs and steps onto the lush White House lawn.

Lybid rushes to her and the two kiss and warmly embrace. Taking her mother by the hand, Lybid leads her up to the President and Hillary and proceeds with the introductions.

Washington. The White House Oval Office. The President of the United States, Bill Clinton, is sitting behind his massive desk, while Hillary Clinton, Lybid Artemida, Secretary of State Madeleine Albright, Sol Liebermann, World War II veteran Alexander Hardale, the American historian Prof. Fairchild, and the Japanese scholar Prof. Yamamura take seats on two sofas that face each other in the center of the room.

A set of documents is spread out on a low table standing between the sofas. The rest of the military and civilian guests take seats along the sides of the Oval Office. Everyone's attention is fixed on the figure of Hanna Vitranenko-Kovhanych, who is sitting just to the right of the President's desk.

HANNA:

> "I would like to explain, first of all, the combat situation in the area surrounding Hitler's bunker, leading up to the last 24 hours in the life of the Fuhrer. The Imperial Reich Chancellery was located in the center of a burning Berlin, near Tiergarten Park and the famous Brandenburg Gate, in an area which included the Nazi Ministry of Propaganda, the Ministry of Internal Affairs and the Reichstag. According to Soviet plans, the Third and Fifth Assault Armies, the Eight Guard Army, the First and Second Guard Tank Armies, all of the Byelorussian Front, were to move towards the very center of the city, the government quarter. The main assault of the Ukrainian Front Third and Twenty-eighth Guard Armies was also aimed at the city center. But the main target was Not the Reich Chancellery; the most important prize and the point on which all these Soviet forces were to converge was the Reichstag building."

Documentary film clips flash on the screen as Hanna relates for her audience the dramatic events of fifty-five years ago.

CLINTON:

"I am thoroughly impressed. You have the strategic vision and memory of a professional military officer!"

HANNA:

"Please remember, Mr. President, that I had the rank of a major in the SS and that my husband and I were taught by the finest of Himmler's instructors in Walsburg Castle, which the SS had appropriated for itself...So, as night fell on that fateful day, 30 April, 1945..."

Hitler's bunker beneath the Imperial Reich Chancellery. Hanna continues her narrative, as the events appear on the screen...

VOICE OF HANNA:

"The atmosphere in the bunker was oppressive and somber, as it might be in a submarine lying disabled on the ocean floor, or if one awoke to find himself buried alive in a scaled burial crypt. The air was heavy with humidity and dust, because in places the structure had crumbling old concrete and plaster. Through the long hours of the night there was usually a still silence, broken only by the generator's hum. Illuminated by bare electric lamps, human faces looked pale and other-worldly. The air that came in through the intake ducts could be warm and stifling, or cold and sticky. The walls were gray, or pale orange in some places, and covered with mold. The monotone of the generator stopped only when it shut off, before coughing and starting anew. The smell of boot leather, damp and sweat-soaked woolen uniforms and coal tar disinfectant hung heavy in the air. And when the sewer backed up it was as pleasant as working in a restroom with a toilet overflowing..."

[TITLE:] "THE NIGHT OF 29-30 APRIL 1945"

Hitler's apartment in the bunker under the Imperial Reich Chancellery.

Hanna's narrative is accompanied by flashbacks to the night's events...

Prof. Haas, accompanied by Rattenhuber, walks up to Hitler.

VOICE OF HANNA:

> "Prof. Werner Haas – a tall, thin, gray-haired man, with a sickly pallor - was the private physician of the Chancellery staff going back to 1933. Because of his experience and reputation, he was summoned to the bunker to look after the Fuhrer's health. Hitler showed him three small glass ampules, which lay separately in a metal case the shape of a rifle shell..."

HITLER:

> "Haas! These ampules contain a fast-acting lethal poison. I received them from Dr. Stumpffegger. How can the effectiveness of the poison be tested?"

HAAS:

> "The poison can be tested on an animal, a dog, for example..."

Hitler thinks for a while, then makes a decision.

HITLER:

> "Call Tornow!"

VOICE OF HANNA:

"Tornow looked after Hitler's favorite pet, a German shepherd named Blondi..."

A corridor in the bunker, located near one of the disabled toilets. Tornow forces Blondi's mouth open. Haas places one of the ampules inside and crushes it with surgical pliers. A few seconds later the dog begins to shake uncontrollably and within a minute is dead. Moments later Hitler walks up and, staring with his empty eyes, looks over the dead body of his pet.

VOICE OF HANNA:

"The poison was then tested on a second dog. The black puppy, however, struggled against the effects of the toxin and refused to die...

HITLER:

"The poison is not as effective as I was led to believe by Dr. Stumpffegger. The cyanide causes a lot of agony before death..."

An SS hand pulls a trigger, sending a bullet into the head of the puppy...

In the garden of the Reich Chancellery Tornow throws the bodies of the two dogs into a shallow pit...

In the bunker Rattenhuber and Haas confer...

RATTENHUBER:

"Haas! What is the poison in the ampules? Does it cause instant death?"

HAAS:

"The ampules contain potassium cyanide. Death is instantaneous."

May 5, 1945. In the garden of the Reich Chancellery, near the entrance to the bunker, Soviet troops have dug up the bodies of Hitler and Eva Braun, both burned beyond recognition. The soldiers, their officers looking on, also pull out the bodies of two dogs, unearthed by a bomb blast.

VOICE OFF-CAMERA, READING FROM A TEXT:

"Reporting... Besides the charred remains of a man and a woman, who could not be immediately identified, the corpse of two dogs' corpses were discovered and dug up. The first is a German shepherd (bitch), dark-gray coat, large, with a collar. No wounds on the body. The second- a small puppy, black, no collar. The roof of the mouth is broken, blood in the area. We were not able to identify whom the dogs belonged to nor the manner of their death. Near the dog's corpses were found: a glass test-tube, dark color, burned pages torn from a printed book, bits of paper with handwriting, an elliptic metal medallion on a thin chain, 18–20 cm. long, engraved on one side with the words 'Keep me with you,' 600 German marks in banknotes of 100 marks each, an elliptical metal tag with the number 31907..."

May 8, 1945. Buche, a suburb of Berlin. Morgue of Red Army Field Surgical Hospital No. 496. In an operating room Soviet medical specialist are dissecting the corpses of the two dogs dug up in the garden of the Reich chancellery.

A woman doctor is taking notes, as a senior medical examiner, dressed, as she is, in a white smock and wearing a gauze facemask, is dictating. Medical personnel, as well as uniformed officers, are standing about, listening intently...

PROFESSOR:

> "Finally, about the two dogs. Note that they were buried under the corpses that presumably belong to Hitler and Eva Braun. Exhibit No. 3: large German shepherd...

> Write this down: a tall German shepherd, with long ears, dark stripe along the back, sides light-colored. Note the two slivers from a thin-walled ampule on the tongue. Chemical analysis has shown traces of a cyanide compound. No wounds. Exhibit No. 4: a small black dog. An entry wound in the head. Also, an exit wound. Write down that no foreign objects were found in the dog's mouth. Chemical analysis, however, has established the presence of cyanide compounds. The finding is that death was caused by cyanide poisoning and lethal trauma to the head."

One of the officer's present leans to whisper something to the doctor.

COUNTERINTELLIGENCE OFFICER:

> "What does this mean?"

MEDICAL EXAMINER (also whispering):

> "You see, it has all the earmarks of a test poisoning. Obviously, one of the dogs was given a crushed ampule, the other had an ampule forced down its throat and then shot..."

The night of 30 April - 1 May, 1945. The underground garage of the Reich chancellery. In the brightly lit garage SS officers are getting drunk, using the hoods of the luxury cars as makeshift tables. SS security chief Rattenhuber, accompanied by several officers, remarks as he walks by.

RATTENHUBER:

"Everything is going fine! Hitler has tried out the poison on his pet, and Blondi is no longer with the living. The suicide of the Fuhrer is but a matter of time."

VOICE OF HANNA:

"The news about the death of Hitler's dog seemed to enliven the SS guards...".

More bottles are uncorked. Vasyl and Hanna, in the midst of the SS men, have a couple of opened bottles of champagne thrust into their hands.

SS LT. COLONEL:

"I drink to Blondi! Let's drink to the memory of the Fuhrer's dog!"

An SS Haupsturmfuhrer sidles up to Hanna and Vasyl and attempts to embrace them.

HAUPTSTURMFUHRER:

"I can no longer contain my emotions! Thanks to Blondi's death we all now know that the Fuhrer is determined and getting ready to take his own life. Or, more accurately, he is determinedly being readied to take his life. Ha-ha-ha! We are all glad that Hitler - and there is no doubt in our minds - that Hitler will go through with his suicide and then we will be able to focus on the very serious task of saving our own hides.

Because of him we have been stuck here! It is obvious that he wants to pull us all into the grave with him!"

SS MAJOR:

"I wish he would hurry. As soon as the Fuhrer does away with himself, we shall all be free!"

SS PRIVATE:

"And we 'll all scatter to the wind!"

An SS aide walks up to Vasyl and Hanna.

AIDE:

"You are wanted by Partigianos' Bormann!"

The aide leads them through the kitchen

n to Hitler's bunker. All along the way they witness its denizens celebrating in a drunken stupor.

AIDE:

Shameful! The Fuhrer is still alive and they are already dancing around his still-empty coffin! This is a shame upon the entire nation! Their celebrations have gone so far beyond any bounds that they pay absolutely no attention to any orders to control themselves!"

VOICE OF HANNA:

"In Bormann's office we found Goebbels, Ekkart, SS Gen. Rattenhuber, the chief of defense of the government quarter SS Brigadenfuhrer Monke and Stumpffegger.

The lights in the office flicker as, high above, the earth shakes from an artillery cannonade.

VOICE OF HANNA:

"This Nazi elite was so absorbed with the issue of Hitler's suicide that we walked in without anyone paying attention to us."

BORMANN (excitedly):

"We must see to it that the Fuhrer - our deity, the living god of the Third Reich - leaves this world with courage, by shooting himself. Hitler must remain in the memory of Germans as a man who died in Berlin with a marshal's baton in his hand, leading his soldiers into battle. I shall personally orchestrate a most important matter: to lay the groundwork for a legend about the Fuhrer's future return!"

GOEBBELS:

"The Fuhrer's death should be shrouded in as much mystery as possible. And if we could arrange it so that his body does not fall into the hands of the Allies, and his death is kept a deep secret; I guarantee you... We'll be able to 'speculate' when, in a year's time, or two or three, we're asked whether Hitler really did die. Like Jesus Christ, perhaps? Eh?"

BORMANN:

"I am glad that, for all those who will have no doubts about Hitler's dying, we will be able to create a myth that the Fuhrer died a hero's death while leading his troops into combat or, at the very least, died according to the code of honor of a Prussian office, by shooting himself, as opposed to the cowards that end their lives by taking poison. I do expect that the Fuhrer has already shot himself..."

Somewhere, seemingly directly above them, there is a series of mighty explosions that make the bunker shudder. Bormann lets out a long sigh of resignation.

BORMANN:

"Our Imperial Chancellery will be nothing but ruins."

Ekkart takes advantage of the pause in Bormann's monologue.

EKKART:

"Pardon me, Partigenosse, but the Fuhrer will delay things to the last. He cannot rid himself of the thought that he will die and we will deceive him and not follow him in death. The Fuhrer wants to outwit us. With promises and putting off his suicide he will try to prolong things until finally the Russians storm the bunker."

Ekkart abruptly turns to Vasyl and Hanna:

EKKART:

"And what do you think?"

VASYL:

"The Fuhrer is bluffing. He is trying to fool everybody with this pseudo suicide. He really wants the rest of us to precede him into the afterlife..."

HANNA:

"The Red Army within a day at most will put a noose so tight that no one will leave here alive. And Hitler, having outwitted you, Partigenosse, will be reveling in the mass deaths, as we suffocate in these narrow corridors when the Bolsheviks blast open the reinforced entrances and bring their flamethrowers in..."

The Nazis drops their heads and say nothing.

Washington. The White House Oval Office. Hanna continues her narrative.

HANNA:

"Ekkart insisted that we get some sleep, as we were quite exhausted. Bormann allowed us four or five hours to rest. Going from the bunker back to the underground garage of the Reich Chancellery, we were struck by the change in the SS guard's attitude. They were visibly irritated and surly, no doubt because through the entire terrible night they had nothing that would indicate that the Fuhrer's eagerly anticipated suicide had actually taken place. They felt that Hitler, by delaying his own demise, had cheated them!"

As Hanna continues, her recollections are visualized on the screen.

One of the drunken SS explodes in anger, smashing a bottle against the concrete wall of the Chancellery garage.

SS GUARD:

"Why is the Fuhrer putting this off? We'll all die because of him!"

COMMANDER:

"Just don't panic!"

SS GUARD:

"It's time for him to do what he must do!"

COMMANDER:

"They know that! Don't panic!"

VOICE OF HANNA:

"With Hermann Ekkart leading us to the small room where we were to get some rest, we passed through Prof. Haas's underground hospital. What we saw there shook even Vasyl, who had witnessed many a horror in his young life. The room held ever 500 wounded, many of whom were dying under the scalpels of young, inexperienced doctors or long-retired surgeons who were desperately trying to recall buried skills..."

Hospital in the bunker under the Imperial Chancellery. It is a place of pain, of moans and screams of the wounded and the dying. A medical officer is shouting at two orderlies.

MEDICAL OFFICER:

We must have more room! Start carrying the corpses out to the street! The stench in here is unbearable!"

FIRST ORDERLY:

"I am not going to leave the dead to be blasted apart by artillery!"

SECOND ORDERLY:

"We don't want to end up just like them, because of you! The war is ending!"

FIRST ORDERLY:

"We want to live!"

Ekkart, Hanna and Vasyl manage to find Prof. Haas in this hellhole.

EKKART:

"I came to get your opinion on the poison...'

The doctor washes his hands in a basin.

PROF. HAAS:

"I'm listening..."

EKKART:

"I need the absolute truth. Hitler is convinced that the poison kills slowly and is not about to risk taking it by mouth? Is he correct?"

HAAS:

"And what, our Fuhrer will not shoot himself, as the honor of a German soldier demands?"

EKKART (smiles):

"Understood."

Ekkart turns around and leads Hanna and Vasyl out of the hospital.

EKKART:

"Hitler is afraid of this poison; more precisely, he's afraid of the painful and slow kind of death that it almost guarantees. Even the pup hung around and had to be shot. And who's going to shoot the Fuhrer to put him out of his misery?

Hanna and Vasyl lie down to sleep in the underground room...

HANNA'S COMMENTARY:

"Vasyl and I were totally exhausted from lack of sleep and quickly fell into a deep and nervous slumber. By the way, in doing so we went against Hitler's orders. The Fuhrer had commanded that on this night no one was to lie down to sleep. Hitler started to burn papers. He didn't want to die alone. He wanted everyone in the bunker to die with him.

But how could he make sure, if he was already dead? So, guess what was in Hitler's mind when he was giving poison capsules to his secretaries? I know: everyone was afraid that the Fuhrer would demand they carry out a mass suicide right before his eyes. And then, after seeing that they were indeed on their way to the other world, he would join them.

And what was it that Goebbels, Bormann, Rattenhuber, the secretaries and the SS men were all afraid of? That Hitler would nag them to commit mass suicide and then, having gotten rid of them, flee from the burning Berlin. In truth, by distributing the poison capsules to his underlings in the bunker, Hitler was forcing them to kill him, for they themselves desperately wanted to live! What a shame that Shakespeare wasn't around!

He would have written such a tragedy about this, outdoing Hamlet or King Lear!"

CLINTON:

"To be, or not to be? That is the question...' And King Lear no doubt never even dreamed of the horrors that played out in that bunker... What happened next? How long did you sleep?"

HANNA:

"Around 6:00 AM Hitler summoned Gen. Wilhelm Monke, who was in charge of the defense of the Chancellery. Hitler wanted to know where the Soviet troops were deployed at that moment..."

Hitler's bunker. The Fuhrer nervously holds his head in his hands, as Monke describes the battle situation for him.

MONKE:

"Soviet units have occupied the Friedrichstrasse Metro station and the Adlon Hotel on Wilhelm Strasse. Russian troops are advancing down Vos Strasse towards the Chancellery..."

HITLER:

"This means that by tonight they will begin their assault on the Reich Chancellery!"

MONKE:

"Precisely, my Fuhrer! The battle for the Chancellery will begin no later than midnight. We will be facing the spearhead of all the Soviet front forces simultaneously, because they will surround the Chancellery from all sides. It will be defended by approximately 700 SS and 80 security personnel. I think that when the Russians send in their flamethrowers tomorrow morning, we will all be burned alive or will suffocate from the smoke!"

VOICE OF HANNA:

"Monke was deliberately trying to mislead Hitler into thinking that there really was no time left for escape. This was a cunning attempt to push Hitler to suicide, to cause him to panic, to convince him that if he failed to kill himself in time, the Soviets would inevitably capture him. In reality, the Soviets at this time had only reach the Anhalter Metro station and not the Friedrichstrasse station and really had not advanced to anywhere near the Imperial Chancellery from any side."

Hiler keeps his hands wrapped around his head.

HITLER:

"I'll never let the Russians take me alive!"

VOICE OF HANNA:

"But Hitler did not want to die. Having destroyed millions of lives, he almost hysterically insisted on his right to life. He did not want to take Monke's word for anything, Hitler crawled out of his 'Pharaoh's tomb' to the street, in order to see for himself whether the noose had in fact been tightened around the Chancellery and that he really must get on with the task of dying alongside Eva Braun. Or, whether he had, perhaps, still a few hours of living left."

Hitler, wearing an overcoat and a beret, dragging his feet and hanging onto his aides, his eyes bloodshot, slowly makes his way up the stairs from his bunker to the Reich Chancellery. But there, instead of the grand surroundings of the main hall, he is greeted by unrecognizable ruins, with the roof caved in. The scene is lit by the light of a rising Sun, explosions, flares and rockets, and the flames of a devastated Berlin.

VOICE OF HANNA:

"To live? Or to die? The sounds of combat reaching the Chancellery did not seem to Hitler to be so close as to require him and Eva to rush to kill themselves right at that moment."

Without straying far from the door leading to the bunker, Hitler takes in his surroundings. The military officer standing next to him points to something, but Hitler, lost in thought, pays him no mind...

VOICE OF HANNA:

"To live? Or to die?"

An SS with a camera appears amidst the ruins. Delighted with his luck in happening upon such a rare sight, he takes the photograph.

VOICE OF HANNA:

"It was the last photo of Hitler alive..."

Washington. The White House Oval Office. The First Lady interrupts Hanna's narrative.

HILLARY CLINTON:

"What a shame that you went to sleep! Every minute of your witnessing the events of that day is just so important for our understanding of history!"

HANNA:

"I regretted it myself! We slept through an important ceremony, when Hitler was saying farewell to the people in his inner circle. It is really a shame that Vasyl and I were not able to witness it. I have always regretted not staying awake for at least another 24 hours."

A guest that was not previously heard from speaks up.

EIDHALT:

"Do not feel bad. The farewell ceremony was well documented by one famous eyewitness!"

BILL CLINTON:

"Dr. Theodore Eidhalt, professor of military history, from Berlin!"

EIDHALT:

"It is an honor to be in such distinguished company! A colleague of Dr. Haas, Prof. Ernst-Günter Schenk, who ran an operating room in the basement of the Imperial Chancellery next to the bunker, was urgently summoned to this ceremony and became an invaluable eyewitness. Approximately at 2:30 in the morning Hitler walked into one of the rooms in the bunker, where about twenty military and civilians had formed a line, and walked up to each one in turn and shook his or her hand. Standing about a meter from the Fuhrer, Schenk was able to clinically observe Hitler's every move. Hitler's bunker. The Fuhrer, putting on the face of one who has irrevocable decided to end his life, goes through the scene of bidding farewell to residents of the bunker. Schenk stands in the middle of the group bunched together in the small room where the ceremony is taking place."

VOICE OF SCHENK:

"I, of course, knew that this was indeed Adolf Hitler, and not one of his doubles. His head was uncovered and he was dressed in his once spotless gray military tunic over a green shirt and black pants, the simple uniform he had worn since the first day of the war. A gold party insignia was pinned to the left breast pocket, next to the Iron Cross from WWI. But the person inside that damp, smelly uniform, smeared with grease and bits of food, was not the same. I stood at attention a step away and one stair higher. When I looked down at him, I saw how hunched over he was, how slumping his shoulders. They seemed to twitch and tremble. His head seemed withdrawn like a turtle's, almost hidden between his shoulders. He reminded me of Atlas holding up the sky, except that he seemed on the verge of being crushed by his invisible burden. All these thoughts blew through my mind one after another, all in the span of 30 seconds, no more. Then there was a pause in the proceedings, because Hitler was fumbling with the two sheets with the short address that had been prepared for the occasion by his aides.

"Hitler's eyes were like pale-blue porcelain - no, gray rather than blue- and looking at nothing and nowhere. The whites were shot with blood. No discernible expression creased his face. The heavy bags under his eyes testified to many a sleepless night, but Hitler was far from the only resident of the bunker that suffered from this condition.

"I can still envision him like this today, even though the entire scene took all of four or five minutes. Deep creases led from his rather large and meaty nose to the corners of his mouth, which was tight, the lips nervously pressed together. His handshake was cold and limp, like holding a dead fish, and transmitted no feeling whatever. It seemed like nothing if not a reflex action, so mechanical, though, perhaps, intentioned by some semblance of warmth in the farewell. When he mumbled something incoherent about his 'gratitude,' I was at a loss as to what my reply should be. Then he apologized for having summoned us at such a late hour. I should have said at least a trivial thank you, my Fuhrer." "I was genuinely moved, reacting the way any physician would have reacted, with at least some sympathy. But it was much too late - no doctor on Earth would have been able to do anything for him. At 56 years of age the Fuhrer was a ruin, his movements largely paralytic, his face a sallow mask of yellow and gray. I was certain that this was a body that had already started to rot."

Washington. The White House Oval Office. Eidhalt is finishing reading the document from his folder.

EIDHALT:

"Here, Ladies and Gentlemen, is, I believe, the most valuable insight from Schenk, from a clinician's point of view: 'And now I knew that there would never be a St. Helena's Island for Adolf Hitler. This was a devastated island of a man, who had at most a year or two to live, three at the outside. He must have felt this, as is often the case with people suffering a terminal illness.'"

LYBID:

"Thank you, Professor. At our earlier readings we had already heard recollections about the Fuhrer as a person with end-stage Parkinson's disease. Hitler was already beset with a fatal illness; why did he need to hasten his end, as Bormann and Goebbels urged him to do?"

FAIRCHILD:

"The reaction of those present at the farewell ceremony was interesting. When Hitler left, what do you think they did? They went into the bar and started to drink and to dance to records. In fact, they danced until dawn! The noise and music reached Hitler in his room, where he just couldn't bring himself to end his life, and so he angrily demanded that they stop. And so, they stopped."

MADELEINE ALBRIGHT:

"Mrs. Hanna. Your narrative was interrupted during the episode where you and your future husband collapsed from fatigue and slept through Hitler's farewell ceremony..."

HANNA:

"Yes."

ALBRIGHT:

"At what hour did you awake and what was happening in the bunker at that time?"

As Hanna replies, the events she describes unfold on the screen...

HANNA:

"Ekkart did not want us awakened. We were dead tired and nothing could have woken us up. Not even the slamming of the heavy steel doors by the SS guards, surly and on edge, like everyone else in the bunker. Hitler still had not killed himself. There were alarming-for the Nazis - reports that our 'Ivans' were moving steadily closer. That they were at the Stadmitte Metro, all but 200 meters from the bunker. It was highly dangerous to venture out into the Chancellery garden. These reports made the already tense atmosphere almost unbearable. Still, it was strange to see the Hitlerites in the bunker on the edge of a nervous explosion. There was wailing heard from all corners of the structure and even outright weeping. While all this was going on Vasyl and I were in deep slumber, dreaming the dreams of the innocent. We woke up almost simultaneously, very late, sometime before dinner. And it was precisely at dinner time on April 30 that the SS guards received the order to pick up their provisions at the Imperial Chancellery..."

30 April, 1945. The basement of the Imperial Chancellery. Vasyl and Hanna walk quickly past the line of SS, who wait to receive their rations.

VASYL:

> "Hanna! Let's wash up in the lavatory here, rather than
> in the lower bunker."

They walk up to the toilet, which has a long line of SS at the door. One of
them pounds his fist on the door.

SS MAN:

> "Get your ass up off the pot, swine! Shouldn't have
> stuffed your face with all those sausages!"

A second SS joins the first and also pounds angrily on the door.

SECOND SS:

> "There's a line out here, pig! Get your butt out of there
> or I'll personally drown it in the toilet bowl!"

Vasyl and Hanna stop. Hanna is obviously ill at ease at the idea of standing
in the toilet line with all the men.

The presence of the woman seems to anger the guards even more and they
slam the toilet door with their fists. Suddenly, the door flies open and out
steps Hitler in his usual dress, the Iron Cross hanging from a jacket pocket.

FIRST SS:

> "Adolf! You have kept us waiting for a half-hour! And
> we have duty!"

Hitler smiles feebly, then retracts his head between his shoulders.

HITLER:

> "Pardon me, Gentlemen. I have constipation..."

SECOND SS:

>"I'll unplug that constipation of yours with this hand grenade up your ass!"

The SS man takes a grenade with a long wooden handle from his belt and waves it under Hitler's nose.

HITLER:

>"I would be willing to discuss..."

SECOND SS:

>"Discuss what? The conquest of Lebensraum?"

He points with the grenade to the toilet bowl.

FIRST SS:

>"Get going, asshole, or you'll get a bullet in the back of the head!"

The SS men, disdain and hate on their snarling faces, roughly turn Hitler around and give him a big shove in the back. The Fuhrer pulls his head in and disappears down the corridor.

HANNA:

>"This was one of Hitler's doubles. His body, dressed in a suit for an escape through enemy lines, was found by Soviet counterintelligence at 2100 on 3 May 1945 among corpses in a drained pool in the Imperial Chancellery garden. There is a deafening explosion overhead; dust rains down from the ceiling and the walls shake.

VOICE OF HANNA:

"At 1300 Soviet troops had opened a massive artillery bombardment of the Reichstag and the Reich Chancellery. The only relatively safe place for an SS soldier was the upper bunker, which was packed with guards. The atmosphere was suffocating, the tension palpable. The SS, like rats, had gathered in the Chancellery basement from every crevice in the complex. Shouts are heard: "Sounds like hellfire up there.""

Vasyl and Hanna go from the basement to Hitler's bunker. In the canteen they come upon a drunk Hermann Ekkart sitting at a table with a rowdy group of SS officers who have a card game going.

EKKART:

"Got some sleep?"

VASYL:

"Why didn't you wake us up?"

EKKART:

"What for? Goebbels insisted that the two of you, as outsiders and non-Germans, not take part in the Hitler ceremony. Slavs should not desecrate the final moments of our Fuhrer with their presence!"

The SS men who are listening in laugh derisively. Vasyl and Hanna tense up.

EKKART:

> "This does not mean that you are in any danger. Not a hair on your heads will be harmed; you are, after all, personal messengers from Reichsfuhrer Himmler. And the SS belongs to him."

Vasyl and Hanna feel the tension leave their bodies.

EKKART:

> "On the other hand, Hitler's doubles might as well be saying their final prayers. Bormann gave the order to liquidate them all. They're in the Chancellery basement, awaiting their fate. I am inviting you to partake in a procedure we call 'special treatment.'

> Maybe you'd like to knock off a couple of Hitlers, for memory's sake?"

VASYL:

> "Why don't you just bring us up to date on what the situation is?"

As Ekkart speaks, the events come of life in Vasyl and Hanna's imagination...

EKKART:

> "SS Gen. Rattenhuber maintained contact throughout the morning with Bormann and Stumpffegger, with whom he had a long, secret conversation. Rattenhuber is in the bunker, his face dark and scowling. He harangues his staff, decrying the lack of discipline, but he refrains from any decisive action, aware that the entire scenario could collapse. Goebbels, frightened out

of his mind and knowing what Rattenhuber and Bormann discussed, tried to hide in his room. He started reading a book that happened to be on his table, when Hitler appeared at his door, and is sitting there now. He is torturing Goebbels with one of his tiresome monologues, which we all know and love, sucking his blood out of him, like a vampire, one drop at a time..."

Goebbels' room in the bunker. Hitler's eyes are tearing, yet still full of demonic power. Spittle whitens the corners of his mouth. He throws his clenched, twitching righthand fist forward, then waves it in the air, repeating, "Treason, treason," and swearing vengeance upon her who betrayed him - the weak - willed German nation, which lost the chance to achieve the greatness he had promised her.

Goebbels, his mouth agape, is forced to watch with terrified eyes as Hitler careens from one wall to another, waving a thick wad of papers with the energy of a man possessed.

The documents fall out of his hands two and three sheets at a time, dancing in the air before alighting on the table or the floor. Goebbels tries to calm down the Fuhrer, whose sallow face betrays his deathly fright and panic.

HITLER:

"Joseph! Finding myself in this trap, I finally understood that Germanarix did not kill himself. No, these are all fabrications by Iordan, who, in his chronicles, hid the truth from many generations of Germans. Germanarix did not fall on his sword. He was no Nero! Germanarix was killed by his followers. Vennitarex killed him, in order to take his throne for himself!"

Hitler's mad rantings continue for another half-hour, but, for Goebbels, what seems like an eternity.

VOICE OF HANNA:

> "The deafening artillery barrage presages the storming of the Reichstag. At 1430 the figure of infantry sergeant Meliton Kantariy was seen on the building's second floor, waving the red flag. Scenes from the storming of the Reichstag by the soldiers of the Red Army..."

Washington. The White House Oval Office. President Clinton interrupts Hanna's narrative.

BILL CLINTON:

> "It would seem that we are approaching the final moments of Adolf Hitler and Eva Braun..."

Basement of the Reich Chancellery. April 30, 1945. Vasyl, Hanna and Ekkart descend to a lower floor and go to Bormann's room. They see him speaking in a hushed voice on the phone. His shoulders are tensed, his elbows raised forward, as if to shield the receiver and the words coming in over the wire. Stumpffegger stands hunched over a table, sucking whiskey from a glass normally used to obtain urine samples and looking glum.

BORMANN:

> "It's time! Rattenhuber! The hour has struck! The Bolsheviks have captured the Reichstag and we are next on the list! We cannot put this off any longer. I order you... to act!"

EKKART:

"Finally!"

The fateful hour. A phone rings and the duty officer in the bunker picks up receiver.

The Rattenhuber is speaking in a voice trembling with tension.

RATTENHUBER:

"These are my orders! Everybody, with the exception of the designated persons, is to leave the lower bunker immediately and not return there. They are to stay either in the upper bunker or in the passageway to the Imperial chancellery and there await further instructions."

Three SS men drop down to the lower bunker to see the order carried out. The secretaries- some of whom had been drinking, other playing cards or sleeping- hurry towards the stairs, all the while complaining about the lack of information.

SS MEN:

"Schnell, schnell! Everyone upstairs!"

Ekkart, Vasyl and Hanna walk out of Bormann's room into the corridor and see a mass of people surge to the stairs and up. Linge is in the middle of the corridor, insisting on relieving his deputy, Kruger, who had another two hours of duty left. Kruger's pro-testations are cut short by a curt command from Bormann, who has stuck his head out of the door to his room. He nods to Linge, who smiles in appreciation and calmly watches Kruger make his way to the stairs and out of sight. Linge then turns around and walks up to Bormann. Out of earshot of anyone in the vicinity they exchange a few words Li takes a blanket from a nearby shelf and places it on a chair in the corridor.

Ekkart takes Vasyl and Hanna by a shoulder.

EKKART:

> "I suggest we go up to the canteen and drink to the Fuhrer's glorious death!"

HANNA:

> "I want to stay and witness..."

EKKART:

> "And I order you to vacate these premises! If my friend Gerhard Sievers is still alive, God forbid that he should think you had a hand in any of this! Besides, don't forget about Goebbels' prohibition!"

Ekkart, pushing them gently yet firmly in the back, guides them up the stairs from the lower bunker to the upper.

The atmosphere in the canteen is one of celebration. Drunken SS officers are dancing to the music coming from a record player. Ekkart, as the senior officer in the room, clears one table, offers chairs to Vasyl and Hanna, and sets out on a new bout of drinking. Glasses and bottles appear and Ekkart, in good humor, pours champagne for the young Ukrainians.

EKKART:

> "Germany shall rise from the ashes! Bormann has already transferred billions of the National Socialist Party's treasure to other countries, especially to Switzerland. Our SS banker friend, Ludwig Strauss, has

spent the past three years shuttling almost daily between Berlin and Geneva and Zurich with suitcases in hand, building - in the chaos that is the international banking system - a Fourth Reich, a financial Reich, in place of our Third Reich, which is falling as we speak. Hitler's death does not really change anything. The only people who need Hitler are the true fanatics, like our mutual friend Garhard Sievers, or that old idiot there!"

Ekkart points to a middle-aged SS lieutenant colonel, who has stood up from behind a table with a cup in his hand.

LT. COLONEL:

"Our Fuhrer is getting set to leave us..."

In the lower bunker Linge opens the door to Bormann's room and whispers a cryptic phrase in his ear: "The deed is done!"

He turns around and, a disturbed look on his face, runs up the stairwell and on to the Imperial Chancellery, shouting, along the way, the shocking news: "The Fuhrer is dead!"

When Linge reaches a massive door, one of the cooks, Constanzia, sticks her head out of the kitchen and asks: "And what about Eva, Heinz?" Linge looks at her with incomprehension before opening the door to the bunker of the SS, where he continues to shout: "The Fuhrer is dead!"

In the canteen SS officers greet the news with palpable relief.

COLONEL:

"Finally!"

CAPTAIN:

"It has happened! Heil, Hitler!"

He throws his head back and gulps down half a glass of schnapps.

MAJOR:

"Anybody have any details?"

VOICE OF HANNA:

"Talk among the officers died down the moment Rattenhuber, visibly shaken by the news, entered the room."

RATTENHUBER:

"The Fuhrer has shot himself, like a soldier! Eva Braun has taken poison!"

VOICE OF HANNA:

"Hitler's personal pilot, Bauer, who had come in with Rattenhuber, avoided all conversation and didn't seem interested in hearing any gossip."

Ekkart looks at his wristwatch.

EKKART:

"Everything is on schedule. Let's go below, or we'll miss him being taken out!"

In the lower bunker Ekkart, Vasyl and Hanna join some of the highest officers of the Reich.

VOICE OF HANNA:

> "Axmann, the Fuhrer of the Hitler youth, had come down to the lower bunker and joined in the chorus: 'Hitler has died an honorable death, as an officer and a gentleman, shooting himself, after taking poison, just in case!"

The Nazis crowd around the exit from the bunker to the Reich Chancellery garden.

Among them are Bormann, Linge, Burgdorf, Goebbels, Gunsche, Kempka, Rattenhuber, Stumpffegger, the commander of the SS guard Franz Schodle and Havel.

RATTENHUBER:

> "The Fuhrer has left us and now we should carry his body to the surface."

Hitler's corpse, wrapped in the blanket, with his legs in the black trousers sticking out, is heavier than the SS officers expected. They grunt as they lift it.

Then two more officers carry Eva Braun's body up to the emergency exit.

An SS guard, Erich Mansfeld, leaves his post on the guard tower to look at the suspicious commotion around the bunker. He sees the legs sticking out of the blanket and the second body, which, as he would recall later, obviously was that of Eva Braun.

A funeral procession of sorts follows the bodies. The corpses are finally laid next to each other face up in a shallow hole dug out of the sandy soil a few meters from the entrance to the bunker. Gunsche and Linge drench them with gasoline from a canister. Gunsche pours gasoline on a rag and lights it, then drops it on the ground. The two bodies immediately catch fire.

SS guard Hermann Karnau watches the scene from the Chancellery garden – the bodies burning, the procession watching. Soviet artillery roars somewhere in the distance and seconds later shells explode unexpectedly nearby. The mourners rush to the bunker, leaving the two bodies alone with the flames.

VOICE OF HANNA:

> "Rattenhuber would later complain in the bunker that the storm of artillery fire did not allow the mourners to pay proper last respects to Hitler and his wife. Not even a state flag could be found to cover their remains. Soviet artillery shells rain down upon the Reich Chancellery garden. The wind blows around the stench from the burning bodies of the Fuhrer and Eva Braun and into the emergency exit from the bunker; the Nazis there slam the door shut. Assault on the Reichstag building. Fighting rages on the first and second floors."

VOICE OF HANNA:

> "At 1800 fresh troops were brought up to reinforce the units storming the Reichstag. It was pitch black when a group of Red Army soldiers fought their way to the roof and planted there a flag of the Military Council of the Assault Army of the Byelorus Front. The red banner first flew over the Reichstag building seventy minutes before dawn, signaling, in effect the fall of Hitler's Reich..."

Washing ton. The White House Oval Office. Hanna has finished her narrative.

BILL CLINTON:

"So, from what you as an eyewitness have told us, there is no doubt that Hitler was killed, together with Eva Braun..."

HANNA:

"Yes. And the Nazi leaders and their SS guards during the night of May 1 – May 2 also killed Reich Minister of Propaganda Goebbels, his wife Marta, their six children, and Field Marshal Krebs."

BILL CLINTON:

"Astounding!"

"Hitler was doomed. There was no way he could have survived. On April 29 the Youth Reichfuhrer Axmann guaranteed Hitler's safety, assuring him that the finest of the Hitler Jugen were putting up a fierce resistance in the neighborhood of the Imperial Chancellery, ready to die in order to save the Fuhrer. Axmann was trying to convince Hitler to leave Berlin. But Bormann wanted Hitler to stay and laid out a different plan. Have a battalion unexpectedly break out through the blockade to join Wenke's army, urged Bormann, knowing all the while that Wenke had been crushed and was retreating west with the remnants of his troops."

ALBRIGHT:

"So, Bormann was betraying Hitler, pure and simple?"

HANNA:

"Yes, Madam Secretary! And consider Hitler's wedding ceremony. What Goebbels and Bormann, who orchestrated the entire scenario, had in mind was to prepare Hitler psychologically and sell him on the idea of second grand ceremony and theatrics - his 'heroic' departure from life. I personally heard how Goebbels and Bormann tried to convince Hitler that his suicide would be like the last scene in the spirit of a Wagnerian opera and the ancient German sagas. A shot...poison...Eva, the faithful wife, the heroine of the epic, killing herself on the grave of the Leader - these were the cheap symbolism and theatrics those closest to Hitler used. And when he started to resist, they killed him!"

BILL CLINTON:

"It seems that in the innermost Nazi circle this was the way Bormann and Goebbels were orchestrating their way to the top..."

HANNA:

"That is correct, Mr. President. Goebbels and Bormann killed Hitler out of a desire for power. All indications are that they even falsified his testament, according to which leadership of the party and the Reich was passed on to Doenitz, Goebbels and Bormann.

In actuality, this was an absurd, farewell flight in Bormann's and Goebbels' political careers and a 48-hour intrigue on the highest pinnacle of the Nazi Olympus. They, with Doenitz, proclaimed themselves a

Roman triumvirate. But in this scheme Bormann and Goebbels thought it convenient to act under the apparent mantle of Hitler, down to the final minutes. I personally was a witness when at 1835 that is, three hours after Hitler's murder - Bormann handed Doenitz a telegram which said that Hitler named the admiral his successor, instead of Marshal Goering. Formal documents confirming this were, supposedly, on their way. In Bormann's radio telegram there was not a word about the Fuhrer's death. So, the following day Doenitz sent Hitler a radio message which began with the words, 'My Fuhrer, my dedication to you is immutable...' At this same time Hitler's body was already burned beyond recognition in the garden of the Imperial Chancellery..."

FAIRCHILD:

"I can corroborate what Madam Hanna has said about all the lying! What was being spread was nothing but lies! On May 1, 1945, on orders of Goebbels, an obituary was issued, supposedly from Hitler's personal office, in which it was said: "Our Fuhrer, Adolf Hitler, today...'- note, Mr. President, on May 1 they are saying 'today,' whereas Hitler had been killed the day before- 'Adolf Hitler today, this afternoon, at his command post in the Imperial Chancellery, while fighting to his last breath against Bolshevism, died for Germany!' In his first message the newly crowned chancellor of Germany, Admiral Doenitz, said: "Our Fuhrer, Adolf Hitler, is dead. The end of his struggle and his errorless and direct life's path was culminated by his heroic death in the capital of the German Reich!' But, as we now know, Hitler lifted not a finger to defend his office in the Reich Chancellery. All of that was a lie!"

YAMAMURA:

"And how could Bormann, the Party, and Goebbels, who, besides being the minister of propaganda, was also the Gauleiter of Berlin, refuse to evacuate its civilian population-three million people – leaving them in the hell of the battle for the capital? And on top of that, Mr. President, refusing even to evacuate 120 thousand children under ten years of age from the combat areas of Berlin! So who's actually to blame for the death of so many civilians?"

HANNA:

"Hitler's death took place under conditions of total disarray and lack of preparedness. The cremation of his corpse, the chaos, the primitive nature and the total apathy surrounding the ceremony, is evidence that no one really planned his death on April 30, least of all Hitler himself. It is obvious that the SS did not know how to do it right and that they didn't bother to consult with the appropriate specialists on cremation. And so the bodies of Hitler and Braun were not burned completely, but only the skin and outer tissue. Afterwards, the orgy in the bunker, the theft of the Fuhrer's valuables and personal things and Eva Braun's dresses and intimate wear. The secretaries put those on under their Nazi uniforms, as they prepared to flee the bunker. And Eva's luxurious furs, stolen from her wardrobe... Or the priceless works of the Old Masters, which a domed Hitler's suite in the bunker... The murders in the bunker, which were explained away by their perpetrators as suicide, the concrete pool in the garden of the Chancellery filled with bodies.. All of this needs to be meticulously investigated, Mr. President"

ALBRIGHT:

"I think it is time to put an end to the propagandistic myth about Hitler's suicide, which has served only the interests of the Nazis, and to unmask the entire Hitlerite clique as the band of killers they were. And cold-blooded killers of one another, like spiders in a jar!"

CLINTON:

"I have decided to order the Justice Department to begin gathering documentation to verify the information you have given us here today, Madam Hanna, about the murder of Hitler and Eva Braun by the Fuhrer's inner circle..."

HARDALE:

"I am so glad that, finally, we will get at the riddle that has most perplexed me in my long professional career, that of the death of Adolf Hitler!"

BILL CLINTON:

"Madam Hanna! You will be the chief witness in this inquiry..."

HANNA:

"Thank you, Mr. President!"

BILL CLINTON:

"And now, I invite all those present here to dinner!"

The White House dining room. Waiters are hustling around a long, exquisitely set table, at which are seated the participants of the latest of the "Hitler Readings."

BILL CLINTON:

"I'm watching my weight. But this roast beef..."

HANNA:

"I actually got to taste some of the pastry that was a favorite of Hitler's..."

MADELEINE ALBRIGHT:

"In the Middle East..."

The atmosphere around the table is lighthearted and spontaneous...

HARDALE:

"And just three hours after we landed at Normandy- we weren't even dry yet – we were given ice cream! That's not something one forgets easily!"

ALBRIGHT:

"Tell us, Madam Hanna, why did Hitler at first forbid you to marry your now deceased husband and then just before his death gave his permission?"

HANNA:

"Hitler had calculated, by the stars and other indicators, that I would be the one who would bear my beloved Swan..."

Hanna gently places her hand in Lybid's palm and her sparkling blue eyes shine with a mother's deep love...

HANNA:

"According to Hitler's plan everything was to evolve like it did in Germanarix's story, with the exception that the SS would have total control over events. In that ancient era Germanarix was unable to marry Lybid Swanhilda and beget with her the Universal Anti-Christ. Professor Fleischmann - God rest his soul - told me that Hitler did not want to marry Eva Braun. He was waiting until the day predestined and foretold by the horoscope, when I and my Vasyl would conceive his future wife..."

LYBID:

"Whose future wife? Hitler's?"

HANNA:

"What is so strange in this? Why do you think Hitler kept Prof. Fleischmann at his side, with his reincarnation tables?"

LYBID:

"Hitler was planning to marry me?"

HANNA:

"Yes. Because Eva Braun insisted on her right to be Hitler's lawful wife, the Fuhrer, together with Bormann, concocted the doctrine of resurrecting Germany's biological potential – as they termed it - after the war. In other words, they proclaimed the law on bigamy. Hitler explained his vision to Bormann in this vein: that after the war Germany would have three or four million women without male partners. This meant that the birth rate would fall precipitously. 'Just imagine,' Hitler said, 'how many divisions would be lost in 20 to 45 years!' So,

Hitler came to the conclusion: 'We must see to it that those German women who are not able to find husbands after the war enter into lasting relations with married men, in order to bear as many children as possible.' He envisioned that these arrangements would have the same official recognition as marriages. And selected men – obviously, those who are physically and emotionally developed- would, according to Hitler's plan, have the right to be married simultaneously to two women, with the second wife also having the right to bear her husband's surname. The document also stipulated that the state would severely punish anyone who criticized the project.

Now, Fleischmann claimed that the only reason Hitler came up with this grotesque plan was on account of Eva Braun, who, by her marriage demands, stood in the way of his following the footsteps of Germanarix and his quest of marrying the future, at that time yet unborn, Queen Lybid Artemida. I think that Hitler had all this in mind when he gave us the rank of major in the SS and made us Knights of Greater Germany. And, of course, made Germans out of us Ukrainians, issuing official documents that recognized us as Aryans, which, in any case, we are and not he and his henchmen. He saw Vasyl and me as his future in-laws, because he planned to marry you, in about 16 to 18 years' time!

Lybid gasps and is left speechless. As are all the guests...

BILL CLINTON:

"Once again, it shows that life is so much stranger than fiction!"

Just then a tall distinguished man walks into the room in the company of a Marine guard and comes up to the President.

PATRICK VALE:

Greetings, Mr. President! I am very grateful for the invitation to today's event!"

BILL CLINTON:

"Ladies and Gentlemen! I wish to present to you Prof. Patrick Vale of the Sorbonne!"

VALE:

"Good evening, Ladies and Gentlemen!"

Vale looks around the table and bows slightly in the direction of faces he recognizes...

LYBID:

"I have heard of you, Prof. Vale. Are you not the author of the article, "William Jefferson Clinton: The French Years,' which appeared in the New York Times and on PBS? IF I recall correctly your research focused on statutes of the French Civil Code that supposedly allow residents of countries and territories that in the past were protectorates or colonies of France to receive French citizenship, if they so desire. And I believe you also pointed out that, on the basis of this statute, President Clinton, could, should he be so inclined, run for president of France. After a certain period of time from the end of his term in the White House, of course!"

Vale is seated at the table and spreads a napkin on his lap.

VALE:

"You are absolutely correct, Your Majesty! As we know, two hundred years ago the present state of Arkansas was part of the Louisiana Territory. And, therefore, President Clinton, as Arkansas' native son, has every right to become a naturalized Frenchman and declare his candidacy for president of France!"

ALBRIGHT:

And, take it from me, very many Frenchmen and, probably, even more Frenchwomen, would be for that idea!"

HANNA:

"And what about you, Mrs. Clinton? Would you like to live in the Palace d'Elysses?"

HILLARY CLINTON:

"Well, for that the first thing my husband would have to do is to learn French..."

HANNA:

"Mr. President! You are such a good person; the French would be happy to have somebody like you!"

LYBID:

"Hillary, you and your husband would become a worldwide phenomenon if you declare your candidacy for the presidency of the United States and your husband runs for the office of president of France! You could make it a kind of family busines..."

HANNA:

"And what about you, Mrs. Albright? Would you serve as Foreign Minister, if Bill Clinton was the President of France?"

ALBRIGHT:

"Well, I suppose I could be his press secretary. Unfortunately, I'm not from Arkansas Anyway, I am actually looking forward to the day I am no longer secretary of state. Then I can get behind the wheel of my own car and drive. Something which I haven't been able to do for the last seven years. You know, secretaries of state are not allowed to drive their own cars. So, I would have to take some driving lessons, get my license and then I could become an ordinary housewife."

LYBID:

"I would like to propose a toast: to Bill Clinton, the future President of France!"

VALE:

"And I would like to add something very important: unlike the United States, France places no limits on the number of terms one can serve as president and there they treat their presidents with much greater respect!"

LYBID:

"I would like to announce the creation of the Lybid Artemida Foundation for the Election of Bill Clinton President of France, the Defense of Democracy and Promotion of the United Nations!"

All present rise and raise their flutes of California champagne...

September 17, 2000. The White House South Lawn. The double rotors of Marine One are beating the air. Two guards are standing at attention at either side of the stairs. Hanna Vitranenko-Kovhanych, accompanied by most of the guests at the Hitler Readings, is walking up resolutely to the aircraft.

LYBID:

"Mama! If only you knew how desperately I have been missing you!"

HANNA:

"I missed you terribly, also, child! But I have a garden to tend and a house to keep and chickens to feed... I promised you that I would come and personally tell the American president what I know. I didn't promise to become a permanent guest at the White House! At my age... I know you understand."

LYBID:

"But Vitaliy is there, he's looking after the house! And you can stay a while and see America!"

257

HANNA:

"Your brother is there all by himself. With nobody to even provide him some company. I didn't want to leave him alone even for a single day. Oh, America, America... It's a little late for me to see America. Forty years ago, would have been a different matter. It was interesting for me to be able to tell people about the truth I witnessed with my own eyes. But to play around in America... But I am very grateful to the President of America for his hospitality. He is a very fine person..."

BILL CLINTON (to Hillary):

"Now just think that a half century ago this woman, who is hurrying home to plant her cabbage and raise her chickens, was deciding the fate of the leaders of the Third Reich. And of post-war Europe, it turns out!"

October 3, 2000. Washington, D.C. Against the familiar Washington skyline, an army of construction workers is hustling about an armada of trucks, bulldozers, excavators and other earth-moving equipment. Hundreds of well-dressed people have gathered on the fenced-in construction lot, next to a huge tableau, titled "Site of the future first Temple of Lybid Artemida," and depicting a majestic, sparkling building of onyx, in the form of an opened lotus flower. A full-scale model of the future temple, made of papier-mâché, towers over the assembled crowd of believers, well-wishers and sponsors and the surrounding buildings."

The Avatar stands at a podium set up in front of the model of the temple, his right hand resting on the Gold Tablets of Lybid Artemida.

AVATAR:

"Today is indeed a great day! A day that will go down in history! Today we are beginning the construction of the first Temple of Lybid Artemida, the first such temple in the past 3000 years. Today I was told by holy men from all over the world that this is the fulfillment of one of the prophecies of Nostradamus, who in "Stanza 74" of Book Nine wrote:

"The murderer secretly flees the city of Fertsod,

The slaughtered bull lies black in the field.

Artemida's mantle rises to the clouds,

And volcanic ash covers the dead.

"In Old French the stanza goes like this:

IX / 74

"Dans la cite de Fertsod homiside,

Fait et fait beuf arant ne macter,

Retour encores aux honneurs d'Artemide,

Eta Vulcan corps morts sepulturer."

"There is also a different translation of the stanza:

"In the city of Fert panic and mayhem rein,

Many bulls, bound, are slaughtered,

They will once again return to venerate Artemida,

And offer the dead to the volcano..."

AVATAR:

"The prophecy is fulfilled! We have returned to Lybid
Artemida, just as we did 3000 years ago! We are building
the temple of Lybid Artemida! We shall now perform
the sacrificial ritual, so that there be not a repeat of the
tragedy of the ancient past, when Herostratus, desiring
eternal fame and a place in history, burned down the
temple of Anemida in Ephesus, which had been one of
the Seven Wonders of the World. For this Herostratus
paid with his life. So that a new Herostratus, a modern-
day Herostratus, does not destroy the fruits of our labor,
our new temple, we have erected a sacrificial temple of
Lybid Artemida, which we shall burn according to the
rite of Ahni, the Sun God! The Karma of the Temple...
The ersatz temple will burn, but the true Temple shall
stand forever!"

The towering temple model burns, like a volcano spewing flames and ash
to the heavens, while the Avatar stands against the background of the
sacrificial pyre and turns in the Gold Tablets of Lybid Artemida...

AVATAR:

"Lybid Artemida punished Tarasiy and Kalisto. And
then what happened? She herself was called to the
Areopah to face judgment..."

The Sun, a life-giving Sun, burns brightly in the sky, and sends forth its
flares, which hurtle towards the Earth, like thoughts intent on
impregnating the minds of men...

TITLE: "LYBID, 3000 YEARS AGO..."

Scenes from the life of Her Majesty the Queen Lybid Artemida. The trial at the Areopah.

On the high hills on the Right Bank of Dnipro-Slavuta, covered with the Sacred Groves of mighty oaks, stand the temples, their myriad precious stones sparkling in the Sun. From there one can see the vast expanse of Dnipro-Slavuta and Galley Bight, where the ancient river spills into the valley between the hills above Kyiv. Its surface is covered with ships and boats as far as the eye can see, their sails like a vast flock of swans gathered from around the world and beating the air with graceful wings.

From a temple that towers above the lush green of the Sacred Groves one can see a huge royal barge, its proud crimson flag flying in the wind. Its billowed sails carry it into Galley Bight, accompanied by an array of smaller battle vessels. It is Lybid Artemida, coming, at her father's command, to stand trial.

Lybid, dressed in a modest white tunic and her royal crimson cloak, stands at the prow of the barge and watches as the Kyiv hills loom ever larger before her and the watery passageway, covered with sailing ships and galleys, narrows. Vessels on both sides try to pass the barge, as thousands of smiling eyes, both on ship and shore, look at her. For to that day the tradesmen, craftsmen, sailors and other common folk along the Dnipro have not even seen their beloved princess.

The Volkhv Mudroslav walks up to Lybid and stands behind her.

MUDROSLAV:

> "Holy Kyiv City! And we have arrived at your father's...
> I really am in awe of you, Princess!"

LYBID:

"Why is that, Lord Mudroslav?"

MUDROSLAV:

"Your father's court may sentence you to a horrible death, but you are calm as the Dnipro's placid waters. Are you not afraid?"

LYBID:

"If the Areopah decides that I acted in accordance with God's law and to preserve the might and sovereignty of Great Kyiv Rus, then, most probably, I have a long and fruitful life ahead of me. That's if I am judged by the laws of God and the state. And if according to human law, common law, I have perpetrated such heinous crimes that I deserve to die, then my own father should have me burned alive, as an example to the people! You must know, Lord Mudroslav, that I have already sentenced myself according to God's law to liberty and life, and according to man's law to death in the sacred fire!"

MUDROSLAV:

"I will be praying for you, child!"

The royal barge enters Galley Bight, where its further path is blocked by a mass of boats.

The barge's captain runs up to the prow.

CAPTAIN:

"Drop the sail! Oars in the water!"

The royal barge's sail drops, baring the mast. A hundred oars roil the water. The captain, standing alongside Lybid, shouts to the crews of vessels cutting in front of the barge.

CAPTAIN:

"Make way! Get out of the way!"

LYBID:

"I have never seen so many white sails in my entire life!"

CAPTAIN:

"There is nothing strange in this, Princess. Winter is just around the corner and barges and barques have come from all over the world to carry away our grain before the ice starts to form on the mighty Dnipro."

MUDROSLAV:

"You see, my child, from time immemorial the Kyiv hills have looked down upon this brisk trade. Merchants have been coming from many countries- Byzantium, Gothland, Poland, Lithuania, Greece, Persia and others. The vessels at the mouth of Galley Bight are so numerous that people can cross the Dnipro without a bridge, just by walking from one ship or barge to another!"

As her barge passes vessel after vessel, Lybid's curious eyes take in the scenes of the bustling life on the Bight and the Royal City Canal that falls into it.

MUDROSLAV:

> "Our grain, the gold of our land, is loaded onto the ships and barges for the long journey along our great rivers, which are another source of our riches. And, thanks be to Dazhboh, transportation by river is much cheaper than by horse or oxen. Grain is our treasure and our rivers are our treasure. What is just our Dnipro worth, in gold or in poods of grain? Is it any wonder that our people have named it the 'Nurturer' and the 'Father'?"

The Dnipro at this point is so jammed with vessels that it seems like some of the barges, unable to find a place on the water, are crawling up on the shore.

Mudroslav directs Lybid's attention to a barge from which huge millstones are being unloaded to the dock.

MUDROSLAV:

> "Look, child. The foreign traders have no idea how something so heavy can be brought to market. It's on the Dnipro, the Don, the Volga and on other rivers of Great Kviv Rus that millstones are transported to be sold."

Mudroslav shouts at a trader.

MUDROSLAV:

> "Say, my good man, where are the millstones from?"

TRADER:

"From the Dazhboh quarry, in the upper reaches of Moskva River, Lord!"

MUDROSLAV:

"Your millstones are, perhaps, the best I've seen! May Dazhboh bless you!"

LYBID:

"And why the best?"

MUDROSLAV:

"The millstones on the Moskva are made of flint, which is harder than just about any other stone and mills the grain cleaner and so the flour is whiter. Millstones do not damage the grain, just prepare it for our human stomachs!"

As Lybid's barge moves on, the barque with the millstones falls behind. Lybid's attention is drawn to a line of poorly dressed men who carry sacks of grain onto a huge barge at a loading dock.

MUDROSLAV:

"Look there - a wagon train, cart after oxen-drawn cart, carrying grain to the harbor. Those brawny teamsters - salty sweat pouring down their faces, their shirts wet upon their backs - load the grain onto the barges. Winter will soon be upon us and those fellows with the veined arms and strong backs want to earn as much as they can, in order to feed the young in their large families."

Lybid overhears the words of a luxuriously dressed merchant, who is bragging to his colleague.

MERCHANT:

> "The grain I bought- it's diamonds, not grain! Not a speck of dirt, so clean it glitters. I paid a hryvnia for each sack!"

Mudroslav shouts to the merchant, who doffs his hat in deference to the princess and the volkhv.

MUDROSLAV:

> "You best get a move on, good man, because the price of grain on the Greek market will fall by a fourth in a week's time. There was a rich harvest this season on the Don, the Volga, the Oka, the Kama..."

MERCHANT:

> "Thank you, my Lord! Glory be to Dazhboh that he has blessed Great Kviv Rus with such fruitful expanses! Glory to Dazhboh!"

MUDROSLAV:

> "Glory forever!"

The grain barge soon recedes in the distance.

LYBID:

> "So many grain ships! Do our people really live so well?"

MUDROSLAV:

"All the people can't be traders. Someone will always live-in want and misery. The great number of ships and grain barges, as many as the eye can see - these are also a source of livelihood for our people. Wherever there is shipbuilding timber- on the Dnipro, the Volga or some other river - beginning in late March, when the last ice floats down with the current, the trees are cut down, bound into rafts and sent downstream. And then the shipbuilders' axes sing merrily along all the rivers of Great Kyiv Rus- it's our skilled craftsmen building grain barges. And what is all of this for?"

LYBID:

"Please, tell me!"

MUDROSLAV:

"Princess, see how many foreigners stand on the docks? Now answer me this: who gathered here in the harbor these bustling masses of workers, who bent their backs and weighed them down with nine-pood sacks of grain?"

LYBID:

"Who?"

MUDROSLAV:

"Hunger!"

"But is there hunger in Rus? The earth has given a bountiful harvest of grain; the boundless golden fields of ripened grain are like clouds rolling in the wind! Wherever you look golden seas of grain promise a rich and carefree life for our people!"

MUDROSLAV:

"What you say is true, Princess! The harvest has indeed been generous and your wise and just father - may Dazhboh grant him long life - will sell much of it abroad, to exchange the golden grain for gold metal! That is why you see so many greedy foreign speculators crowding the docks!"

Mudroslav points with his withered, crooked finger to the groups of merchants, dressed in various clothing.

MUDROSLAV:

"Those are Byzantines! And those are Franks! Over there are Arab traders! And Egyptians over there. And there you see Jewish merchants negotiating with Rus middlemen. Like greedy blackbirds setting down on a field to pick its golden fruit, so, too, have these innumerable foreign dealers gathered together to trade for Rus' main riches, her grain! And the main reason this is happening is that your father has decided to sell these riches for gold, for there is trouble in Europe! The Goth king Germanarix has sent his armies to subjugate various free peoples and this means that Rus itself will have to ready her forces without delay, because otherwise it will soon be forced to tear our industrious people away from the plow!"

LYBID:

"And send them to die?"

MUDROSLAV:

"Unless you agree to marry Germanarix, child! For as long as King Germanarix continues courting you, without success, our people will have to prepare to survive this winter without grain, which your father, for the sake of gold, is sending down the Dnipro to Byzantium and even Egypt!"

LYBID:

"And what will our people eat, if not the grain they raised with their own hands?"

MUDROSLAV:

"Why, fish, thank God! Fish!"

LYBID:

"Fish?"

MUDROSLAV:

"Our rivers abound with fish! And for that divine reason this living bounty is very cheap and whenever grain is scarce our fishermen save the farmer from a hungry winter. Fish has a place of honor on a peasant's table. In some places it completely replaces bread. Even the poorest can find salvation in fish, be it of the leanest and worst sort."

CAPTAIN:

"Salted perch, sturgeon, pike and other species of fish from Dnipro, Volga, Ural and Don waters save the entire population from hunger, not just those people who live on our great rivers They feed even those who live by themselves deep in the forests and on the steppes! If bread, Princess, is our gold, then fish in the rivers is truly our living silver!"

Lybid's barge has entered the Korchevatsky Channel, which winds among the hills and leads to the center of the Royal City and the very heart of Rus.

CAPTAIN:

"We are now on the watery road to Paradise on Earth - Svarha, where the foot of any commoner may not step. Where the sacred mountain Aryana is surrounded by water from all sides. Aryana, to which the gods descended and begot our people!"

A sleepy Atalanta, who had stood guard all night, has joined Lybid, Mudroslav and the barge's captain in the prow of the vessel.

On shore stands a military checkpoint. The soldiers have gathered to greet the royal barge, shouting: "The Princess! The Princess! Our Swan has taken wing!"

A heavy forged chain, stretched across the natural channel drops in the water just before the bow of the royal barge is to cut across its line. The vessel glides smoothly into the arm of the Dnipro that leads into the Garden of Iriy.

But what is that? Lybid sees a group of children playing on the shore, their clear voices ringing in her ears and reaching into her heart. The children are playing...her, Lybid Artemida.

271

Several young boys, dressed in bearskins, are dancing a circle dance around an older girl dressed up as a princess, and singing: "Lybid, Princess! We're raised on wild honey and bear's milk! Allow us Kalisto to marry and command not Atalanta to kill us suitors, for we may yet be of use to you."

SECOND GIRL:

> "I will run you down like a lynx, you stupid bears, and
> tear out your throats like a wolf!"

The boys scatter, shouting happily, while the girl chases after them, swinging a stout stick.

ATALANTA:

> "My God! That is it!"

Here Lybid's inner strength fails her and she begins to sob uncontrollably. Then a cry that she can no longer keep inside breaks out of her chest. Lybid bites her knuckle, trying to subdue her deep sorrow, but in vain, for her tormented soul cannot overcome the sharp pain brought on by the killing simplicity of an innocent children's game...

Areopah, the majestic oaken temple of the High Court of Rus. Lybid - followed by Mudroslav, Lyubomyr, Atalanta, her nymphs and others who accompany her - walks through a dense crowd of Kyivites to the Temple. Hundreds of people reach out to Lybid, shouting their greetings and encouragement, but her soldiers push them back from the Temple steps and she walks into the building of the High Court. The Temple hall is enormous. Beneath one wall stands the golden royal throne and eleven chairs. On opposite side is a long bench. Lower-ranking Volkhvs crowd around.

MUDROSLAV:

> "The Areopah... The Aryan Hilltop. My heart can't stop
> pounding. And your divine father will arrive soon...
> The trial of a daughter of gods, Princess, can only be
> conducted by the gods themselves, headed by your
> father... Twelve gods will soon sit down in these empty
> places! And seats on the benches will be taken by twelve
> high Volkhvs and each one will watch carefully so that
> the twelve living gods act justly and in accordance with
> the will of the Almighty!"

A thunderous roar from the excited throng outside signals the arrival of
the twelve Volkhvs, headed by the White Volkhv. They solemnly walk
through the crowd and into the hall.

WHITE VOLKHV:

> "Greetings, Princess!

LYBID:

> "Glory to Dazhboh, Lord!"

The White Volkhv, a wily politician, who knows how to maneuver in
order to increase the power of the Temple in the life of the nation.

WHITE VOLKHV:

> "Daughter of the Sun! I was shocked at what you did! I
> do not know whether this was a great evil you
> committed or a great good. I shall be dispassionate."

He diplomatically walks over to his seat.

Another roar from the crowd enters the hall through the windows and doors of the temple: "The King has arrived! The King!"

The Great King, Boos Apollo and ten other members of the royal family walk up the Temple steps. The King is explaining something to Boos, who nods in reply.

KING OF KINGS:

> "I convinced your mother not to come. I told her: 'Maya, do not go. It will only break your heart."

BOOS:

> "And what about my heart, Father? Doesn't it matter that it will break?"

The King unexpectedly spies Prince Palant among Lybid's soldiers, who guard the entrance to the High Court.

KING OF KINGS:

> "Ah, Palant! How you've grown!"

PALANT:

> "Glory to Dazhbohl"

BOOS:

> "I am happy to see you, my friend! I hope to see you at dinner this evening! We'll talk!"

Boos Apollo gives the young man a friendly pat on the shoulder and follows his father into the hall.

The trial proceeds. Lybid stands with her head held high before the twelve siting gods, among whom Boos Apollo is tormented by the plight of his sister. Their father sits glumly, then turns towards Lybid.

KING OF KINGS:

> "Murder! A savage murder, which has upset royal courts all over Europe! I am very angry! Among the Byzantines, the Franks, the Goths – you are spoken of as the witch of death! How do you dare live, when you tortured and killed an innocent maiden and a prince who was in love with you since the age of nine! And you - my daughter! Monster!"

Royal palace. Lybid's mother, Zlata Maya, paces around the chamber, nervously wringing her hands. A lady-in-waiting enters the room.

MAYA:

> "I am about to faint from anxiety. What is happening there?"

LADY-IN-WAITING:

> "They are allowing her to plead her case. She is speaking now..."

The trial. Lybid is shocked into indignation by her father's words and goes on the offensive. The faces of the Volkhvs burn with embarrassment, as they witness the royal family's shame...

LYBID:

> "I know, Father, you seek vengeance because I killed your unborn child! Your fatherly heart cries out. You think: What would he have been like? Or she. But you

would have just as well spit at Tarasiy. And I loved him! I loved him from the time we were children! And I was forced to kill him, following your command, to marry a foreign ruler, a man I do not love but one who is convenient to you and to my country. Meanwhile, you were having your fun with Kalisto! No fool like an old fool! My father the libertine! Why am I here? Only because you, Father, desired the forbidden charms of a young virgin Kalisto! Why were you, for the pleasures of her young body, willing to cast a shadow on MY royal innocence? Yes, where was your famed kingly wisdom when, with your dalliance with my nymph, you risked raising doubts about my maidenhood, which I felt it my sacred duty to safeguard for the sake of my beloved country? What did you gain with your exploits between the sheets? So that in all the royal courts of Europe there would be whispering that my virginity is a sham and that my famous nymphs are but fairies of depravity and debauchery? What about THEIR honor? Do we not raise them to marry into royalty and nobility in all of Europe? You are a debaucher... Of those beautiful and innocent creatures, those future mothers of note... You have almost destroyed their value on the European market of brides of noble blood, by branding them with the sign of Kalisto! I am not a murderer! I have saved the honor of the country! Yes, I had to commit these brutal killings, executing Kalisto, who had dishonored her maidenhood, and my beloved Tarasiy, who lusted after my body, so that no one in the world would have any doubts whatsoever about my own royal innocence, doubts that might later undermine the authority of my husband, be he king or emperor. Doubts that he is my first!"

The faces of Lybid's relatives in the hall betray their sympathy to the young woman.

LYBID (shouting):

> "That he is my first!"

The Volkhvs whisper their concern among themselves.

LYBID:

> "I achieved what I set out to do: my famous nymphs, my bold warriors and my kingly suitors all over Europe now feel a fear! Because of what I did no one will ever dare laugh at my future, lawful husband! And no one will ever dare laugh at you, my beloved Father!"

KING OF KINGS:

> "I am moved by your righteous words, my daughter! But what are your words to me? I could have become a father once again!"

The King loses control over himself and groans in pain, unable to reconcile his conflicting feelings.

KING OF KINGS (shouting at Lybid):

> "I lay with Kalisto but one time! I was filled with a joy I hadn't felt since my youth!

> But I never thought she would become pregnant from that first time! Or that you would have her killed in such a grisly way! That you would kill the mother of my future child!"

The absolute ruler suddenly looks around the hall and proclaims:

KING OF KINGS (in a threatening tone of voice):

"That was not meant for anyone to hear!"

But it has been heard by the sovereign s many relatives...

BOOS (with anger in his voice):

"Father! Father! You are, without doubt, divine, and you are our judge, not we yours. By the divine right of kings, you are free to choose for yourself any women on Earth whom you desire! But to trade away your children's right of primogeniture, the rights of succession to your absolute rule over Rus, and to replace them with children yet unborn and conceived outside a sanctified marriage...! Father, I am distraught and ashamed! Our entire family is greatly saddened! And I feel great pain for our mother!"

ANOTHER RELATIVE:

"We are a family! We do not need any other new-found brothers and sister, nephews and nieces! We will not allow our rights to be redistributed to any newly acquired children!"

The King, thrown off balance by the unexpected angry reaction of the royal family, gives in to a wave of momentary despair. Overcome by a feeling of helplessness, he places his head in his hands...

Lybid hears the Volkhvs talking animatedly among themselves and senses that they have been powerfully affected by what has transpired.

VOLKHVY:

"The royal family will not share... The rights of succession... And there was no way of knowing who might have been born... The downfall of all of Rus... A son, a daughter, a harlot to bring shame to the Sovereign... A dynasty has its own laws..."

Lybid moves to take advantage of the prevailing mood among the high priests.

LYBID:

"Kill me, Father, if you want to keep dishonoring our divine mother, if you wish to continue your debauchery!"

BOOS:

"Lybid! Sister! You are a hero!"

The White Volkhv, nodding in response to what he hears from his priests, has made up his mind

WHITE VOLKHV:

"I see that Lybid... You are right!"

The White Volkhv rises from his chair, leaning on his staff. His voice unexpectedly thunders, as if borrowed from a god of thunder, so that it sends shivers down the spine of even the mightiest of kings...

WHITE VOLKHV:

"O Great Sovereign! I am a servant of Dazhboh! And therefore, I shall say this straight to your eyes. Rejoice, O Divine One! Accept it! The Almighty, in His justice and acting through the hands of your daughter, has prevented the birth of brothers and sisters who would have been alien to these golden children of yours!"

Oh, how craftily the White Volkhv builds the Temple's relations with the successors of the Sovereign of Rus! The priest's speech is flawless, striking all the right chords...

WHITE VOLKHV:

> "The Almighty has seen to it that your new, future children - children, who, unfortunately, were conceived, or, were yet to be conceived, outside of lawful marriage; children alien to all your progeny from the blessed Queen Zlata Maya - would not be born! So that in days to come they would not kill, while fighting for power over the land of Rus. So that the land would be spared the fratricidal wars between them, the unblessed, and your divine, lawful, glorious successors, who sit here among us! O great and just Sun King!"

Outside the Areopah the throngs are restless, in anticipation of what the proceedings inside will bring. Suddenly, there is a roar as the doors fly open and out steps a radiant Lybid Artemida.

LYBID (shouting):

> "Innocent!"

The masses of Kyivites rejoice, men throwing their caps up in the air. A mighty chant goes up: "Lybid! Lybid! Lybid!"

Behind Lybid stand the faithful Atalanta and her nymphs.

Lybid's soldiers use their shields to push the people aside, making a path for the Princess through the crowds. Lybid, her head held regally high, walks in triumph past her people, who extend their hands, trying to touch at least the hem of her clothing.

Lybid nods left and right as she passes by.

LYBID:

> "Thanks be to you, good people! Glory and thanks be to Dazhboh!"

Among the soldiers who guard Lybid and who allow her to pass through the throngs is Palant. As soon as Lybid, Atalanta and the nymphs walk by, he stands behind her, spear and shield in hand, and shouts, so loudly that the crowd falls silent. The only other sound is the cawing of the ravens in the trees nearby.

PALANT (in a challenging voice):

> "Princess, halt!"

Lybid abruptly stops and turns to face Palant. All within earshot are stunned at laudacity of the young prince. Shouts go up: "How dare he!" "The insolence!"

PALANT:

> "Halt..."

LYBID (insulted and angry):

> "How dare you stop me, Palant?"

PALANT:

> "By the right of honor!"

Lybid's soldiers, hands on the hilts of their swords, step in between the two. Those with a spear in their hands aim it at Palant.

PALANT (to the soldiers):

> "You think I am afraid? I am as much a warrior as any of you! But then you are not warriors – you're a pack of faithful, well-fed dogs!"

LYBID:

> "Palant, my friend, what is it you want?"

PALANT:

> "I loved Kalisto! You are a murderer, yet you came out of the Areopah absolved of her murder! A family affair, they decided! I wanted to marry Kalisto, even if she was pregnant by your father. She and I would have raised a real future king! But you killed her! How dared you destroy my happiness? I don't want you to live!"

The crowd surrounding the two howls with anger. The soldiers grip their swords more tightly.

ATALANTA:

> "I will kill you, Palant!"

Atalanta draws her sword but is grabbed from all sides by Volkhvs.

LYBID:

> "Atalanta, don't you dare! Palant is my friend!"

PALANT:

"No, I am no friend of yours! You are the murderer of my ... Betrothed? Of my wife!

You are not the White Swan! You are a black vulture which ripped apart my little dove. Kalisto! Oh, you are a goddess from a line of gods. And the gods are allowed anything – to kill their friends and their servants... If you eat something that doesn't agree with you, if your mood is spoiled by something or other..."

LYBID:

"Palant, why these lies? Why do you slander me!"

PALANT:

"In my grief I have found my own truth. And anything I say is the truth!"

LYBID:

"Come to your senses, Palant! I am your friend!"

PALANT:

"You are my enemy! You killed my future family! The gods are allowed anything? But the gods are immortal and eternal! And you? Your entire divine family are not gods, for you are mortal, you fall ill, you grow old, like all of us. We burn your bodies on a sacred fire and the ashes we bury in the soil! So, if you are mortal, then how can you be gods, and I not a god? If your father can sleep with my future wife and make her pregnant, why can't I make you pregnant? As if I were not your equal..."

Lybid is flush with anger...

LYBID:

"And, so, you desire my body, Palant?"

PALANT:

"I spit on the will of the Areopah, which has determined
to let you live!"

At this time the Volkhvs, headed by the White Volkhv, come up to the
pair. A part of the crowd that has pressed in to be near Lybid immediately
tries to move away.

Shouts are heard: "Farther away from sin..." "Tomorrow, at the market..."
"The neighbors must hear..."

WHITE VOLKHV:

What is this my old ears hear? Palant has raised his
voiced against the gods and dares to question the
decision of the Areopah?"

PALANT:

"Areopah? I laugh at your farce!"

LYBID:

"Palant, do you remember the oath you swore when we
were both nine years old?"

In Palant's mind a scene from the past appears - the Volkhv Mudroslav
introduces him to Lybid, just before they are to set out on a long journey...

MUDROSLAV:

"And this, Princess, is Palant..."

LYBID:

"Palant... Will you be loyal to me, Palant?"

PALANT:

"Until the day I die!"

LYBID:

"And if you betray your devotion to me?"

PALANT:

"Then you can take my life! I will have no regrets!"

LYBID:

"Swear it!"

PALANT:

"I swear it!"

LYBID:

"From now on your life belongs to me! Until the day you die!"

The scene fades from Palant's memory...

LYBID:

"... Your life belongs to me! Until the day you die!"

WHITE VOLKHV:

"Palant, you have betrayed your oath! A servant does not criticize his master! He endures every slight until his death... But you, Palant, dared to accuse the daughter of the gods, to blame her in front of everyone here. Your bitter words, your subversive example – that one can criticize the gods - should they become an infectious plague in Holy Rus? So that every commoner and peasant decide that he can act likewise, and a thousand Palants, who, like you, rose from the swamp of ignorance, would bring her to her knees with your disobedience? Whoever here heard your infectious words has already passed them on to another, or two, or ten, implanted your lies in the minds of a thousand illiterates. Rumors about your rebellion against the princess will spread like a putrid stench all over Great Rus and thousands of fools will want to bathe in your infectious swamp...You must die for this, Palant!"

MUDROSLAV:

"And the uplifting news about your ignominious death should be brought to all corners of Rus!"

WHITE VOLKHV:

"Die, Palant!"

At these words the king's soldiers and the young Volkhv disarm Palant, and seize him by his arms.

LYBID:

"Stop!"

Everyone looks at Lybid with dismay.

LYBID:

> "Palant should not be slaughtered like a pig for its meat.
> The rumor that we killed him in revenge for his true
> words, that we killed him in a cowardly way, will spread
> all over Rus!"

WHITE VOLKHV:

> "With his unfounded accusation right to your face he
> threw down a challenge to our state, a state which is just
> and fair in all things! He has used you, Princess, to
> justify his claim that, although he is not of royal blood,
> he has the right to sit on the royal throne. He wants to
> upset the caste system. He, the son of a prince, but not
> of a king!"

ATALANTA:

> "I will kill Palant in a fair fight!"

LYBID:

> "For all of Rus to say that I hid behind your back?"

WHITE VOLKHV (to the soldiers):

> "I order you to take the loyal Atalanta and lock her up
> in a dungeon, until this issue is resolved! So that by her
> presence she does not interfere with the will of the gods"

The soldiers and the young Volkhv disarm Atalanta.

ATALANTA:

"I will be silent! Like a fish in the water!"

WHITE VOLKHV:

"Yes, you will! Now, lads, take her to a 'dungeon,' for she is not a traitor but our hero!"

SOLDIERS:

"Take her where?"

WHITE VOLKHV:

"To her mother and father! And along the way praise her as a hero, so that everyone may hear that she is being honored! And then guard the home, explaining to all that you are an honor guard, because she is worthy of the highest praise for her courage and noble deeds! Let it thus be done!"

Atalanta is led away.

WHITE VOLKHV:

"Who will fight for the honor of the gods of Rus?"

LYBID:

"I will fight and kill Palant in fair combat!"

WHITE VOLKHV:

"Then let it be today and let it be before sundown. Let it not be at night, when the powers of darkness hold sway. Under the Sun and not the Moon. And in the presence of your father!"

The sacred oak grove. The duel to the death between Lybid and Palant. A royal grandstand has been set up on the ceremonial grounds, which are encircled with idols of the Slavic gods. Royal guests have begun to fill the grandstand, while the Volkhvs are busy preparing the setting for the coming spectacle. Throngs of Kyivites are tightly bunched around the list.

Palant is guarded by soldiers of the King so that he does not escape. The young prince paces back and forth like a caged animal. Meanwhile, Lybid is down on one knee, praying inside a ceremonial circle of Volkhvs, who perform the ritual of Dazhboh's blessing before combat.

WHITE VOLKHV:

> "Protect her, Almighty Dazhboh, in this combat to the death, for the terrible Palant stands there with a sword in his hand! Your power, O Dazhboh, shall be with her, daughter of the Sun, just as the Powers of eternal darkness now stand alongside Palant!"

The priests have built a pyre for the one who will be killed in the duel. A Volkhv with a torch stands alongside.

The King of Kings, Queen Zlata Maya and Boos Apollo have arrived at the grounds, accompanied by the highest nobles. The King walks up to Lybid.

KING OF KINGS:

> "Why do you insist on this deadly duel, my daughter?"

LYBID:

"I shall myself kill Palant for insulting you, his living god! Do not tell me, Father, that you have warriors in your realm that will chop him up into little pieces. This is a matter for me alone to resolve!"

QUEEN MAYA:

"Walk away from this, my little Swan!"

LYBID:

"And shame Rus before the world? Allow it to think that Palant was right?"

KING OF KINGS:

"I will not be able to live if Palant kills you! I should forbid you to fight. It would be better if I order Palant executed for treason! It would be..."

LYBID:

"Father! Your guilt burns my flaming heart more painfully than my internal fires burn. I shall fight to save the honor of our family from the rumors that infect Great Kyiv Rus like the plague. And if you forbid me to fight, I shall kill myself, in order to escape the shame!"

KING OF KINGS:

"Then take my sword!"

The king gives a sign and from behind him servants carry out a gleaming sword...

LYBID:

"The Sword of Ariy?"

Lybid takes the weapon and walks up to a wide tree.

LYBID:

"This hornbeam tree is as strong and as hard as iron!"

Lybid swings the Sword and the meteorite metal slices without resistance through the tree. Everyone anticipates what will happen next. The tree stands as it did before, until a breeze picks up and the giant totters and topples onto the list. Those standing in its shadow just manage to escape. Raves sitting in its crown take flight in a cawing cacophony. Women in the crowd gasp in awe. A look – the realization of impendis doom - crosses Palant's face.

VOICE IN THE CROWD:

"The Sword of Ariy!" "Ariy's Sword!"

Lybid returns the weapon to the king.

LYBID:

"Father! Why did you give me the Sword of Ariy? It would be the same as killing a harmless fly. To kill a defenseless man - a victory like this will bring me only dishonor! I shall fight with an ordinary sword!"

KING OF KINGS:

"You are nothing but a headache, my daughter! You ARE my headache!"

Palant lets go a sigh of relief, while the King, in despair, puts his head in his hands.

KING OF KINGS:

> "Palant! I will spare your life if you kill my daughter in fair combat. But if you surrender and allow her to kill you, then know this - I shall have your entire family put to the sword - your mother, father, sisters and brothers..."

PALANT:

> "I shall kill Lybid, O King!"

KING OF KINGS:

> "And I shall forgive you! Fight for your mother and father, for your entire family, Palant!"

The despairing ruler goes and sits on his throne in the center of the grandstand. Trumpets blare. Boos Apollo and Volkhv Mudroslav walk up to Lybid.

BOOS:

> "I shall be praying for you, dear sister!"

MUDROSLAV:

> "I bless you for battle, child!"

Lybid and Palant stand opposite each other, swords and shields in hand.

WHITE VOLKHV:

> "For Dazhboh!"

Palant and Lybid charge at each other, a battle cry on their lips. The air is filled with the ringing of swords and the clanging of shields. The fierceness of attacks and parries, the ferocity of the two combatants, drive the crowds surrounding the list and the royalty and nobles in the grandstand to a frenzy of trepidation and excitement. Abruptly, the weather turns: heavy clouds blot out the Sun, lightning bolts split the sky, thunder rolls, A fierce wind comes from nowhere, whipping around a drenching rain.

Lybid and Palant continue their struggle to the death, falling and getting up, sinking into the thick mud. Suddenly, a clap of thunder deafens the gathered, as a bolt of lightning comes down from the sky and strikes Palant, traveling along his armor and into the ground. He screams and falls. Shrieks from the terror-stricken crowd break through the howling of the wind and the pounding of the downpour...

Soldiers and priests run up to the fallen prince and remove his helmet, revealing his smoldering hair and his bulging eyes.

WHITE VOLKHV (to Palant):

> "The Great Perun has rendered his judgment! He has smitten you with his fiery arrow. But, still, you are alive! This means that the Great Perun wants you to live – in order to walk the land of Rus and, to the end of your days, tell everyone you meet about the injustice you have done to Lybid Artemida, the lies you told about her. Teach the people with your shame, Palant, and you will be forgiven by Almighty God and our great king! Choose life!"

PALANT:

> "I will not submit! I will not!"

He jumps to his feet and shakes his fist at the heavens.

PALANT:

"I do not fear you!"

WHITE VOLKHV:

"You fool!"

PALANT:

"O powerless god of thunder! I laugh in your face! Go ahead, gather your clouds! I fear you not!"

LYBID:

"Do not blaspheme! I can forgive anything, but not blasphemy against God! Die, Palant!"

Lybid lifts her sword high, but before she can strike, Palant retrieves his weapon from the mud and blocks the blow. Metal rings, sparks fly... Lybid finds unexpected strength, ducks Palant's swinging sword and, turning from the side, plunges her own into her erstwhile friend's midsection...

LYBID:

"How fortunate that your mother is not here to fitness your death..."

Palant gasps for breath, his eyes staring straight into Lybid's. Lybid draws her sword out and with one downward stroke cleaves his forehead. The dead prince's body collapses into the muck.

The rain keeps on falling, the wind shrieks around the people stunned into silence by the witnessed terminal violence.

WHITE VOLKHV:

> "Burn him! Give him up to the fire!"

Several young priests pick up Palant's body - blood still spurting from his head - carry it over to the funeral pyre and light the flame. Despite the downpour, the fire soon reaches toward the leaden sky and consumes the body of the prince who would be king...

And three millennia hence a sacrificial fire similar in its might and ferocity consumes the model of Lybid Artemida's temple in Washington, as an entranced crowd listens to the Avatar's narrative and sees itself on the Sacred Field, witnesses to the noble Palant's ignoble end...

Lybid, covered in the blood of her childhood friend and mud and soaked from the rain, breaks down in uncontrollable and mournful sobbing. The king walks up to her and gently takes her in his arms...

KING OF KINGS:

> "To love you, my daughter, my life. I love you with gentleness and trepidation. Go ahead - mourn, sob, cry out all your future tears, so that in moments of the deepest sorrow in days to come, your eyes be as dry as the driest desert..."

As he speaks, falling snow mixes with the rain and the surrounding, darkening grove is soon covered with a white, glistening powder...

KING OF KINGS:

> "You are grown now; your childhood is behind you. Time for you to marry in order to continue our line..."

Constantinople, capital of the Byzantine Empire. The window of the palace looks out onto a seascape the Golden Horn harbor, filled with sailing ships. The emperor of the Byzantine Empire, the mighty Theodorex, paces the floor. He is clearly agitated and speaks rudely to the high nobles gathered in the chamber, who stand in silent fear in his presence.

THEODOREX:

"Snow in the Golden Horn! This is the first time I am a witness to such a miracle. It's obvious there has been some kind of profound change in nature... But what was it I was talking about?"

The nobles are quick to respond.

NOBLE:

"You were pointing out that you are the emperor of the mighty Byzantine Empire and that this, of course, should carry much more weight than the name of the Goth king, Germanarix!"

THEODOREX:

"Oh, yes! So, what have my high ambassadors been doing? I have conquered Byzantium with my sword, but I lost Gothland and the lands of the Franks. Only a dynastic marriage between Kyiv and Byzantium will lead to the creation of a military power that will stand up to the Goth-Frank alliance. Unless Germanarix tears the glorious Lybid Artemida away from me. I want her brother to become my devoted brother as well. What does the ambassador write about Lybid and Boos?"

COUNSELOR:

"The ambassador writes: The purest love and the closest friendship unite brother and sister. She deeply loves her mother, the Queen Zlata Maya, and woe to whomever dares to insult her or cast aspersions on her honor. Apollo and Artemida will ruthlessly destroy them with their golden arrows."

THEODOREX:

"He is quite eloquent, that envoy of mine..."

COUNSELOR:

"Everything is quite simple: Lybid and Boos will not allow their father to sire any more children, so that they do not lose their right of succession to the throne. That is another reason they are so protective of their divine mother. They will not allow their father to take another wife, nor anything else that might have an effect on the dynasty. That is the guarantee of their ascending to the throne after the death of the King of Kings."

THEODOREX:

"Counselor! What I need from you is some concrete, practical advice! The mightiest power in the world today is the Empire of the Rus-Anty-Scythians, with its capital in Kyiv, the City of Kings. Byzantium is, of course, a super power, but it is still second to the mightiest empire of them all, the land of the Anty. That is why this capital of mine- once conquered by Kyiv - is called Byzantium. 'Bis-Antiy,' or "New Antia." My great empire is but a copy of their mighty super empire."

COUNSELOR:

"An empire can be enlarged by two means only, my Emperor! Either by a successful marriage or a successful war..."

THEODOREX:

"I do not want war with Kyiv Rus. The blood of millions will needlessly fill the rivers and the seas. And it is a war we cannot win, I am for a lasting, eternal peace! But a victorious peace! I want to be peaceful as a dove, but as cunning as a serpent. I want to marry Princess Lybid Artemida. Why have not my envoys completed negotiations with Kyiv for a royal marriage? Or are you waiting for Germanarix to wisk her away? If the king of the Goths succeeds in marrying Lybid Artemida, he, and not I, will become king of a world empire. And if I make her mine, then I will leave Byzantium, sit on the throne of Kyiv and unite two of the mightiest states on Earth!"

COUNSELOR:

The situation in Kyiv has changed. There is a change in the status of the bride-to-be..."

THEODOREX:

"I am afraid to hear what you are about to tell me. God forbid, the Maiden has...lost her innocence... "

COUNSELOR:

"No, my Emperor, that is not possible, not without a lawful marriage. After all, she is the goddess of wisdom. The change is of a different nature..."

THEODOREX:

"What nature? Why do you torment me?"

COUNSELOR:

"High politics! Lybid Artemida has accomplished her first major military feat, a victorious duel! She fought a battle to the death with the most accomplished of all the warriors of Rus, Prince Palant. She killed him, her childhood friend. The King of Kings was so excited he renamed her the Maiden Athena, in place of the Maiden Artemida. And what is paradoxical, but also natural for the ruler of a world empire, he ordered the nations over which he holds sway to venerate her in both these hypostases simultaneously, as Lybid Artemida and Lybid Athena."

THEODOREX:

"My future father-in-law has understood that his daughter's youth is gone. Another way of seeing it is that the young girl Lybid Artemida has been reborn as the mature marriageable fruit, Athena Pallada. It was very wise of him to divide her into two hypotheses - that of the young maiden Artemida and the warrior princess Athena Pallada, a woman to be venerated in all the temples of the land. Childhood is one thing; the age of marriage is quite another. How wise is the king! And how mighty are the Scythians, that they can force the nations of the Earth to worship them in legends and myths... My marriage with Lybid will make me the mightiest emperor in the world!"

COUNSELOR:

"O munificent Sovereign! Because it is the Scythian custom to have all events of state presented to the people in the form of myths and epic ballads, heralds have already started spreading this legend all over the empire of the Rus. As I have already informed Your Majesty, the King of Kings convinced his wife, the Queen Zlata Maya, not to take part in the trial of their daughter, so that her ears would not hear what transpired, including the part about Kalisto's pregnancy. The legend that was born of this is thus: that Zeus put the goddess Maya to sleep, by feeding her sweet morsels, and then swallowed her; soon afterwards a daughter was born..."

The Imperial Counselor unrolls a scroll and looks at the text...

COUNSELOR:

"I will read..."

Theodorex lets his active imagination take over...

COUNSELOR:

"Sometime later Zeus began experiencing an excruciating headache. He summoned his son Hephaestus and ordered him to split his head open, so as to rid him of the pain and din inside. Hephaestus swung his ax and with a mighty blow cleaved Zeus' skull open. And out of the head of the Wielder of Thunderbolts emerged the mighty warrior goddess

Athena Pallada. In full battle array, a shining helmet on her head and a spear in her hand, she stood before the astonished Olympic gods. She lifted her spear menacingly and let out a war cry that rolled far across the heavens and shook the very foundations of Olympus. Athena's blue eyes burned with a deep wisdom and she shone with a strange, compelling might and beauty. And the gods honored the favorite daughter of Zeus, born from his head, the protectress of cities, the goddess of wisdom and knowledge, the invincible Athena Pallada..."

In his imagination Theodorex sees a frightening vision: lightning sears the dies, thunder rolls and the wind whips snow and rain around the mighty Athena Pallada, standing tall and reaching the heavens...

TITLE: "LYBID, 3000 YEARS HENCE..."

January 1956. A concentration camp near Magadan, the U.S.S.R. In the office of the camp commandant an inmate couple stands before him, the wife holding their sleeping infant daughter in her arms. The commandant gets up from his chair and looks down at the face of the child.

COMMANDANT:

> "I am happy for this infant. This is as it should be. How beautiful she looks, sleeping the sleep of the innocent. She doesn't even know that she was born in a camp, she doesn't know about lies, betrayal, envy and greed..."

The commandant abruptly turns to his secretary.

COMMANDANT:

> "You're dismissed! Leave us!"

SECRETARY:

> "Yes, Sir, Comrade Major!"

COMMANDANT:

> "And don't listen in by the door, or I'll tear your ears off!"

The secretary leaves and closes the door behind him, but the commandant opens it and checks in the hallway.

COMMANDANT:

> "Go! Go!"

He closes the door, walks up to the parents and looks once more at the sleeping Lybid.

COMMANDANT:

> "Anything can happen... Though Comrade Stalin once said that there is no such thing as miracles, I have witnessed some strange happenings in my lifetime. I remember when Czar Nicholas II, Nicholas the Bloody, ruled over all of Russia. But something happened forty years ago and within a year there was not a trace left of his Romanov dynasty, a dynasty that had ruled for 300 years. And in his place, for over a quarter of a century, a former convict and political exile by the name of Stalin sat on the Kremlin throne. Joseph Dzhugashvili-Stalin, born of a poor Georgian family in the dusty little town of Gori, ruler of the huge empire that is the Soviet Union. And our other famous national heroes? Peasants, mostly! CO miners or railroad men. Our Nikita Khrushchev, General Secretary of the Communist Party of the Soviet Union, can barely put two words together. Used to be director of a club! Can anybody tell me those are not miracles? So, your daughter could very well herself climb to the Kremlin heights! What if you are amnestied and, sometime in the future, rehabilitated? Where will you want to live after your release? You know you won't have the rights that all Soviet citizens enjoy. Instead of a passport, you'll get pieces of paper for identification purposes only. And that's the way it will be for at least five years."

HANNA:

"We will go back home to Ukraine, to Great Rus. It waits for us. I long to see my dear parents, who have suffered so much..."

COMMANDANT:

"You yourselves won't have it easy there. Nor here, for that matter. But your daughter - what was her crime? I'm getting up there in years and I've seen much in my life. And yet I look at you and I wonder. I think about how unjust it was that the troika sentenced two innocent heroes to such torment..."

VASYL:

"We've sometimes wondered – who were the judges?"

COMMANDANT:

"Well, yes... It's like I said; let's leave it at that..."

The commandant falls silent, a hint of fear crossing his face.

VASYL:

"Commandant, Sir. Everything has its price and we - Hanna and I-are paying a heavy price for the freedom of our Motherland. I firmly believe that all of this was not in vain and that our divine daughter will complete our mission. I believe that humankind will ultimately come to understand its great purpose of peace on Earth."

HANNA:

"May God forgive all the people with malice in their hearts and darkness in their souls and give them the wisdom to put a stop to all these cruel and senseless wars and to begin building a paradise here on Earth..."

COMMANDANT:

"I believe that your daughter will play a key role in that future."

The camp commandant leans over the child, smiling.

COMMANDANT:

She may be destined for great things. It could happen that one day all of mankind will 'Oooo' and 'Ah!", sit down, scratch their heads and say, 'This woman changed the world!' If it does happen, do not hold against me any of what happened to you here. I hope your daughter does not take vengeance on me. I will be old by then and retired. Have her take pity on me!"

VASYL (a wide, guileless smile lighting up his face):

"Don't worry, Leonid Artemovich..."

HANNA (her sparkling blue eyes smiling upon the official):

"We promise..."

COMMANDANT:

"I look at the two of you and something deep inside me roils and burns. The injustice that has gripped the world! You are such beautiful people, inside and out.

306

Your souls radiate such goodness, such warmth! How could those troikas condemn you to such a fate? And I don't comprehend how, after all that you have endured, you haven't become bitter, as if all that evil didn't touch you at all."

VASYL:

"Oh, it has touched us. After ten years in Siberia and Magadan, I have no feeling in my feet, due to frostbite. I spit up blood from my lungs. I paid with my health for the good I did for various demons. Everything has its price. Except the things we treasure most - those are priceless. No matter what we endured, the thing we received- the birth of this little one - has no price."

Vasyl tenderly kisses tiny Lybid's head, then looks at Hanna, who knowingly glances back at him.

HANNA:

"We are alive, my dear Vasyl, but our suffering Ukrainian people have paid with seven million lives in artificial famines alone. And how many have died in concentration camps and in the struggle for truth and the freedom of Ukraine. For that reason, we must live and look to the future and raise the daughter that the Lord has blessed us with. We won't be sullying our lives with memories of the ugly past, of the injustices dealt us by the atheists. We don't have time for that. We don't have time to complain. Let's remember how much Jesus and Krishna had to endure. How they were persecuted. But there is none greater than Almighty God and everything will be the way He wills it, He and not some insane cretin."

In her thoughts Hanna goes back to May 9, 1946, the dreadful day of her arrest.

Cherkassy Region, Katerynopilsky District, the village of Zalizniachka. A young, blue-eyed beauty, with long, luxurious hair, is in the kitchen, preparing supper. She takes a big pot of steaming, fragrant borshch off the stove, sets it on the table, sits down in a chair and awaits her beloved parents coming home. There is a knock on the door.

HANNA:

> "Come in, please, the door is unlocked; there is no need for such formality in your own home. Father, is that you joking this way? Or is it Mama?"

Another knock, and Hanna gets up to open the door.

HANNA (opening the door):

> "Come in. I said the door is open."

A middle-aged stranger, red-haired and freckle-faced, stands on the threshold.

STRANGER:

> "Good evening. Does Hanna Hnativna Vitranenko live here?"

HANNA:

> "Yes, she does. And you have come at just the right time. I came just a few hours ago from Uman to visit with my mother and father for a few weeks. I can't wait to see them. They're still at work, they work so hard. I thought it was they, joking around."

Hanna feels a sudden, inexplicable pain squeezing her heart.

STRANGER:

"May I come in?"

HANNA:

"Yes, yes, do come in. Please forgive me for not inviting a guest inside. I guess I got a bit confused. I miss my parents so much, so I've come to visit them and celebrate Victory Day with them. And then it's back to school. I want to finish my education as soon as possible, so that I can go to work and let Father and Mother go into their well-earned retirement. They have been working so hard for so long. Time for them to enjoy life a bit."

STRANGER:mnhgmjhr

I'm not from around here and got somewhat lost, going from the station to your house. I have something to give you from your friend Maria. Zamkovenko, I think her name is."

HANNA:

"Maria?"

STRANGER:

"Pardon me, I haven't introduced myself. My Name is Ryzhov, a friend of hers..."

HANNA:

"But my friend's name is not Maria; it's Hanna, just like mine."

RYZHOV:

"Yes, yes of course. I guess I'm somewhat tired. Been traveling all day."

HANNA:

"Then perhaps you would like to eat something. I just came and only had time to cook up some borshch. Hoped to knead some dough and make some varenyky, but there isn't time before my parents come, which should be any minute now. So, please stay and sup with us to celebrate Victory Day, modestly, but from the heart."

RYZHOV:

"I am in somewhat of a hurry- I want to catch the last train to Kyiv. It'll be dark soon and I don't know the way."

HANNA:

"Then you sit down and have something to eat, whatever the Lord has provided. You needn't wait for anybody. I'll show you the quickest way to the station - it's not very far – then have supper together with my parents."

Hanna pours a bowl full of steaming, red Ukrainian borshch and places it in front of Ryzhov.

RYZHOV:

"That there is beautiful-looking borshch you've prepared.... And delicious, too!"

HANNA:

"While you eat you can tell me how my dear friend is doing in Kyiv.

RYZHOV:

"Well, alright. [coughs]. But maybe we'll discuss that on the way to the station?

HANNA:

"That's fine. I suppose there will be a little bit of time."

RYZHOV (looking at his watch):

"It's time. We should be leaving."

Hanna glances at Ryzhov's large bowl and is surprised to see that he has already drained it.

RYZHOV:

"Why don't you throw something on; it's evening and somewhat chilly."

HANNA:

"Why? I'll be back in a few minutes. And if it does get chilly, I'll just run and warm up. [She lets out a girlish laugh.] I am so happy to be home with my parents again, the mast wonderful parents in the world, here on the sacred land of the great Shevchenko, that I am ready not only to run its length and breadth but also to kiss every last centimeter!"

RYZHOV (coming out of the house):

"I see that you love Ukraine very much..."

HANNA:

"Yes, I cannot live without it and will do anything so that my land and my people no longer have to suffer, so that there be no more famines, which I have had the misfortune of witnessing. You yourself no doubt remember that horrific time, when people were driven to eat other humans? Hard to believe, is it not, that such things could happen in Ukraine, the breadbasket of Europe?"

RYZHOV:

"I lived in Moscow and saw or heard nothing of this."

HANNA:

"Well, we've come to the burial mound. It was raised by people carrying earth in their hats. See how tall it is? Just go straight and you'll come to the station. And I'll be on my way home..."

Unexpectedly, Ryzhov draws out a concealed revolver and aims it at Hanna.

RYZHOV:

"Get your hands behind your back and head for the station."

The Chekist Ryzhov leads Hanna to the Zvenyhorodka station, and from there takes her by train to Kyiv, to an underground dungeon of the NKVD. There they torture the innocent Ukrainian beauty, demanding that she sign the confession that would seal her fate. They keep her in a dungeon crawling with rats, starve her, finally putting her before a troika. The three-man tribunal sentences the young Ukrainian patriot to ten years in concentration camps in Siberia and Magadan, without the right to correspond with her loved ones. Thus, Hanna Hnativna Vitranenko was taken from the land of Shevchenko, while her mother, Frosyna, with tears in her eyes begged the NKVD vampires to let her see her beloved daughter one more time, and to give her a piece of warm clothing and a bit of food. It was all for nothing.

Meanwhile Vasyl Petrovych Kovhanych, under guard of the NKVD, set out on a long journey to distant regions of Siberian Russia. The courageous widow, Domna Andriyivna Kovhanych, cried for her only son, as did his little sisters, Yalynka and Natalka, and his many friends. And all of Ukraine-Rus wept, as her best and brightest, the flower of the nation, were carried off to face a death from starvation, freezing cold and torture, just because they were proud to be Ukrainians and wanted their people to be happy in their own land.

Hanna remembered her mother and father- blue-eyed, both of them - and her brother Dmytro in their village of Zalizniachka, and the spring on its outskirts, from which flowed cold, clear water, as pure as the tear that rolled down her cheek and dropped on the face of little Lybid Halia Kovhanych.

VASYL (tenderly wiping Hanna's face):

> "Don't cry. Let our enemy's cry. We will laugh, for we will survive everything and we will win. It's not for nothing that we are together again, even if it be here in Magadan..."

Hanna and Vasyl smile at each other and snuggle up even tighter around their infant daughter. The three concentration camp inmates form something unfathomably strong and magnificent.

The concentration camp commandant is moved.

COMMANDANT:

> "I don't know why I should be surprised. Gold, wherever you may toss it, will never rust, but will remain a noble metal. And so, it is with noble people."

HANNA:

> "And in fifty years' time all this filth will have no meaning. Yes, it's as my husband says: "The hero is not the one who strikes another, but he who endures the blows!""

COMMANDANT:

> "I wish for your daughter... Maybe this is trite and, perhaps, beyond the realm of the possible, but I wish for her that she will one day speak to all of the world's leaders, right there at the UN, and will proclaim how mankind should live! The way we live now - it's not right, it's not the way human beings should live!... And the Sun looks down on us from its perch high in the sky

314

and thinks, "What an absolute travesty! The complete idiots! God Almighty!"

The major abruptly takes off his hat and, before an astonished Hanna and Vasyl, crosses himself October 8, 2000. UN headquarters in New York. The first day of the World Summit of heads of state and heads of government. A warm autumn Sun greets the presidents, prime ministers and other dignitaries representing over 200 countries, as they step out of their limousines in front of the UN General Secretariat Building. The police keep vast throngs, including hundreds of journalists, behind security barriers. Television trucks jam the surrounding streets, their antennas forming an urban forest. Camera crews and reporters from the major networks protect coveted space near the entrance to the building. A red light goes on a Beta SP and CNN viewers all over the world begin receiving a report from the scene.

ZIMMERMAN:

> "Good afternoon, everybody! This is Allen Zimmerman, reporting live from the UN building in New York! A sensational development in this, the unofficial capital of the world community, as Queen Lybid Artemida has once again shown her unique ability to influence global events. She has convinced the leaders of the world to gather at the United Nations to discuss the issue of the Sun. And they have gathered here in the United States without the bureaucratic red tape that usually accompanies such meetings. It is possible that the presidents, prime ministers and royalty have been influenced by the World Congress of Masons, which took place at the Metropolitan Opera Building in July 2000. At that convention the decision was made to appropriate not less than 100 billion dollars to organize an expedition to the Sun. And so, the world's leaders have answered the intriguing call of a woman said to be

the reincarnation of a queen who nineteen hundred years ago conquered the entire ancient world. The world's most influential leaders, representing practically all of the countries of the world and billions of their citizens, will be collectively deciding issues that will determine the destiny of mankind... CNN cameras have been placed at all the key points in the UN building. And now, for a report from inside the General Assembly Hall, we go to our correspondent Ruth Mazembe, Ruth, if you will!"

Ruth Mazembe, an African-American journalist, appears on the screen. As she speaks the director cuts from one camera in the hall to another, illustrating her narrative...

MAZEMBE:

"Thank you, Allen, and good afternoon, Ladies and Gentlemen! I consider it an honor to be able to bring to you the inside story of this unique international gathering, so representative of the world community! You can see the steady stream of presidents and kings, as they come into the hall and head for their places. The arrival of each head of delegation is announced by the playing of the national anthem of his or her country, many of them are long-time personal friends and there is a sense here that this can add to the very positive atmosphere that one feels forming here, that might help build a consensus on the issues of utmost importance that will be addressed here. We see black embracing white, a Japanese politician embracing his Indian counterpart, a German warmly greeting a Jew. Delegates from every continent and every country - North and South Americans, Europeans, Asians, Africans, Australians, leaders of island states. Most are dressed in either Western business suits or tuxes, but there are quite a few who have come in the national dress of their countries... You hear in the background the national anthem of Australia in honor of the prime minister of that country Down Under, played by the U.S. Marine Corps Band. Now I see that some of the parliamentary delegations have also started to arrive, with the senior member of each group carrying a banner with its affiliation-'German Bundestag,' 'Israeli Knesset,' 'British House of Commons...'"

There is a cut-away from inside the hall and Allen Zimmerman again appears on the screen.

ZIMMERMAN:

"Ruth, we just received a report that among those present inside the UN Hall are members of some of the world's wealthiest and most powerful families. Bill Gates is said to be here, Bill Allen and Warren Buffet, as well as leading members of the old-money families - the Rothschilds, the Morgans, Rockefellers, DuPonts, McCormick. And even super stars of the arts and the entertainment industry...'"

The live camera is again on Ruth Mazwembe inside the General Assembly Hall...

MAZEMBE:

"Yes, many of the most influential people on Earth are gathering here, whose faces are universally recognized. Our viewers can see for themselves, as our cameras pick out one after another. But what I want to come back to is that everyone here, from the president to the parliamentary delegates to the celebrity guests, have come to hear one amazing woman and to set a course for mankind's relationship with the Sun. And that woman, Queen Lybid Artemida, is on her way now..."

A long black limousine is making its way along the streets of New York, as a police escort on motorcycles and in squad cars leads the way and brings up the rear, lights flashIng. Inside the limo Lybid, dressed in a sparkling imperial robe, and Sol Liebermann are watching the CNN broadcast from the UN Building.

LYBID:

> "I am so tired, Sol! It seems that from June I have been practically living inside this limo. It will be five months soon. And it seems like nothing changes. This TV set shows pretty much the same things, the same journalese, except that now we have Ruth Mazembe in place of the late Phillip Gorsky, who will say-The conscience of modern civilization is reflected in to what extent we can look directly, without blinking, not only at the Sun, but into each other's eyes, as well."

Lybid and Liebermann look at the TV monitor, where the CNN reporter is again on the screen.

RUTH MAZEMBE:

> "The conscience of modern civilization is reflected in-to what extent we can look directly, without blinking, not only at the Sun, but into each other's eyes, as well. Just a year ago, some of the most skeptical..."

LYBID:

"Sometimes I feel so worn out, Sol, that I doubt whether I can bring this work to fruition. And it seems that my heart will stop beating from an almost deadly sadness before I am able to fly to the Sun. I feel so alone!"

LIEBERMAN:

"When Robert Oberfell and Betsy Rosenberg died you felt as though the little world you had created for yourself through your relationship with them, though short-lived but very real, also died. I am painfully aware that I have failed you, in that I am not Robert Oberfell and you have not been able to replace him in your heart with me..."

LYBID:

"Believe me, Sol, it has also been very painful for me that I have not been able to see you as a replacement for Robert. I sometimes catch myself expecting that the door will open and Robert will get in, sit down opposite me, in the place where you are now sitting, and will say something funny. Or something encouraging. But believe me, Sol, I am sincerely grateful to you for your dedication. Even if you are not Robert Oberfell, you are, for me, my Sol Liebermann."

The TV screen shows a wide shot of Lybid's motorcade.

ZIMMERMAN:

"And now the moment we have been waiting for! I believe the advance cars of the motorcade of Her Majesty the Queen Lybid Artemida are approaching, as

319

thousands of people all around me are holding their collective breath in anticipation..."

Inside the limousine the TV monitor shows a push-in on the entrance to the UN building, then a close-up of the motorcycle police escort and the line of squad cars whizzing by.

Finally, Lybid's limousine is seen driving up to curbside, the camera finally fixed on the door from which the Queen is expected to emerge.

LIEBERMANN:

"Any second now... Get ready! Olafson will open the door... God be with you!"

Secret Service agent Swen Olafson opens the door from the outside and Lybid Artemida, her smile as warm as the Sun, the gold and precious stones in her garments reflecting its blinding rays, steps out onto the curb. The crowds erupt with a joyous, welcoming roar.

ZIMMERMAN:

"Ladies and Gentlemen! Truly like a radiant Sun Lybid Artemida appears before our eyes!"

A storm of applause greets Lybid as she walks into the General Assembly Hall. The audience is on its feet and turned towards her. As Lybid walks past them down the center aisle, the men bow slightly. The UN Secretary General meets her at the podium, kisses her hand, then approaches the microphone.

SECRETARY GENERAL:

"As the Secretary General, I welcome you, Your Majesty, in the name of the United Nations Organization!"

Another standing ovation follows, as president and ordinary delegate alike heartily applaud the woman who has brought them together for the convocation. The orchestra plays a flourish. Everyone sits down, as Lybid is escorted to a special chair to the right of the podium.

SECRETARY GENERAL:

> "I proclaim open the world summit of heads of state and heads of government of the member states of the United Nations Organization. And in doing so I wish to direct the attention of the world community to the fact that you, Your Majesty, have already created your main miracle - you have brought us all here together to pay you homage in the name of the peoples of our planet and to hear your plans for a flight to the Sun. The 100 billion dollars that are to be appropriated in this fiscal year for the expedition are a symbol of the victory of a new way of looking at the way our world is governed. A spiritual revolution has taken place, without which those 100 billion dollars might as well burn up on the Sun. And now I would like to recognize the President of the United States, William Jefferson Clinton. President Clinton has played the determining role in the organization of this summit by inviting all of you - presidents, prime ministers, monarchs and other high representatives of the nations of the world- to respond to Her Majesty's initiative to convene this summit. Thanks to President Clinton, his inexhaustible energy, all mankind, Your Majesty, is preparing for your flight... And now, I ask the Honorable William Jefferson Clinton, President of the United States of America, to come to the podium!"

The audience rises spontaneously in a standing ovation as Bill Clinton comes up to the Secretary General, shakes his hand and makes his way to the rostrum. Waiting a few moments while the distinguished gathering sits down, the U.S. president begins his address to mankind.

PRESIDENT CLINTON:

> "Mr. Secretary-General, Your Majesties, Your Excellencies, dear guests, ladies and gentlemen! I welcome you all in the name of the people of the United States of America!
>
> I welcome Her Majesty, Queen Lybid Artemida, in the name of our children, whose future will be decided by her expedition to the Sun. If you, Your Majesty, bring back to them the Sun's Blessing, if you find there indeed a Royal Planet, then we shall proclaim, 'Paradise Found!' Or we might say the Sun is, after all, nothing but a sphere of super-heated gasses and 100 billion dollars of irreplaceable resources contributed by all of mankind will have burned up uselessly in the rocket engines of your space ships. Preparing for today's address I asked my staff to compile some information about the Sun. And this is what they put together..."

President Clinton reads from a huge electronic tableau displaying the text of the study...

PRESIDENT CLINTON:

> "Modern astronomy confirms that the Sun is nothing but a sphere of heated plasma, which has kept burning for millions of years, fueled by hydrogen and helium. The Sun is moving in the direction of the Hercules Constellation with a speed relative to the nearest stars- of 19.5 kilometers per second. Its distance to the center of the Milky Way Galaxy is 28000 light years. Distance

to the center of the plane is 50 light years It turns around the center of the galaxy at a speed of 250 kilometers per second and the comolets journey around the center takes 200 million years. The Sun's age is estimated at 5 billion years. As a star the Sun is classified as a yellow dwarf. And although its density is only 1407 times the density of water, its mass is 332,946 times the Earth's mass. The average diameter of the Sun is 1,392,520 kilometers. The Sun's mass represents over 99% of the total mass found in the Solar System.'"

Clinton looks around the hall to see what kind of effect the data has had on his audience...

CLINTON:

"Do we dare believe that the Sun is truly our god?

LYBID:

"And where should we seek God? In our own Solar system, where our obvious god, the Sun, is everyday visible to our eyes? Or should we reach directly into the Universe?

Modern occultists claim that their god, with whom they constantly interact, is the entire Universe! They direct the sight of hundreds of millions of people away from the Sun and into the depths of the Universe and it doesn't even occur to them that the distances astronomy deals in are truly incomprehensible! Let's think about this. The accepted measure of distance is the light-year, the distance that light travels in the course of a year.

To get an idea of the distances that we are dealing with let us recall that the light from the Sun takes but eight and one-half minutes to travel to the Earth, a distance of 150 million miles. The Moon is but one light second away from us. The entire Solar system is but a few light hours across. The nearest star is a bit over four light years away. The radius of our galaxy is about 100,000 light years, and includes no fewer than 100 billion stars. The distances to other galaxies are on the order of millions of light years. Our 'neighboring' galaxy, Andromeda, is about 2.5 million light years away from us. The most powerful telescopes on Earth allow us to look at the most distant galaxies, separated from us by 10 billion light years. Though the 'information' that comes to us might be about stars that faded many million years ago, modern-day astronomers painstakingly enter them in astronomical charts and catalogs as if they exist to this day. Can we believe such a cosmos? A cosmos in which half of what we can see through our telescopes today is dead and changed into cosmic dust? A cosmos in which the light from distant stars is like the letter from a person who died long before you were even born, in a city that no longer exists! So where should we be looking for God? In the far reaches of a deceitful cosmos or right there on our Sun?"

CLINTON:

"I would encourage the distinguished leaders present here to take part in this intriguing discussion. I propose that we begin with questions which would explain to our peoples the essence of the expedition to the Sun."

The U.S. president walks off the podium, satisfied at having created an atmosphere that is conducive to Lybid's plans.

SECRETARY GENERAL:

"Your Excellencies! I invite you to address your questions to Her Majesty Queen Lybid Artemida..."

One after another the world's leaders put their questions to Lybid, bending slightly towards the microphones built into the backs of the chairs immediately in front of them.

FRENCH PRESIDENT:

"If the Sun is our god, then what, astronomically speaking, is the Universe's equivalent of the Supreme Being?"

LYBID:

"The Sun, as a part of the infinite body of the Universal God, is, in and of itself, a typical star. And the rest of the stars which we see in the night sky are also suns, some of which have their own planetary systems. Stars do not exist in isolation but are part of gigantic circular structures which we know as galaxies. Beyond our own Milky Way are countless billions of other galaxies very similar to our own in that they are usually in the form of a disc. The Andromeda Nebula is a typical galaxy, which appears to the unaided eye as a bright spot in the night sky. Galaxies in turn form clusters. Our telescopes have allowed us to conclude that the Universe is filled with galaxy clusters, millions of them, more or less evenly spread out in space. This, in fact, is the Universe. And the Universe is our Almighty God, the Supreme Being. But the Sun, within the body of Almighty God, the Supreme Being, is our god! And I would like to speak here only about It!"

JAPANESE PRIME MINISTER:

"How difficult will it be for your expedition to actually reach the Sun?"

LYBID:

"The Earth revolves around the Sun on an elliptical orbit with a circumference of 939,885,500 kilometers. So, its distance to the Sun varies. Orbital velocity is also no constant, varying from 105,450 km. per hour to 109,000 per hour. The average distance from the Earth to the Sun likewise varies, averaging out to almost 150 million kilometers. So, our flight should take place at a time when we are closest to the Sun. Moreover, the trajectory of our return flight is calculated so that we would not be trying to catch up with the Earth through space, but so that our Mother Earth would catch up with us as we travel away from the Sun. As we see there on the electronic display."

AUSTRALIAN PRIME MINISTER:

"From the point of view of our technological capabilities, how far is the flight lo tike Sun for us?"

LYBID:

"It is far enough so that, in the words of an ancient saying, 'not one bird can fly there.' According to a belief of the ancient Aryans, the 'Land of the Divine,' that is, the Sun, could only be reached on the sacred bird Harud. In the Hindu 'Questions of Milinda' the answer to the question, 'Is it far from here to the world of Brahma?' was: 'Very far. If a rock breaks away there, then, traveling 48,000 yodjan in a day, it will reach Earth in four months.' Well, 48,000 yodjan is more that 80 million kilometers. The ancients also passed down some interesting information about the dimensions of our Central Planet: Kulun Kullustuur lived in a land that was 'brilliant white' and it took a crane eight or nine years to fly around. If a crane flies with a speed of 40-50 kilometers an hour, then we arrive at precisely the circumference around the Sun's equator. If measured around the photosphere, this comes out to 4,300,000 kilometers. As you see, the data passed down to us by our ancestors is amazingly accurate!"

PRESIDENT OF UKRAINE:

"The Ukrainian government studied several days' worth of your speeches and testimony. We didn't sleep, we didn't rest and we didn't eat. You have opened up for us a most interesting world, the world of a thinking Sun. However, we are very concerned about the obvious danger for your spaceship from solar flares. We are afraid for you, afraid that the Sun would use its flares as a fiery weapon against you. For example, we are not able to tell, looking through a telescope, whether or not the flares are part of the Sun's air defense system, used against spacecraft violating the sovereign territory of the Sun state. That's one. And secondly aren't you afraid of burning up in the Sun's corona?

What if there are unknown laws of gravitational pull that bring us down from heights greater than the reach of solar flares. Thirdly. We all know that the corona extends more than ten solar radii. Up until 1931 the only time that the corona could be seen was during total solar eclipses as a pearly white halo around the sun's disk, which was covered by the Moon. After the invention of the coronagraph the Sun's corona could be seen at times other than eclipses. Modern technology allows us to look directly at the Sun and when we do observe it, we see clearly the details of its structure."

LYBID:

"Our ancestors knew the structure of the Sun even without the coronagraph!

According to Aksimander, the apeiron was divided into cosmic heat and cosmic cold. The wet and cold core was enveloped in a flaming layer. This corresponds to the Hindu belief that all worlds are surrounded by a layer, beyond which are the world waters 700,000 yodjan deep. The waters are surrounded by fire, the fire by air, the air by wisdom, the wisdom by the divine substance."

PRESIDENT OF GEORGIA:

"That is correct! But how do you plan to reach the Sun if at any given second you risk destruction from one of the innumerable solar flares? The average height of the flares above the surface of the Sun is 30-50,000 kilometers, the average length is 200,000 kilometers and the width-5000 kilometers. To hell with the flares, anyway! In the end, your spaceship will splash down into an ocean of fire and will burn up in that blinding crematorium! So how do you plan to set the spaceship down onto the Sun's surface?"

LYBID:

"We will use windows to the Sun. In other words, a gateway through the corona. They are there, with a radius of 200,00 kilometers! An Icelandic saga tells us:

'Afterwards, they saw another island, a smaller island, which was surrounded by a flaming, rotating wall. In one place in that flaming wall there was an open door. Every time that, with the rotation of the wall, the door was opposite the travelers, they could see through it the entire island and everything that was there, including all of its inhabitants - there was a multitude of people there, beautiful of face, in luxurious clothing, feasting, with gold cups in their hands...' Obviously, there are many distortions in this, due to the imperfection (relative to today's) in the ancients' conceptual system. But, you know, what they are talking about are sunspots. The saga implies that, using the sunspots, we can draw a map of the Sun. That same opinion was held by Herschel the Elder. He claimed that the spots on the Sun are temporary openings in the clouds, through which we can see the dark surface of the central core. Herschel the Younger explained sunspots in the following manner: they are tremendous whirlwinds, rising through the atmosphere. Both Herschel's were correct. A sunspot is nothing but the eye of a storm in the Sun's atmosphere. It is clear that any storms would develop only in the upper layers in the corona, Sunspots are holes in the corona. The bigger and more powerful cyclones reach down to the lower levels. And those areas where turbulence is suppressed and is not illuminated by the intense radiation of the upper layers, we see as holes and spots. Therefore, in those calmer areas we have a greater chance of peering deeper inside the Sun. And, finally, we will see for ourselves that 'multitude of people there, beautiful of face, in luxurious clothing. feasting, with gold cups in their hands...' So, the sunspots - these are the eyes in the storms in the Sun's atmosphere, that is, the windows or the 'holes.' It is through one of those "open doors' that we will guide our spaceship. And if it doesn't burn up, we will obtain a picture of the surface of the Sun planet."

EGYPTIAN PRESIDENT:

"Are there any depictions on Earth of the surface of the Sun?"

LYBID:

"I believe there are, in the form of small globes found on the north shore of the Black Sea. They are not similar to globes of Earth. By the way, please note that, for some reason, the area of islands is quite small. Getting ahead of myself, I will say that a map or a globe of the Sun should to some extent remind us of Earth, the laws of planetology are consistent and apply to all heavenly bodies. The most massive islands or continents should be located at diametrically opposed meridians. There should be a North-South asymmetry - the area of continents (or islands) on the northern hemisphere should be greater, and they should be located at the middle latitudes, while the southern hemisphere should have a lesser area of islands and they should be concentrated near the south pole. In other words, all planets are pear-shaped."

KING OF SPAIN:

"How were you able to calculate the optimal course for the Sun?"

LYBID:

"We were able to find a suggestion in a remarkable Norwegian fable, 'East of the Sun. West of the Moon'. In the fable a sorcerer decides to leave his cheating wife. She vows to find him. He tells her: "The trouble is, there is no path to that castle. It stands east of the Sun and west of the Moon and no one on Earth knows the way there'. Let's look at a diagram showing how Robert Karim described the beauty of this fable."

A diagram appears on the electronic tableau, showing the trajectory of the proposed fight. Close-up of the diagram.

LYBID:

"If take-off is during daytime, we should fly to the east of the Sun, if during nighttime - to the west of the Moon. In both cases the direction will be opposite to the rotation of Earth. The velocity will decrease and the spaceship will begin to descend to the Sun".

PRESIDENT OF IVORY COAST:

"Tell us, Your Majesty, are we to understand that you plan to land the spaceship directly on the Sun?"

LYBID:

"Not at all! Given the present level of space travel technology, our crew would burn up in the Sun's corona. What I have in mind is that we will fall from Earth directly to the Sun, thus saving fuel by turning off the engines.

Cut-away to TV screen...

ZIMMERMAN:

"Ladies and Gentlemen! This is Allen Zimmerman, reporting for CNN from the headquarters of the United Nations in New York. At this moment in the UN General Assembly hall the heads of state of member nations have signed an agreement pledging 100 billion dollars to fund an international expedition to the Sun in the near future. Inside the hall is my colleague Ruth Mazembe".

Ruth Mazembe appears on the screen, her report illustrated by cut-away to one of a dozen cameras positioned throughout the hall.

MAZEMBE:

"Good afternoon! I'm Ruth Mazembe, reporting to you live from inside the General Assembly Hall of the United Nations. It is my great privilege to be here at this historic session, during which the leaders of 160 nations signed an international agreement to fund the most ambitious project in the history of mankind. You see on your screens the agreement passing, for their signature, from one head of state or government to another. It was indeed a propitious decision to have the world's leader come together to debate and sign the document that will pave the way for mankind's journey to the Sun. I cannot imagine the agreement being signed by each leader on a separate occasion. The contributions to the project are, of course, not equal, but are based on each nation's ability to pay. For example, Kuwait, despite its size, will pay 9 billion dollars, while Latvia, the tiny republic in the Baltics, will invest only 30 million. The biggest share of the cost will, of course, be borne by the United States."

The following scenes show the various characters who played a part in the modem saga of Queen Lybid Artemida watching the report on their television sets at home or in the office. The screen shows a replay of a part of the address of President Clinton...

CLINTON:

"I am proud to say that I was the first to sign the international agreement..."

Inside the UN hall Lybid and the Secretary General are standing side-by-side at the podium.

SECRETARY GENERAL:

"In the name of the United Nations Organization and the world community I announce the decision of the summit of the leaders of the member states of the UN to award to you the honorary humanitarian title of Queen of the United Nations. Millions of minds on Earth wrestled with the riddle of the prophecy, by what means you would conquer the world. In the tablets and in the oral tradition of all the peoples of the Earth it was said that when you return to this world, you, as Athena Pallada, would subjugate all lands and begin to rule over all peoples. Today that riddle is solved-you have indeed conquered the world, though not as the queen of war, but as the queen of peace! All the peoples of the Earth have come to you of their own volition, as you have indeed won over 6 billion hearts with the power of your all-conquering love!"

The Secretary General hands Lybid a plaque, as the audience rises in a standing ovation.

SECRETARY GENERAL:

> "In the name of the United Nations allow me to give to
> you, as a memento of your work for the benefit of all
> mankind, an exact copy - inscribed on plates of gold - of
> the Gold Tables of Lybid Artemida."

Four huge UN employees, their backs slightly bending from the weight of
the load, walk up to Lybid and place at her feet a marble stand holding the
tablets with the prophecies of Lybid Artemida, each golden, glistening
page separated from the next by a sheet of the softest leather.

There is a shot change to a television screen showing a news broadcast.

NEWS ANCHOR:

> "The mayor of New York has announced that there will
> be a grand firework display this evening in honor of the
> gathering of world leaders at the United Nations..."

The television screen shows the mayor being interviewed in his office,
interspersed with shots of positions all over the city, where workers are
preparing for the fireworks show...

NEW YORK MAYOR:

> "According to my instructions there will be 170 separate
> fireworks displays, each one honoring the leader of a
> member state of the UN who signed the historic
> agreement today at the United Nations. This will be the
> grandest fireworks extravaganza in the history of the
> world. The first display will be in honor of the Secretary
> General of the UN, the last - to honor Queen Lybid
> Artemida. There should be 162 displays altogether, of
> course, but I decided to add eight more to get an even
> number of 170. The great city of New York dedicates

them to the memory of the U.S. astronauts who died in the pursuit of solving the mysteries of space. The fireworks display will be launched simultaneously from 100 different positions all over the city, each one representing a billion dollars of the total sum of 100 billion dollars pledged for the ambitious project of a manned space flight to the Sun.."

Lybid, with President Clinton on her left and the Secretary General on her right, walks down the center aisle, through the lobby and out into the night, followed by the participants in the UN summit. The sidewalks, streets and banks of the East River are filled with hundreds of thousands of revelers. Their eyes instinctively turn to the sky as the first explosions of the fireworks show light up the sky. Mouths open, they stand transfixed by the multi-colored patterns of exploding meteors...

CLINTON:

"We did it, you and I! It wasn't for nothing that you had yourself immolated 3000 years ago, in order that you and I meet again. I often dream about Byzantium and our first meeting on the sacred Bear Mountain in Tavrida in the land of Kimer, which you in Ukraine today known as the Crimea..."

LYBID:

"If it had not been for you, Theodorex, today's victory for mankind would not have been possible. I am sincerely indebted to you. But, Bill, you do agree that for the first time in your life you have been fortunate in your choice of a wife. And that, secondly, you are the ruler of an empire much more powerful than during your past lifetime as Theodorex. How can one compare Byzantium with the United States of America!"

SECRETARY GENERAL:

> "Enough of this talk about the past, my dear Mr. President and Your Majesty! I beg you - be very careful about resurrecting the past. Before you know it we'll have Germanarix on our tail! I do not want Germanarix - who thrice tormented mankind as the king of the Goths, as Napoleon and then as Hitler - to torment us yet again. Today we have atoned for everything. The past is no more! We have arrived in the new millennium! And there shall be a new Earth and a new Heaven!"

In her limousine Lybid, accompanied by Sol Lieberman and escorted by a detail of police motorcycles and squad cars, drives away from the UN building.

LIEBERMAN:

> "Congratulations on your final and irrevocable victory today! The issue of the 100 billion dollars funding for your expedition is decided!"

Lybid silently nods. This is no longer the enchanting queen that just captured the hearts of the most powerful men and women on Earth. Sitting beside Lieberman is a weary, though strikingly beautiful, woman, who is bereft of any feeling of joy, apparently forever.

The television monitor in the limousine passenger compartment shows a news broadcast, with a montage of the events at the UN. The Secretary General is seen handing Lybid the signed international agreement and bestowing on her the honorary title of Queen of the United Nations.

NEWS ANCHOR:

> "The Sun has finally been given a price! One hundred billion dollars! The biggest one-time targeted

international investment in man's history. Wall Street has already bestowed its own honorary moniker on Queen Lybid Artemida - "The 100 Billion Dollar Woman' - since she was today elected the chairperson of the International Executive Committee in charge of the fantastic, unprecedented 100-billion-dollar project. Now it's a question of who will gain the most financially from this enormous investment, on Wall Street, in London's City and elsewhere..."

LYBID:

"My God, how I wish this would be my last incarnation on Earth! I would bring this last mission to fruition and never again return to this world!"

Suddenly starting to yawn, Lybid covers her mouth with a royal handkerchief...

LYBID:

"I'm falling asleep, right here in the car! Can barely keep my eyes open! I'm being summoned to the Sun! And you, Sol? Aren't you tired?"

Lybid's facial expression almost betrays her hope that Lieberman becomes her spiritual companion and shares the intensity of her feelings, as Robert Oberfell had. But Sol Lieberman has no inclination to sleep, as if the Sun had no need of him...

LIEBERMAN:

"You go ahead and sleep. I'm not sleepy. I got plenty of rest to keep me going..."

Lybid closes her eyes and, curling up across the back seat like a cat, quickly falls asleep. She dreams that the darkness outside the car window dissipates, the passenger compartment fills with a blinding light and the air inside turns into a pillar of light, which pulls her soul out of her body and carries it towards the Sun. She sees herself floating through the window of the limousine and quickly rising, while the motorcade speeds off into the distance and soon becomes just a line of red and white lights on the shining grid of streets stretching between a hundred skyscrapers burning with a million lights. Lybid is flying. She quickly passes through the Earth's atmosphere and the Blue Planet turns into a diminishing bright spot in the blackness of space. At the same time the Sun looms ever larger above her, a roar, as if from a flaming waterfall, growing in her ears. Or maybe it's the sound of the engine in the limousine in which Lybid fell asleep? The Sun soon envelopes Lybid in its awesome embrace and her consciousness dissolves in a flaming sea of blinding light...

And there she is – in a heavenly grove made bright by a warm, golden glow. From all sides there run to her, their smiling faces radiating joy, the inhabitants of paradise -

those she knows as the righteous. Those that died 3000 years ago and in World War II, those that were killed defending her a few months ago. Her friends and relatives in all her incarnations – her father Vasyl, the Volkhvs Mudroslav and Liubomyr, Kyi, Shchek and Khoryv, Robert Oberfell and Maj. Black, Betsy Rosenberg and Philip Gorsky, Mancuso and McKenzie, Adm. Johnson and Gen. Smith. Many, many people, so dear to her heart. Lybid embraces and kisses them. They cry and they laugh...

TITLE: "FIVE YEARS HENCE..."

September 13, 2005. Washington, DC. Against the spectacularly familiar Washington skyline towers the Temple of Lybid Artemida in the form of an open lotus flower of sparkling onyx.

Inside, under the cupola, where the air glows in the light of a million precious stones, thousands of people sit on bench seats surrounding a podium, listening to the Avatar read a sacred text from the prophecies inscribed on the Gold Tablets of Lybid Artemida.

Behind the Avatar an enormous digital portrait of Lybid looks at the pilgrims, radiating goodness and warmth. The Tablets lie on an altar of gold.

AVATAR:

> "And Lybid said: 'I shall be born in bondage and I will
> die on the Sun, when I fly there for the third time. The
> first time I will fly around the Sun and I will not be seen
> on Earth for a period of five years...'"

As the pilgrims hang on the Avatar's every word, the Temples servants walk between the aisles, distributing small golden tablets, like bibles in a church...

Kyiv, capital of Ukraine. Temple of Lybid Artemida. Temple servants distribute candles on holders, which the worshipers light from the candles of those sitting next to them. The priest reads the sacred text of the Gold Tablets in Ukrainian...

PRIEST:

"I shall leave the Earth on my silver shining chariot and beyond the sky of the Earth a large solar boat will await me, built by Earth people from two steel boats. On Earth there are no such vessels and there will not be for a thousand years... And I will get into that strange boat...'"

New Delhi. Temple of Lybid Artemida. A temple servant gives money to the poor among the worshipers, as a priest reads the text of the Gold Tablets in Hindi...

PRIEST:

"I will sail to the Sun together with my retinue, among which there will be both learned scholars and those who can sail in closed steel boats beyond the sky of the Earth, where there is no air...'"

Beijing. Temple of Lybid Artemida. Chinese dishes are prepared on open fires and temple servants serve them to the multitude of worshipers, as a priest reads the text of the Gold Tablets in Mandarin...

PRIEST:

"The first time I shall not be accepted by the Sun, for the boat that carries us cannot sail through the solar fires. But I will send to the Sun's surface two of my steel envoys, which will have my eyes and my ears, and I shall see all and hear all. But it will be obscure, as if seen in a dream...'"

Egypt. Temple of Abu Simbel on the Nile. Under a huge awning inside the temple tourists and Egyptian worshippers toss paper and coin currency on plates carried through the overflowing crowd by temple servants. An Egyptian priest reads the text of the Gold Tablets in Arabic...

PRIEST:

> "'I shall prove to the people of Earth that the Sun is indeed God's Paradise and that there live on the Sun those that died on Earth. But among Mankind there will be many who will not believe the reports of my steel explorers of the Sun and will grumble that their drawings are made on Earth...'"

Tanzania. Temple of Lybid Artemida. Under a thatched covering built in the mighty shadow of Kilimanjaro, temple servants serve beef skewered on spits to the overflowing crowd of worshippers, as a priest reads the text from the Gold Tablets in Swahili...

PRIEST:

> "'And then I shall fly with my retinue to the Sun a second time, but on a ship the learned scientists on Earth will build in such a way but it will fly in the fires of the Sun and will not burn...'"

Morocco. Temple of Lybid Artemida in the Sahara Desert. A thousand worshippers have filled a huge tent of decorated camel skins, built against the backdrop of an ancient walled city. Temple servants serve them tea, as a Moroccan priest reads from the text of the Gold Tablets in Berber...

Alaska. Temple of Lybid Artemida, built of ice and snow in the form of a huge igloo. The overflowing crowd of worshippers warm their hands over small heaters fueled by whale oil brought up by temple servants. An Eskimo shaman reads the text of the Gold Tablets in Inuit...

SHAMAN:

> ""And the first time I shall be away for five years, but when I return to Earth, we shall all be younger by ten years. And when I travel to the Sun for a second time, we shall be gone from the Earth ten years, but upon returning we all shall have become twenty-five years younger. And the third time, when I shall remain on the Sun, then those from my retinue who shall choose to return home, they will arrive back on Earth as youths and maidens, though they left as mature men and women, and twenty years have passed... I shall say it thus: The Sun gives to each the gift of youth and can keep the righteous from old age, for the Sun is for us the supreme self-generating source of being, the Mother and the Father of time!"

A view of Earth from space, as the voices of the priests come together reading the same text: ""And now, for matters of Earth on the day when I shall fly to the Sun for the first time...'"

Television news magazine. "UN World News" appears on TV screens all over the world, followed by the anchor's voice under video...

First Feature.

TV NEWS ANCHOR:

> "Today, for the first time in history, humans will fly to the Sun! We will become witnesses to a defining moment in human civilization. Her Majesty Queen Lybid Artemida ill lead her international crew..."

The screen shows Lybid presenting the members of the crew at a news conference at the Kennedy Space Center at Cape Canaveral.

LYBID:

"I am so glad that I will have with me the finest astronauts from the United States, Ukraine, Russia, Great Britain, China, Japan, Israel..."

Second Feature.

TV NEWS ANCHOR:

"Semarhl – the god of Fire among the ancient Rus, manifesting himself in the bird Ra-roh. Semarhl, who vanquished the light and dark forces of the Black Serpent! The god of sacrifice by fire, the mediator between mankind and the heavenly gods. And the name given by Queen Lybid Artemida to the space complex that will carry our earthly goddess to the Sun."

The screen shows the Semarhl in orbit looking down on the Earth, a spacecraft the size of an aircraft carrier that includes a landing platform and living quarters for the long journey to the Sun. Two gigantic rockets are located on either side.

TV NEWS ANCHOR:

"The nuclear reactor supplying power to the living complex of the spaceship, its main nuclear rocket engines and the main engine and booster rockets of the Shuttle taken together generate approximately the same amount of power as all the nuclear warheads detonated by the United States, the Soviet Union, Great Britain, France and China in the sixty years of peace that followed World War II! That is the unimaginable power that is seen as necessary to propel the Space Queen Lybid Artemida and her crew to the Sun, and, after orbiting that heavenly body and using its gravitational

pull for a slingshot effect, to ride that peaceful nuclear
fire back home to Mother Earth!"

A graphic representation shows the shuttle locking into the Semarhl's
landing dock, the astronauts on board transferring from the orbiter to the
living complex and the Semarhl, its nuclear engines firing, setting out for
the Sun.

TV NEWS ANCHOR:

"The spaceship has everything necessary to sustain life
during the long journey, including a system of artificial
gravity, a greenhouse, a swimming pool. The boldest
dreams of science fiction writers and Hollywood
directors have taken form in this, the most extraordinary
creation in man's history!"

Third feature.

TV NEWS ANCHOR:

"Today, on the fifth anniversary of the terrorist war in
Manhattan, the sword of Themis, the goddess of
Justice, has come down on the group of conspirators
who planned and carried out the attempt on the life of
Her Majesty the honorary Queen of the United Nations
Lybid Artemida on September 13, 2000!"

Video clips remind viewers of the bloody battle in New York.

TV NEWS ANCHOR:

"The 33 leaders of a fanatical terrorist group responsible
for the bloody events of that day have gone on trial in a
federal court in Washington. DC. Their main leader,
who had boastfully threatened President Clinton and

who had said he was the infamous Nazi war criminal Ekkart, made an unexpected statement."

But the man on the screen is not Ekkart, but a middle-aged man with an Arabic appearance.

EKKART:

> I called myself Ekkart because I wanted to put the national-socialist movement in the United States in a negative light. I wanted to ignite an ethnic war in the U.S. by setting WASPS against German-Americans, and then have them start killing Jews. And then..."

Washington. Ekkart residence. A self-satisfied Hermann Ekkart is watching the report on the terrorist trial, when Gerhard Sievers walks in.

SIEVERS:

> "Feeling good about your brilliant disinformation campaign?"

EKKART:

> "I fooled the CIA, the FBI and the entire National Security Council of the United States of America. I tied Interpol up in knots and I made fools out of British and French intelligence. I deceived the Mossad. Over 300 false witnesses, 18 suicides, 39 real eye-witness eliminated, three quick local wars, 3000 falsified newspaper and television reports! All by myself I did as much as the SS and the Abwehr did in World War II. While living for five years with the fear that all this disinformation will collapse and theMcLarren Senate committee will find my fingerprints in this entire affair..."

346

SIEVERS:

"Our fingerprints, my dear Ekkart. Our entire World Fascist Council of Vengeance and Rebirth!"

EKKART:

"Has Strauss arrived?"

SIEVERS:

"He's on his way from the airport..."

Sievers watches Ekkart's servants take priceless paintings off the walls and pack numerous suitcases.

EKKART:

"How slowly the time drags... Want some whiskey?"

SIEVERS:

"Yes, please."

A servant brings Sievers a drink, as the CNN channel brings the two old Nazis some disturbing news...

TV ANNOUNCER (female):

"This report comes to you from the Washington headquarters of the International Bill Clinton for French President Foundation, which has already gained quite a bit of publicity because of two famous names associated with it, those of former President Clinton and Her Majesty Queen Lybid Artemida, the initiator of the project!"

The TV screen shows the street on which the headquarters of the foundation is located, then the building, dissolving into side-by-side portraits of Clinton and Lybid, with foundation address, phone numbers and website.

TV ANNOUNCER:

> "There are signs that the French people themselves are reacting favorably to the idea of the former U.S. leader running for the presidency of their country. There are also indications that the prestige of the Lybid Foundation is having a distinctly positive impact on the campaign. Here is what its founder had to say at the recent world convention ef the organization..."

Lybid Artemida, standing at the podium before a crowd overflowing the convention center, appears on the screen.

LYBID:

> "I am very pleased to note several very positive trends reflecting an international acceptance of the work of our foundation! The figures are truly astounding! We have collected a record amount of donations during the recent 24-hour 'Help Bill' telethon..."

SIEVERS:

> "Strauss has been negotiating with that damn foundation about being a sponsor, on behalf of Swiss bankers..."

EKKART:

> "Not a bad idea!"

On the screen Lybid is continuing her speech.

LYBID:

> "And we have quite a few examples to follow, the record
> for one-time charitable giving being the donation of
> $500 million, announced on December 12, 1955 by the
> Ford Foundation to benefit 4157 educational and other
> institutions. We are also inspired by the example of the
> chairman of the Shipbuilding Industry Foundation of
> Japan, Mr. Rioshi Sasakawa, who in the period 1962-
> 1984 donated a total of 5,160,450,000 pounds, and of
> the American industrialist Andrew Carnegie, whose
> charitable giving helped finance 7689 church organs
> and 2811 libraries!"

Sievers and Ekkart frown.

EKKART:

> "She has managed to stick her fingers into everything!"

SIEVERS:

> "This is getting on my nerves! Maybe you could put my
> favorite video on..."

Ekkart nods to an aide and the highly trained Nazi immediately turns to
carry out the will of his master. The monitor momentarily goes blank, then
lights up with a scene from a funeral at Arlington National Cemetery.
Under weeping skies, a military band plays a somber march, as family and
friends of the deceased, shielded by umbrellas, have surrounded a coffin.
A minister reads a prayer, as the honor guard ignores the pouring rain.
Finally, Gerhard Gottlieb Sievers steps forward to stand in front of the
mourners.

SIEVERS:

> "Family and friends, Ladies and Gentlemen! Today we
> lay to rest our combat in arms, a hero of the Normandy
> invasion, and, I can say with pride, my blood brother,
> Col. Alexander Hardale. He died tragically last
> Saturday, killed by a wild boar during a hunt. It is
> painful for me to say that we, his friends, left him alone
> in a blind, where we found him dead a few minutes later,
> He went through the entire war and death was
> powerless before him! Germans and Japanese tried to
> kill him, fired cannon and mortars and machine guns at
> him, engaged him in hand-to-hand fighting! But he
> survived and came out on top, a hero! And now, in his
> 'golden years,' killed by a wild pig! A travesty of fate!

For me, an old and experienced hunter, it is indeed shameful to
comprehend that a stinking, ignoble beast, having torn a decorated veteran
of World War II with its tusks, has escaped unpunished into the forest,
there to roam in the thicket and breed. It is doubly painful that another
distinguished Normandy landing veteran, a former Judge Advocate,
Major Abraham Goldberg also died on this trip, his tracks ending at the
edge of a patch of quicksand. Apparently, he chased after the boar to
avenge the death of his comrade in arms, Alexander Hardale..."

Sievers contentedly closes his eyes and listens to the sounds of "Taps' and
the twenty-one-gun salute...

EKKART:

> "I advised you against killing Hardale and Goldberg...
> But I still can't comprehend where you found the moxie
> to get yourself elected secretary of the International
> Normandy Landing Veterans Association..."

SIEVERS:

"I killed them just because they were always boasting
before me how they were Normandy heroes. As if that
gave them the right to everything. My 'blood brother"

Hardale and that Jew Goldberg insulted not some pack
rat who supposedly spent the war shuffling supplies in
a warehouse at Pearl Harbor. By the way, you remember
that it was your idiots in the SS who 50 years ago
concocted for me that cover, absolutely dull and
ordinary and therefore impossible to break. No, it's not
the Hardales and Goldbergs who have the right to boast
about Normandy, but I. Who killed 79 Americans and
English there! Whom Hitler personally awarded
Germany's highest combat medal, the Iron Cross with
Oak Leaves - my fourth! -specifically for my feats at
Normandy. So, they were heroes of Normandy? I am a
hero of Normandy! And that is why I sit with their vets
in that pompous association of theirs. By the way, I also
wounded more than 30 Yanks there during the
invasion, and now I embrace those paraplegics at
veterans' meetings and, in order to get their votes in the
council, I play them with whiskey and Russian vodka..."

Kennedy Space Center, Cape Canaveral, Florida. Launch pad of the
expedition to the Sun. Hundreds of specialists are preparing the space
vehicle. A computer engineers with "Brett Coleman" emblazoned on the
left breast pocket of his white smock takes the elevator to the nose of the
orbiter, walks out on the platform and, surrounded by engineers, into the
cockpit. There, he is approached by an engineer with the name "Scott
Larsen" on his breast pocket.

351

LARSEN:

"Brett! Test the flight software!"

COLEMAN (upbeat):

"That's why I'm here, Scott!"

Washington. Ekkart's residence. Hermann Ekkart is chairing the Nazi council - thirteen "apostles" dressed in black and sitting around a round table, Swiss banker Laudwig Strauss and American Nazi leader Rudolph Hanisch among them.

EKKART:

"Coleman, as the engineer responsible for the on-board computer, will insert my Own program into the mission software, thus turning the space station into the most fearsome weapon in the history of mankind!... You have a question, Mr. Hanisch?"

On board the space shuttle Brett Coleman looks around furtively, then inserts a disc into a computer port and presses a few buttons on the control board. Several lights come on, as the computer begins downloading the new program...

At the Ekkart residence, Hanisch takes time to phrase his question...

HANISCH:

"I don't understand completely, Mr. Ekkart, how you hope to cut off the Shuttle's crew from control of the vehicle... Sir!"

EKKART:

"Thanks to the on-board computer, Hanisch! At the moment the Semarhl's engines start, the computer will change the mix in the air supply system and the entire crew, including God's favorite, Lybid Artemida, will die instantaneously when the nitrogen in their blood boils!"

STRAUSS:

"And then, Brother Ekkart, the software will target specific points on the Earth' surface?"

EKKART:

"That is correct! To destroy the capitals of the countries that were responsible for our defeat in World War II!"

SIEVERS:

"London and Moscow!"

EKKART:

"And, of course, Washington!"

STRAUSS:

"And New York, that abominable disseminator of American democracy, from which you, gentlemen, have already evacuated all your relatives! Plus, the cursed Paris!"

EKKART:

"Now, for us here in Washington to survive, gentlemen, a minute after the launch of the Shuttle we must help my servants move the rest of the priceless artistic treasures in my home and all the documents into my two-story concrete bunker built beneath this residence, literally under your feet. It is a full replica of the Fuhrer's bunker under the Imperial Chancellery in Berlin, with the exception that there is not two but seven meters of reinforced concrete overhead and the most advanced ventilation system in the world. Washington shall be wiped off the face of the Earth by a fiery hurricane, just like Hiroshima and Nagasaki, while we in the bunker will hear only a distant rumble and feel a slight tremor!"

On board the space shuttle, Brett Coleman extracts the computer disc and leaves the cockpit. He stops on the platform for a moment, looking down on the launch pad that is humming with human activity in preparation for the countdown. Squinting in the bright daylight, the computer engineer glances up at the Sun...

A second later he looks away from the blinding light, but the Sun has already sent its hypnotizing spell through his pupils, along the retina and to his brain. Coleman sees himself in the future, witness to the apocalyptic events to come...

Houston. Mission control center. Dozens of space flight controllers are focused on the computer displays before them, looking up periodically at the electronic map of the world that covers an entire wall, on which a moving, blinking light shows the location of the Orbiter.

FLIGHT CONTROLLER:

"Ten minutes into the flight and all conditions normal!"

VOICE OF LYBID (over radio connection):

> "G-forces at minimum. We have gone to weightless
> flight!"

The mission director is calmly pacing among the television monitors and computer terminals, periodically checking on one of the digital clocks on the walls...

VOICE OF LYBID:

> "Initiating docking procedure with the Semarhl... The
> station is right below us...
>
> Approaching docking module..."

Several dozen monitors and a huge wall screen show the transmission from the shuttle's on-board cameras, switching from the scene inside the cockpit to the approaching docking module of the spaceship.

VOICE OF LYBID:

> "Ten feet... Five feet... One foot..."

A picture of the nose of the shuttle entering the docking module covers the entire screen, shaking briefly a second later as the two touch.

VOICE OF LYBID:

> "We have contact!"

Shouts and applause fill mission control, as many of the controllers embrace one another...

VOICE OF LYBID:

> "Ladies and Gentlemen! The Semarhl is saddled! Switching over to station life-support systems. Instruments show flow of oxygen from the Semarhl..."

Pictures show the shuttle crew removing their helmets. A jubilant Lybid stands out...

VOICE OF LYBID:

> "We can all breathe a bit easier now! Getting ready to switch control over to Semarhl's on-board computer..."

Lybid presses several keys to activate computer programs on the spaceship, only to have them captured by the software introduced by Brett Coleman. Suddenly, monitor screens at the Houston Mission Control Center, which had been showing video from the orbiting structure, go blank.

A momentary silence envelops the room, as controllers exchange blank stares...

FLIGHT DIRECTOR:

> "What just happened?"

COMMUNICATIONS DIRECTOR:

> "All control functions from mission control to orbiter interrupted!"

A bespectacled specialist runs up to the flight director with a computer printout.

MEDICAL OFFICER:

"Sir! Oxygen indicator shows computer error in air composition settings!"

FLIGHT DIRECTOR:

"What!?"

MEDICAL OFFICER:

"They're suffocating, Sir!"

Involuntary gasps and groans escape from the lips of the professionals at the Houston Mission Control Center, as they go about their desperate tasks...

NAVIGATIONS DIRECTOR:

"Heads up! Ignition of Semarhl engines indicated. She seems to be moving and gaining speed!"

Something as close to panic as Houston Control has ever witnessed grips its professionals, as the feeling sets in that things are spinning out of their control.

FIRST VOICE:

"The station is leaving orbit!"

SECOND VOICE:

"The station is separating into modules! I have indications orbiter has left the docking module... Semarhl's booster rockets have disengaged and it is moving away from the station. Monitors show separation of back-up reactor from life-support system of station's living quarters! On-board computer of the reactor is up...!"

THIRD VOICE:

"The Firebird-14 satellite detects firing of Semarhl's main booster rockets!"

Space. The orbiter, the Semarhl's booster rockets, the space station's living complex and the nuclear engine are silently moving through the darkness. Upon entering the Earth's atmosphere, the space components become enveloped in ever more flames and smoke...

Houston Mission Control Center. Hardened professionals, some of whom were

at their posts during the Challenger and Columbia tragedies, fight to stave off a creeping panic.

FLIGHT DIRECTOR:

"I need reports on the trajectories! Where are they heading?"

Voices on the quiet edge of despair answer: "Washington!" "New York!" "London!" "Paris!" "Moscow!"

People on Earth look up at the sky, marveling at the brilliantly arching falling stars at the edge of space that secretly carry death to millions below.

The orbiter falls on Washington and its explosion at Ground Zero – the White House - turns the capital of the United States of America into a flaming crater. A fiery whirlwind sweep over the majestic monuments, the Capitol, the Mall with its museums, over the Potomac and past the Pentagon and Langley...

The Ekkart residence. In the bunker below, concrete walls shudder and lights flicker slightly. In a room decorated with Nazi banners and other paraphernalia the host and his comrades sit at a well-appointed table, lustily singing a marching song and lifting steins and wineglasses.

EKKART:

"Much more powerful than I imagined...!"

SIEVERS:

"The blinding beauty that must be topside..."

At the Kennedy Space Center at Cape Canaveral dignitaries and guests look northward and gasp at the crimson cloud hanging over where Washington should be. President George W. Bush shouts at his aides: "Nuclear Armageddon is upon us!"

The first booster rocket hits New York and sends a mushroom cloud rising over the megapolis. Skyscrapers fall like houses of cards, firestorms sweep down walled canyons, and a shock wave snuffs out the lives of millions, as they try to comprehend the sudden cataclysm that has descended upon them.

In Hermann Ekkart's bunker, an electronic map of the world has been set up against one of the walls. A bright red light that pinpointed New York goes out. The walls of the bunker shudder.

EKKART:

"New York is dead!"

The giddy Nazis and neo-Nazis raise their steins and glasses in a "toast" "to New York," as triumphant National Socialist music plays on...

STRAUSS:

"The Fuhrer's dream has come true!"

SIEVERS:

"An end to the Babylon harlot of Jews and dollar idolaters!"

A powerful tremor shakes the foundations of the bunker.

EKKART:

"I think that was no less than a 12 on the Richter scale!"

Hanisch slaps the palm of a hand against the bunker's concrete wall...

HANISCH:

"The Noah's Ark of National Socialism!"

At Cape Canaveral dignitaries and guests again point to the north, where a second and more powerful burst of red light rends the horizon from the direction of New York.

Moments later the sky darkens and a howling wind picks up. President George W. Bush, in despair, shouts at his aides: "Apocalypse! Apocalypse! We have to do something!"

At Mission Control in Houston the engineers and controllers, their eyes filled with shock and tears comfort each other...

The second Semarhl booster rocket hits London and a mushroom cloud rises over the British capital. The Tower and Big Ben. Westminster Palace, the House of Commons are all swept by a fiery broom. Trafalgar Square and Hyde Park burn.

In Ekkart's bunker, another red light goes out on an electronic map of the world.

EKKART:

"London is dead!"

Giddy Nazis again raise their steins and glasses in a "toast" "to London," as triumphant National Socialist music plays on...

SIEVERS:

"A million times more powerful than the V-1 and the V-2!"

At Houston Mission Control a Frenchmen nervously dials a number on his cell phone and speaks to his wife: "Edith, take the children and get out of the city! Immediately! Save yourself!"

In Paris Edith jumps out of the bed she was sleeping in next to their two small children and runs to the window, through which the Eiffel Tower looms in the distance. It's too late...

As the Semarhl living complex falls on Paris, a mushroom cloud rises over the French capital. The Eiffel Tower collapses as if it were made of wax. A firestorm vaporizes Edith and her children, the Louvre, Montmartre, Notre Dame...

In Houston, the Frenchman, still holding the cell phone to his ear, hears only static. He drops the phone and his heart-rending scream mixes in with the din of the chaotic scene.

In Ekkart's Washington bunker a red light that was Paris goes out.

EKKART:

"Paris is dead!"

The celebrating Nazis lift their cups and glasses in a toast "to Paris."

SIEVERS:

"Even the Fuhrer never possessed such divine power!"

At the Kennedy Space Center President George W. Bush shouts to his aides:

"Connect me with Putin!"

In the Washington bunker Ekkart points a finger at a spot on the electronic map.

EKKART:

"In a moment Moscow will be extinguished!"

The Semarhl's nuclear reactor plunges into the heart of the Russian capital, raising a fourth mushroom cloud. The shock wave and fiery tempest raze the Kremlin, together with its palaces and churches, St. Basil's Cathedral, the Church of Christ the Savior, the Rossiya Hotel, the Ostankino TV tower...

Brett Coleman shudders, as if hit by a bolt of lightning... What is this? He feels a hand on his shoulder... Slowly coming out of a trance, he sees himself as he was, standing on the top platform of the Shuttle launch pad and looking up at the Sun.

The apocalypse did happen, but only in the mind of Brett Coleman - an apocalyptic vision of a crime, part of which he has already committed by installing the murderous software into the shuttle's computer...

The colleague that laid his hand on Coleman's shoulder looks at him anxiously.

COMPUTER ENGINEER:

"What is the matter, Brett?"

COLEMAN:

"I am a criminal, Sam! I almost became the most wretched murderer in the history of mankind!"

Washington. Ekkart's residence. The Nazi meeting continues.

EKKART:

"Adolf Hitler was reincarnated as a member of the white race in 1962. He is now 43 years old. I was there at his birth. Our Fuhrer has not yet been consecrated into the secret of his destiny. He does not even suspect that I have been monitoring his every move for 43 years. But when I personally give our Fuhrer the testament, he left for himself, he will remember everything and the bursting activation of his real consciousness will turn him into the true Third Anti-Christ!"

SIEVERS:

"Who is he? What is his name? Where does he live?"

EKKART:

"I will not tell any of you, nor anyone else! Not for anything! Until I myself announce the Fuhrer to the world!"

SIEVERS:

"Enough, Ekkart! Enough of this petty jealousy and bickering over which one of us has the right to call himself Nazi criminal No. 1! Too miserly to share the glory?"

EKKART:

"And what right do you, my brothers-in-arms, have to take the Fuhrer away from me? I alone raised him in total secrecy, dedicating my life to him! I... I am the spiritual father of the neo-Adolf Hitler!"

STRAUSS:

"And I am obliged to hand over to the Fuhrer the 30 billion dollars in gold that he willed to himself! I have to conduct a thorough investigation before handing the wealth of the Third Reich over to him! Or do you expect that I should accept your word that he is, indeed, our Fuhrer?"

SIEVERS:

"Do I understand it correctly that if something should happen to you, you will take your secret with you to the grave?"

STRAUSS:

"I demand that you tell us his identity!"

EKKART:

"You want to trick me into giving up his name! And then what? You'll poison me? Guard my life as you would your own, Gentlemen! IF I die you will never find our Fuhrer, and the neo-Hitler will never come to know about you!"

Suddenly, the program on the television set in the room is interrupted, and a flustered anchor appears on the screen.

TV ANCHORMAN:

> "We have just received some astounding news! We switch you now to the Kennedy Space Center at Cape Canaveral in Florida for this live report, which is bound to shock you!"

Against a backdrop of a shuttle launch pad, an excited reporter is shouting into his mike.

> "The launch of the Sun expedition has just been postponed by four hours!"

The camera pushes in on Brett Coleman, standing in the center of a tight circle of security and NASA officials, journalists from around the globe jostling each other to get as close as possible to him. Coleman is holding a laser disc in his hands.

REPORTER:

COLEMAN:

> "This computer disc holds a program that was to activate the destruction - by the Sun spaceship - of such cities as Washington, New York, London, Paris, and Moscow!"

At the Ekkart home gasps of shock and howls of outrage greet Coleman's revelation,

EKKART (shaking his fist at the on-screen Coleman):

> "You miserable coward! Damn you!"

STRAUSS:

"Mein Gott! The money...the money lost! Traitor!"

EKKART:

"I loathe her! I despise her!"

SIEVERS:

"Settle down! We must think!"

EKKART:

"She is mightier than all of us put together!"

Like a man possessed, Ekkart runs up to the shuttered window through which a narrow beam of sunlight makes its way into the darkened room. He looks through the slit and out at the Sun.

EKKART:

"I hate you! I despise you!"

The Nazis don't understand at whom Ekkart is venting his anger. But the Sun has reacted and (in Ekkart's consciousness alone) explodes in the sky like a super nova in all its magnificence.

EKKART:

"I loathe you! I hate you!"

Suddenly, Ekkart sees in his mind's eye a bright vision 3000 years old: the heretical Palant, on the dueling field with Lybid, holds his arms wide apart, his head raised towards the heavens rent with blinding but cold flashes of lightning.

Ekkart sees Palant from above, falling all the while towards a mouth open wide with blasphemy and finally into the darkness therein...

Standing by the window, Ekkart unexpectedly screams and clutches at his heart. His face starts turning a dark blue and his mouth gasps for air, like a fish thrown out on the bank of a river. He grabs at the Venetian blinds in a reflexive attempt to keep his feet but brings them down with him as he collapses in a heap.

The Nazis rush up to the stricken Ekkart, who is convulsing on the carpet, his eyes bulging, a labored rasp escaping from his throat.

STRAUSS:

"O Lord! A heart attack!"

SIEVERS:

"Call 9-1-1, immediately!"

A dozen cell phones light up, as the Nazis react as if on command, each shouting louder than the next: "Send an ambulance immediately!" "A man is dying!" "Heart attack!"

For a moment Sievers is reminded of the stock exchange after some breaking news, the traders trying to outshout each other...

Ekkart continues to writhe on the floor. Sievers kneels down beside him and looks into his face.

SIEVERS:

"I beg you - don't die!"

STRAUSS:

"Tell us who our Fuhrer is!"

367

SIEVERS:

"Give us his name!"

SIEVERS:

"Tell us where to find him!"

Ekkart grabs Sievers' arm with both his hands and pulls him closer. He tries to speak, but the only sounds leaving his lips are unintelligible.

STRAUSS:

"Give us our Fuhrer! What is his name? His name!"

Ekkart slowly releases Sievers' arm as the last of his strength leaves his body, along with his spirit.

Outside the Ekkart residence an EMS vehicle stands at the curb, its lights flashing. An emergency room doctor and two technicians with equipment rush to the door. They are quickly led to the stricken Nazi. A brief examination, a shot of adrenalin directly into the heart and electric shocks to the chest bring no results...

A police car drives up and a uniformed officer gets out and walks through the front door. The doctor, kneeling over the body, looks up at him.

DOCTOR:

"The old gentleman's heart gave out..."

The police officer looks around the room in stunned silence, his gaze going from one Hitler portrait to another, from Nazi flag to SS uniform to one swastika insignia to another.

Sievers approaches him.

SIEVERS:

"Could I get you something, Officer? A drink, perhaps?"

POLICE OFFICER (ignoring the offer):

"What is this - a private temple to Adolf Hitler, here in the U.S.?"

SIEVERS:

"He was the director of a private museum..."

The policeman looks around at the luggage and boxes in various stages of packing...

POLICE OFFICER:

"Looks like he was getting ready for a little trip..."

SIEVERS:

"He is Prof. Jeb Phobbs, the famous Nazi-hunter, now equally active in the fight against neo-Fascism."

POLICE OFFICER (understanding nothing):

"I see..."

The fight for Ekkart's life continues.

DOCTOR:

"Clear!"

The line on the portable heart monitor stays flat.

STRAUSS (in despair):

> "I am Ludwig Strauss, international banker from Switzerland! I control billions of dollars! You must bring him back to life! I shall donate ten million dollars to your hospital if you bring him back to consciousness, even if it's only for five minutes! I have to ask him something! Mein Gott! You just have to make him able to answer one question!"

Strauss gets out a checkbook, fills out a check, tears it out and holds it up.

STRAUSS:

> "Ten million dollars!"

The emergency medical team members silently look at each other, knowing they've done their honest best without the reward. As they renew their efforts, they are joined by a team from a second emergency vehicle, then a third and fourth...

DOCTOR:

> "Clear!"

Ekkart's body bounces up in the air as the electricity surges through it.

DOCTOR:

> "Turn it up a notch!... Clear!"

SECOND DOCTOR (to Strauss):

> "I'm afraid nothing is..."

Strauss starts writing out another check.

STRAUSS:

"One million dollars each to everyone here!"

Ignoring the madness, the emergency medical teams continue their efforts with calm and discipline, even as they know them to be in vain. Ekkart's lifeless heart refuses to restart, as the defibrillator keeps tossing the limp body up from the floor.

STRAUSS:

"I demand it! Damn it! You want more? I'll give you more!... Thirty million! One hundred million!"

The cop, dumbfounded by the scene before him, shakes his head...

POLICE OFFICER (to Sievers):

"I'll have that drink now. Whiskey, please!"

Kennedy Space Center, Florida. A limousine carrying the president of the United States, escorted by its usual entourage of police motorcycles, Secret Service vans, and other vehicles, drives up to the launch pad, where the shuttle stands ready. Buses carrying members of the flight crew and scores of other vehicles carrying members of the media and guests follow. Laura Bush and President George W. Bush get out on one side of the limousine, Her Majesty Queen Lybid Artemida on the other. They meet in front of the car and walk up to join the astronauts. Members of the media scurry to claim the best vantage points outside the roped-off area.

A CNN reporter, going live, can barely hide her excitement.

REPORTER:

"President of the United States George Bush is personally seeing Lybid Artemida and her courageous crew off on their journey to the Sun. I am reporting directly from the site of a magnificent feast - you have to call it that - put on by Her Majesty herself for the thousands of guests here. And everything that is left will be incinerated in the flames from the giant rocket engines of the shuttle as it lifts off! We are told that this is in keeping with an ancient Rus rite of a sacrificial offering!"

Lybid is coming to the end of her parting speech.

LYBID:

"And, saying good-bye, let us also remember the righteous dead, for they are now living on the Sun we will soon be flying to. And let the wicked burn in hell for their evil deeds, where they shall not know the Lord's forgiveness..."

Ekkart's body is carried to an ambulance, which drives off, followed by the other emergency and police vehicles. Ten of the Nazis, their meeting brought to an abrupt end by Ekkart's death, also depart, leaving Sievers and Strauss standing alone and dejected in front of his home.

Through the open door is heard the sound of a television report...

VOICE OF TV ANNOUNCER:

"We are just minutes away from the launch of the historic expedition to the Sun. I will allow myself to say that all of mankind is holding its collective breath as we..."

STRAUSS:

"So, we are going to let her fly off...?"

SIEVERS:

"And what are the two of us supposed to do? That damned Ekkart! He just couldn't reconcile himself to my fame and so he decided, at the end of his life, to best me just once. And to be known for all eternity as the executioner of Lybid Artemida and in the memory of all Aryan descendants as the last of the Nordic heroes..."

STRAUSS:

"...Who personally paved the way for world domination by Adolf Hitler, reincarnated!"

SIEVERS:

"You are much too perceptive for a banker. Better that you should be the chancellor of a united Germany, or Austria!"

STRAUSS:

"Does this mean that everything is ruined?"

SIEVERS:

"Ruined? The idea itself is immortal as long as there is the Party's gold, Ludwig! It's the money and the gold of the National Socialist Workers' Party of Germany and of the Fuhrer of the German nation Adolf Hitler -the money and not the ideas - that will live forever. And, sooner or later, multiplying itself in the hands of skilled national socialists of a new generation, the Fuhrer's money will become the most influential capital on Earth, defeating the collective wealth of the Jews, the Japanese, and the Chinese. This is my prophecy!"

STRAUSS:

"But what about the Fuhrer? Where are we going to look for the new Adolf Hitler, born in secrecy?"

SIEVERS:

"Nowhere! Ekkart, that vain, complacent fool, greedy for future glory as Hitler's chief apostle didn't leave us so much as a clue about where to begin our search. Kept playing me for a fool, dropping one misleading hint after another. If Hitler was born somewhere in Western Europe, that's 300 million inhabitants. If in Eastern Europe, including the European part of the former Soviet Union, it's another 300 million. You and I would spend hundreds of millions of dollars to conduct a search, knock ourselves out, and probably wind up with either a madman or a con artist who finds out that we need a Fuhrer and are ready and willing to hand all the party's gold to him! He will wring every last nickel out of us and, like an alien element that invades a healthy body, he will infect our international organism with cancer, compromise it and ultimately destroy our sacred National Socialism."

STRAUSS:

"And, meanwhile, the true Fuhrer will be living his life either as an illiterate yokel herding goats in the Swiss Alps, as a drunken waiter in some Biergarten in Austria, or as a thieving auto mechanic in Poland or Slovakia, and no one will ever know that he ls Adolf Hitler..."

SIEVERS:

"I truly believe, I sincerely wish for him... I hope that our Fuhrer, as a minimum, will die as a famed painter, a noted designer, or, better still, an architect of note. May our Fuhrer, in this incarnation, live the kind of life that, because of the great mission that lay upon his shoulders, he wasn't able to live..."

STRAUSS:

"But what if, thanks to his reincarnation memory, he should unexpectedly recognize Adolf Hitler in himself and is thrown into an insane asylum and stuck with shot after painful shot to cure him of himself? And he never gets to read the occult testament that he addressed to himself in 1945, which bestows on him the power to rule over you and me, dear Sievers, and over the rest of the world. His will be the dreary destiny of hundreds of millions of the inhabitants of Europe."

SIEVERS:

"Or of America. Or Africa. We don't know where he is..."

STRAUSS:

In that case there's nothing left for me to do here "

SIEVERS:

"The struggle continues, Ludwig!"

STRAUSS:

"I know. One does not leave the SS..."

SIEVERS:

"Lybid, unfortunately, will triumph. But we shall not surrender! We will throw all of our gold and all of our blood-stained money into the cause of resurrecting National Socialism all over the world, into anti-Semitism and the idea of a World War III for the sake of winning Lebensraum in Eastern Europe for Western Europeans. Return boldly to Europe, Strauss, and await our signal!"

STRAUSS:

"And what about you?"

SIEVERS:

"I will shortly call a lawyer to tidy up Ekkart's affairs and then we will together lock up his building. And in the evening, like the rest of humanity, I will put on some warm slippers, get a glass of warm milk, and in the circle of my large and prosperous family, I will be watching CNN. that wretched coverage of the launch of Lybid's expedition to the Sun. And my loved ones shall not hear the silent grinding of my teeth, as I sit there, helpless to stop her triumphant flight!

Comrades in defeat, Sievers and Strauss embrace.

Kennedy Space Center, Florida. Lybid Artemida's spaceship rises from its launch pad, slowly at first, as if pulling a long flaming tail up with it, then, gaining speed and altitude, begins to loosen the bonds of gravity and heads up into space.

President George W. Bush and thousands of guests sitting in grandstands set up for the occasion follow it with their gaze, until only a brilliant plume remains visible. And when it dissolves into the blinding glare of the Sun itself, their eyes rest momentarily on the Central Planet itself, which seems to flash over its entire surface, as if seen from a low solar orbit, and, to an explosion of the majestic musical theme, throws a title onto the Screen.

EPILOG

September 10, 2010. Television channels all over the world are carrying a newscast from United Nations television.

ANNOUNCER:

> "At the UN today - acclamation for the feat for the ages, the mission to the Central Planet of our Solar System, the Sun, by Her Majesty Queen Lybid Artemida and her heroic crew. Their spaceship landed back on Earth, after a five-year round-trip journey..."

The screen shows the spacecraft touch down on the concrete landing strip.

The next shot shows the President of the United States greeting Lybid Artemida and her crew at the Kennedy Space Center. Bouquets of flowers are handed all around, as reporters, technicians and guests rush about in the harsh glare of television lights.

ANNOUNCER:

> "U.S. President Hillary Rodham Clinton, accompanied by her husband, French President Bill Clinton..."

The credits begin, listing the major roles in the film.]

The newscast continues with a second feature.

ANNOUNCER:

> "The question, is there life on the Sun? has been answered!"

Queen Lybid Artemida is in the chamber of the House of Representatives of The United States, explaining video shot during the Sun expedition. A close-up shows the Semarhl's landing module descending through solar flares towards the Sun's surface. Its camera records a fantastic landscape, described in a crackling radio transmission back to the mother ship: "Below we see some most unusual buildings..."

The camera shows a scene on the surface: the landing module surrounded by denizens of the Central Planet, among whom we recognize Lybid's relatives and friends from all her incarnations - her father Vasyl, the Volkhvs Mudroslav and Lyubomyr, Kyi, Shchek d Khoryv, her grandfather Hnat, her grandmothers Domakha and Frosyna, Robert Oberfell, Capt. Beck, Betsy Rosenberg and Philip Gorsky, Mancuso, McKenzie, holding two shining banners in his hands, Adm. Johnson and Gen. Smith... So many of her friends and loved ones, each one surrounded by a golden glow... But the pictures, unfortunately, are of poor quality, due to the interference from the Sun's corona...

RADIO MESSAGE:

>"This is coming to you direct from the landing module. There is a feeling that the landing here on the Sun was expected..."

ANNOUNCER:

>"It is with a sense of excitement that I recall the words, uttered two thousand years ago by Jesus, the Son of God: 'In the Kingdom of God they do not marry, but live like the angels in Heaven!"

[Credits roll with the names of those in supporting roles]

The third feature begins.

ANNOUNCER:

"The almost 100-year history of the Nazi movement on Earth has come to an end!

In a U.S. Federal Court today in Washington, D.C. concluded the trial of the leaders of the worldwide National Socialist conspiracy of the supporters of Adolf Hitler. Thirteen of the top leaders of the World SS Council sit on the defense side of the courtroom. We were allowed, by special dispensation of the presiding judge, to place our cameras in the court room for the final statement of Gottlieb Gerhard Sievers, considered by many to be one of the most, if not the most, blood-thirsty henchmen of Heinrich Himmler, the leader of the notorious SS. He has been living in the United States, growing old in comfort to the age of ninety, at the expense of the American taxpayer..."

Appearing on the screen, however, is not Sievers, but a completely unknown old man!

FALSE SIEVERS:

"I will keep on living, to the consternation of everyone, and, at the first opportunity, I will resume the killing of Jews, democrats, communists, and Christians!"

The deeply aged veterans in the courtroom shout in anger. The loudest among them is the true Gottlieb Sievers. He is approached by a television producer and asked to follow her out of the courtroom. In the corridor, he gives an interview.

TRUE SIEVERS:

"I am indignant and in the name of all the veterans, the saviors of Europe from the Nazi plague, I want to say that mankind has survived the disease of Hitlerism, racial hatred, and anti-Semitism, which led to the genocide of the Jewish people. Today's ban on the neo-Nazi movement in the world demands from me, as a member of the human race and an advocate of the military heroes of the 20th Century, that I personally do everything in my power to see that the hateful ideas are rejected forever. And I will spend however many billions of dollars it takes, because the blood of the defenders of freedom, spilled in every theatre of World War II, calls for this."

[Credits roll with the names of those in minor roles.]

Fourth newscast feature.

ANNOUNCER:

"We have another sensational report! Ludwig Strauss, a Swiss citizen who is considered the pre-eminent banker in the European Union has been elected chairman of the World Council. As such, he has been given the honor of announcing the introduction of the long-awaited single currency of the United Nations, which is to be known officially as the 'world golden union.' The universal currency is called the child of Mr. Strauss, who is looked upon by many as a genius of the international banking system."

The screen shows a scene from the world mint, where the gold currency is being struck. A distinguished elderly man walks into the picture, solemnly scoops up the heavy, shining coins in his hands.

STRAUSS:

> "The eternal metal - gold - has returned and is once again the ultimate store of material value. Electronic money has disappeared, thanks to the growth of the Internet.
>
> Modern science has proven itself to be powerless against the efforts of cyber-criminals to create untold electronic wealth out of nothing and thus to threaten the very existence of the world trading system. The international payments crisis has shown us that the old, gold-based currencies are infinitely stronger than electronic signals which have no material presence and which cannot jingle sweetly in the pockets of billions of people, or snap crisply when taken out of a billfold!"

REPORTER:

> "And what do you think of the recent article in the Jerusalem Post?"

STRAUSS:

> "I consider it a scandalous, irresponsible bit of nonsense! What docs Nazi gold, taken by Hitler from the Jews, have to do with any of this? Believe me, we international bankers have tried, but have not been able to find even the faintest trace of the gold hoard of the Nazi Party! And was there any gold to begin with? I personally belong to the realists who are convinced that there never existed any co-called 'Nazi gold." This is a myth comparable to the El Dorado legend, a treasure that no

one ever laid his eyes on! But thousands of Spaniards paid with their lives for this myth, becoming the victims of their own gold-lust. Perhaps you have read the published report on my study, where I have proven beyond any doubt that the existence of the 'Nazi gold' is no more than the same kind of myth and provided a list of thousands of seekers for this false treasure that today lie in graves all over the world!"

REPORTER:

"Perhaps you could provide us with a few examples..."

STRAUSS:

"I grieve along with the family of Heinrich Hoffman, who believed claims that the 'Nazi gold' was to be found in the Amazon delta. Well, he did find gold, but it belonged to the notorious narcotics kingpin Pablo Escobar. The unfortunate gold seeker was fed alive to the crocodiles, a video of the bloody episode being sent to CNN. Meanwhile, an unscrupulous journalist and provocateur, Alex Kaufman, from Bonn, propagated the scandalous fairy tale that this gold of Pablo Escobar was, in reality, the gold of Adolf Hitler! For shame!"

REPORTER:

"And what would be another example?"

STRAUSS:

"An expert of the World Bank, Gustav Keiron, was hanged in his hotel suite in Acapulco by Islamic extremists, because he had the misfortune of uncovering the gold of Osama Bin Laden himself! Yes, there were markings of the State Bank of the Third Reich on Bin Laden's gold bars. But gold lasts forever, going from the hands of one owner to another..."

REPORTER:

"All this is quite fascinating!"

STRAUSS:

"No one has ever told the story of gold as the history of mankind! And this has been a grave mistake of human civilization. It is precisely the ignorance of dilettantes that leads to such scandals as that involving Ivan Karpinsky, the émigré banker from Moscow who claimed that the bloody gold of the Communist Party of the Soviet Union, hidden in Indonesia, was, in fact, Hitler's gold!"

REPORTER:

"Revolting!"

STRAUSS:

"That's not the word for it! Take a look at this stream of coins coming from the press. They are still hot to the touch. They are like newborn children that just left the womb of their mother, pure and innocent. There is not and never was any Nazi gold! They should be ashamed of themselves, the amoral political provocateurs who try to equate the noble metal that goes into these exquisite gold coins with the wedding bands and dental crowns of the millions of Jewish victims killed by the Nazis during World War II!"

REPORTER:

"And what is the international gold currency invested in?"

STRAUSS:

"I... that is, our World Banking Council are putting the gold into the charitable projects of Her Majesty Queen Lybid Artemida, which help to feed starving children, fight illiteracy, and provide neonatal care in countries on six continents. I am very proud of our campaign against anti-Semitism and the all-out war we bankers have declared against racial and religious intolerance. I am proud of the crusade we have launched for brotherhood among all the peoples of the planet. But our council places the highest priority on supporting Lybid Artemida's program to send a second international expedition to the Sun, using a base on the Moon.

[Credits roll for the rest of the cast.]

Fifth newscast feature.

ANNOUNCER:

"The Solar Expedition has provided the momentum for the greatest technological boom in the history of mankind. Only four years after the launch of Her Majesty Lybid Artemida's expedition to the Sun, there is a research and tourist complex on the Moon, operated the United Nations! The right to take part in the first civilian research expedition to the Moon has gone to Nobel Prize laureates in the sciences and several wealthy businessmen, who invested over [the word is rendered unintelligible by radio static] billion dollars,"

The screen shows the Moon and a landing module on its shining, desolate surface, figures in white spacesuits moving about it with the light steps characteristic of a low-gravity environment. The splendorous blue-and-white sphere of the Earth looms in the distance.

The Twenty-first Century astronauts gather around a plaque left by the first Earthly visitors, on which is written: "Humans from the planet Earth, from the United States of America, first landed on the Moon in the year 1969 A.D. We came in peace in the name of all of mankind."

The new visitors are putting crystal covers over the plaque and the first human foot-prints on the Moon's surface. Another group is taking photos next to a Soviet lunar rover that thirty years earlier had reached the end of its useful lifespan. The black visors on their helmets reflect the life-giving rays of the Sun.

Unexpectedly, behind them, far off in the distance, a bright object rises from the surface, and, with a change of direction, shoots toward the Sun.

VOICE OVER A RADIO TRANSMISSION:

> "This is Kenneth Armstrong, grandson of Neil Armstrong, the first human to set foot on the surface of the Moon. We have just seen a space ship take off from the direction of the Sea of Rains. This might be visual confirmation of what Lybid Artemida talked about when she said her space ship, the Semarhl, was accompanied on its return flight from the solar expedition by an unidentified space vehicle that somehow did not allow itself to be photographed and which landed at a lunar base in the Sea of Rains. Her Majesty said this was not an alien space ship, but a craft

manned by our brothers and sisters in intelligence, members of the civilization on the Sun."

[Credits roll for graphic artists and special effects.]

Sixth newscast feature.

ANNOUNCER:

"Her Majesty Lybid Artemida has launched a campaign against excesses of the cult of personality that has pervaded the religion that is associated with her name and that has become all the vogue on six continents."

On the screen, Lybid Artemida is shown visiting her temples in different corners of the Earth, finally, a gigantic temple in the center of the Kremlin.

LYBID:

"Why this obsession with size? How do you justify spending three billion dollars and tons of gold on a building? This is not what I asked of you! It would be better by far to use this money to fight the effects of drought or to feed starving children. Or to clean up the lands contaminated by Chernobyl or to drain the Kyiv reservoir that is a cancer on Ukraine and all of Europe, poisoning the air and killing people! This is a crime against mankind! Earlier, there was the insane arms race. Three billion dollars were spent in the U.S., the Soviet Union, in China - on the latest nuclear missile submarine, a technological killer that prowled the oceans, terrorizing the human race with its lethal power.

Then there were the spy satellites and killer satellites that looked down on us from space. And what did you gain by all that? We banned war and all of your weapons;

387

trillions of dollars' worth became worthless junk. And now what new evil have you brought us?"

Lybid continues her painful speech at the site of a huge temple being built on a high hill overlooking Los Angeles.

LYBID:

> "This is insanity! To spend the people's treasure on a pseudo-religion, which you, in your commercial interests, have pushed as the latest in spirituality. Who is going to profit from this? Those who will grow rich from the sale of the sacred name of God and of His prophets! This is profitable to all those unscrupulous financiers, bankers, movie moguls and New Age religious speculators who, without my permission, used my appearance on this Earth to set up a universal, futuristic, speculating, obscenely profitable stock company. Or, perhaps, some kind of neo-orthodox Mafia of the occult, which exploits the mass psychosis of people hoping to find joy in a new religion that promises much. A religion that shamelessly exploits my name, even while I am still alive! I never asked for this! I always did and always will fight against this kind of falsehood and abuse!"

Lybid continues her protest in front of an ultra-futuristic temple at the foot of Mt.Fujiyama outside Tokyo.

LYBID:

> "I am simply a woman! I denounce all attempts to proclaim me as somehow divine!
>
> Everything I have and am I owe to our Heavenly Father! I do not want billions of dollars spent on temples

388

bearing my name, billions that should be spent by nations on building God's paradise on Earth!"

[Credits roll with the names of the rest of the production staff and technicians]

Seventh feature.

ANNOUNCER:

> Her Majesty the Queen of Humanity, Lybid Artemida,
> has today been elected the Secretary-General of the
> United Nations! A great event has taken place in the
> history of human civilization! The Daughter of the Sun
> has become the Spiritual Leader of humanity!"

The screen shows Lybid Artemida before the UN General Assembly. The audience is on its feet, applauding. The previous Secretary-General, Mikhail Gorbachev, takes off the ceremonial sash of office and hangs it over her shoulder.

Lybid walks onto the podium and addresses the assembly. Her face radiates joy, as radio, television, and the Internet carry her words all over the globe.

LYBID:

> "Citizens of the world! Let us unite and work as one!
> There is nothing we can't achieve, if we work together
> in the name of God!"

A smiling Lybid stands in the center of the screen, bathed in light.

The image fades and the names of the producers, associate producers and director of the film roll from bottom to top.

THE END